SHE, YOU, I

SALLY KEEBLE

ELEANOR
PRESS

ISBN 978-1-7392302-0-3

For Jane

PROLOGUE

February 2020

This is where it starts, here in this street where Granny Maisie was born, and stuff happened that kicked off my story.

Behind me there's a wall of happy sounds from kids in a playground. A woman in a track suit walks past pouring her heart into her phone. A man in a red T-shirt ambles towards me with a reluctant dog in tow.

The sun blisters down, and I unzip my bomber jacket. I should be able to feel a heartsqueeze from the past. Instead all I feel is sticky heat. It's February. It's Edinburgh. It shouldn't be hot.

"Mr Reekin' Eejit." Across the road a boy throws a stone at a row of terraced housing. There's a crack as it hits a window. Cheers from the kids crowding against the railings in the playground.

"Bugger off," bellows the man with the dog. The boy gives him a one-finger salute, the kids scream, the man shakes his fist, and then as he passes me, he smiles and says, "Lads," as if I should understand. The dog trails along like this happens every day.

And I wonder for the zillionth time if this trip was a mistake.

· · • • • • • • • ·

Back in the day, when Granny Maisie was growing up here, the street was lined with tenements steeped in misery and coal dust. She lived in one of them, a skinny girl with bright red hair and a cast iron will. I've got the red hair, but I'm not so tough. Unlike her, I can still cry.

Aunt Julia says it was poverty and war that made Granny the way she was. But I say no, there must have been something more that killed off her emotions so long before the rest of her died.

"Skye Stanhope, just like your mother, always arguing," Aunt Julia says. And when I say, that's not true either, she adds. "I should know, I was her sister."

But I'm nothing like my Mum. Isla, her name was—she would toss her head and tell me, "Be a badass, babe." Me. The least badassy of any of us. Not that I really know for sure. My imaginings and my memories of Mum are all mixed up now. Which is why I came here, to start from the beginning of our story and find the truth. About why Granny ran away to war and why Mum died.

I cross the street to where the boy was standing. The houses are yellowy brick with new front doors. Neat fences mark out each patch of garden. The air's full of Sunday lunch smells. Everywhere's suburban tidy, except for one place where the window's cracked and grass sprouts through rubbish that stinks like it's from last year

Something presses against my legs and there's the ratcheting sound of a cat purring. It sidles away up the concrete path and sits on the doorstep and eyeballs me. Then a curtain twitches in the front window and a grey face peers out. It's round. Not fat round, just round round. What hair there is looks grey too, plastered down so it's barely visible, apart from providing some definition to the face.

I step up the path and the playground noises behind me dissolve, so now it's just me and the cat on the doorstep and the face in the window which lights up like a lantern. A smile. No teeth. Just a gummy smile, like a baby's. I take another step and the eyes shine at me—beam—like they know me, except I've never seen them before. Now I'm so close, I can almost hear a wheezy breath and smell the sourness of a sad life.

A scrawny hand appears above the windowsill and waves. I wave back. The curtain falls, the face disappears. Then the front door creaks open, and a figure emerges. The face is the same. The body beneath it is swamped in baggy trousers and a cardy that could once have been beige. A very old man totters out and blinks like he's unused to daylight. He shuffles towards me, his slippered feet can't keep pace with his excitement, and then I hear his piping voice.

"I knew you'd come back, Maisie."

"SHE"

1935 - 1964

Chapter One

September 1935

She was safe under the bed. Metal strips above, bare boards below, her father's tin trunk behind—name, rank, number engraved on its lid. "All you need to know about a man," her father said. A blanket hung over the edge of the bed. Maisie lay behind it and clenched her fists against her chest to keep in the fear.

Tonight was bad.

"Floozy!"

"No!"

Shouts from the kitchen. Them fighting. She curled up and squeezed her eyes shut, covered her ears to make it stop. Anything to make it stop.

"You're my wife."

A scream from the kitchen ran through her body. And then another, and another, until the whole night became a scream. She tried to block it out, but she couldn't. It was inside her ears, inside her head. She was the scream. And then it stopped. She took her hands from her ears and listened. Nothing. Silence.

Maisie lifted the blanket and peered into the room. Gaslight from the street spilt over the tattered strip of net curtain nailed across the window. It glinted off the broken mirror above the empty fireplace, touched the two best chairs on their square of worn carpet, and lit up the locked front door out to the landing of the tenement.

In the far corner was the door into the other room, the kitchen. A spindly table stood next to the door, with a piece of lacy cloth draped over it, "To hide its legs," her mother said. On it was a china figurine of a man in a kilt with a lamb around his neck and a dog at his feet.

Beside the figurine was a photograph in a round frame of pleated cloth. Her mother, Flora, her hair swept up into a chignon and set with glittery jewels—only glass, she said—sat on a chair and behind her stood a soldier, uniformed, his face unmarked, handsome, with jet-black hair and a wide moustache that curled up at the ends like a smile. Her father, Simon. One arm was crocked behind him, the other stretched along the back of the chair, cradling her mother, and the greys of their clothes swirled around the whites of their faces and blended into the beige of the fabric that enclosed them.

The night the glass in the frame got broken wasn't as bad as this.

Then the shouting started again. The door from the kitchen rattled. Maisie gasped from the fear of it. The fighting was coming in. She scrambled behind the tin trunk, wedged herself between it and the wall, and made herself as small as possible.

"You're nae but a floozy." The door slammed back against the wall.

Maisie squeezed her eyes shut.

"Please Simon." Her mother's voice.

There was a clatter and the sharp sound of china breaking. Maisie's eyes sprang open into the darkness, and she would have cried out, but bit her lip to keep the sound in.

"The child." Her mother, pleading.

"Whose child?" She heard a smack. She knew that sound. Hit flesh.

The room shook, the iron bed clanged against the wall. The floorboards shuddered. She wrapped her arms around her head.

The fighting moved away, back into the kitchen. She unwound herself and listened. Their voices, their footsteps. Both of them in the kitchen. Quiet now. Perhaps it was finished.

Then something grated on the kitchen floor and there was another scream. One long wail. She felt the pain of it, pressed her hands against her stomach to make the hurting stop.

Something hit the kitchen wall—not china, a pot perhaps. If only it would stop. She heard footsteps come back into the room, quieter now. Just one person. A muffled sound, someone panting. Not her father. The door slammed shut.

She waited. Perhaps finally it was over. But it was never over, only left off sometimes, like when she was at school, or playing with her friend Nancy. Then she pretended to forget. Or when she was asleep. Yes, then she could forget. Except even then, he was still there, inside her head.

"Let me in." His voice. The brass doorknob squeaked. Him turning it, trying to get in, pounding on the door. Him.

"Flora. Open this door."

"You'll kill me."

"You do as I say."

"No."

A kick on the door. "You'll be sorry."

Maisie held her breath for what felt like forever, until her head spun, and she thought she might faint. Or burst. Yes, perhaps she'd burst, and then what happened? She let go and felt the space between her face and the tin trunk fill with hot air. Her feet were stone cold, and she rubbed them against each other.

"Go to bed, Simon." Her mother's voice.

"Don't you tell me what to do."

"You must be tired."

"Tired. Why should I be tired?" The door handle rattled. "You make me tired." Sobs from the other side of the door, followed by a whimpered, "Please." Her father.

Inside the room was silence. Thuds from the kitchen. Then nothing.

Maisie crawled out from under the bed. Gaslight caught her on the floor, an eight-year-old girl, scrawny arms and legs luminous in their whiteness poking from a shift cut from one of her mother's worn-out dresses, a pale pointed face, from which shone two blue eyes, not soft childish blue, but fierce turquoise, and above them a bush of red curls that burnt defiance. Her mother sat on the floor with her back pressed against the door into the kitchen. The best chairs were knocked over, the round table was on its side, the figurine in pieces. Flora's legs were straight out, her arms flopped at her side, her eyes shut. Like a doll. Or dead. What if her mother was dead? Maisie felt her heart stop.

"Were you hiding under the bed again, Maisie?"

Her mother was alive. She could breathe again. "Yes, Mam."

"Get back in and I'll come and lie with you a bit."

Maisie climbed into bed and pulled the blanket around her shoulders. Flora picked up one of the best chairs and placed it against the door, wedged it tight under the doorknob. Then she walked over to her daughter's bed and lay down beside her. Maisie burrowed her head into her mother's warm softness and breathed in the sweetness of her that was caught in her woollie and felt her insides go whoosh with the safety of it.

"You don't need to be afraid. He'd never hurt you," Flora said.

"I'm sorry about your figurine, Mam."

Her mother stroked her hair. "He's not a bad man, your Da. He's just... not well."

Her mother kissed the top of her head and Maisie felt the pain in her stomach melt away. She stretched her arms into the coldness of the room and reached around her mother's neck to pull her face close enough to kiss.

"Your hair's wet at the back, Mam." She rubbed her fingers together and felt the warm stickiness. "It's blood."

"It's just a wee hurt. It'll be all right. You sleep now."

She kissed her mother and cuddled against her. She felt her body grow light as if it would float away.

A click. Maisie's eyes started open, and she sat bolt upright in bed. Her mother was gone, and the best chairs were upright facing each other again on their patch of carpet. The round table was back by the kitchen door. The picture was sitting on it. She couldn't see the broken figurine. The grey light creeping over the windowsill would bring a new day. There was still time to sleep.

············

Maisie sat on her bed in her Sunday clothes and watched her mother doing her hair in front of the mirror above the empty fireplace. Flora's hair was braided into two plaits. She twirled one round, pinned it over an ear, and patted it into place. Then she checked it in the mirror, and repeated the process with the other plait, turning her head from side to side and tweaking her hair to cover the bruise on her temple. Maisie saw how Flora smiled at herself between the cracks in the mirror, but she also saw how, at the back of her mother's head, a patch of hair was missing and the raw skin wept.

"D'you want me to make it look better behind, Mam?"

"No, pet, my hat will cover it."

Flora put on her coat and then held the hat up above her head—a cloche, greyish on top, but still light blue under the rim where the weather hadn't spoiled it yet—and, following her image in the mirror, lowered it slowly over her forehead, wincing when it reached the bare patch at the back. Then she took her long pin with the pearl at the end and fixed the hat in place. Its blue matched the colour of her eyes, and her auburn plaits peeked out below the rim, nestling against her china-white skin and rosy cheeks. To Maisie she was like a princess, a figurine, to be put in a cabinet and admired and not broken.

Flora turned and smiled. "How's that?"

"You look beautiful, Mam."

Flora took her gloves off the mantelpiece, twisted her wedding ring around on its finger, then pulled the gloves on.

"Now, lassie, you get yourself ready. It won't be doing for us to be late."

Maisie wriggled off the bed as her father came in from the kitchen. Simon filled the doorway in his big black coat, the one he made himself, weaving the seams together so it would last as long as he did, as he told her every Sunday.

"Pull your socks up, Maisie," he said. "The child's skirt needs attention, Flora. It's too short."

"Yes, Simon." Flora smoothed down the collar of Maisie's coat and pulled a brush through her hair until the girl's eyes prickled and she said, "Ow Mam," and then Flora settled a beret on her daughter's head, tucking the curls under to make it stay put. "There, you look a picture."

Simon pulled out the keys that he kept on a chain in his pocket and unlocked the front door. Then he slid back the bolts with a clang and held the door open while Maisie took her mother's hand and went out. On the landing, she heard the muffled noises of her neighbours starting their day, their voices mixing with the smell of sour sweat and coal fires that escaped from under the doors to join the stench from the toilet by the stairs. She looked over the metal bannister down two stone flights of grey dankness and then up to where, between the railings on the landing above, a small white face appeared.

"There's Wee Jimmy," Maisie waved up at him. "Hello Wee Jimmy. I'm off to the kirk wi' my Mam and Da." A little hand came out between the railings and waved back. The boy's face didn't change.

"He's a daftie." Her father pulled the door shut and the rattle of his keys in the lock echoed around the stairwell. Then he walked along the landing, past the neighbours' front doors, past the stinky toilet and started down the stairs. Thwack, his leather boots hit the stone steps. Maisie's footsteps and her mother's pattered behind.

Outside, she breathed in the clean air, filled her lungs with the freshness of it. She took her father's hand and rubbed his palm with her fingers the way he liked, so he looked down at her and smiled. Her mother took her other hand, and they set off along the road, the three of them holding hands like everything was all right. As they turned at the corner, Maisie saw a small grey figure with raggedy shorts and bare feet duck into a doorway behind them.

"There's Wee Jimmy again."

Simon turned and shouted down the road. "Be away with ye, Wee Jimmy. Go home."

They walked up the hill towards the church, through the grey chasm of the tenement blocks, up to where the houses started—creamy stone houses with gardens in front.

"Respectable," Flora said.

Magnificent, Maisie thought of the painted front doors and shining windows and the rose bushes with their last lush blooms nodding pink and golden over the garden walls. Ahead of them, Nancy jumped out from her front gate onto the pavement.

"Hello Maisie," she called, and waved until her mother took her with a disapproving hand and pulled her away up the hill.

"Snooty," Maisie's father said.

Lucky, thought Maisie. If only she could be like Nancy Gillies, Nancy's mother laughing with Nancy's father, the girl being pulled along, peeking back over her shoulder, and winking. Her friend was wearing a new felt hat. Scarlet. It made her look grown up.

At the church door, the usher nodded and said, "Mr Munro," handing her father two brown hymn books. Her father stood back to let her mother go first and Maisie walked down the aisle beside her beautiful Mam, the church vaulting above them like in heaven, with her Da, the war hero, following behind. She wished it could always be like this. The three of them all right together. Always. They sat in an aisle halfway up the church, and her father passed her Mam a hymn book and her Mam gave it to Maisie to look up the hymns listed on the wooden board beside the towering pulpit.

Two rows ahead and off to one side, a man turned around. His black jacket sat exactly on his shoulders, his red hair was dulled with oil and slicked back from his sandy face—an undamaged face. He had a generous smile which lit up eyes that were fixed on Flora. Maisie saw her mother's cheeks pinken, saw how she raised a gloved hand to adjust her cloche hat and smiled like she did when this same man met them walking back from school of a weekday or fetching their errands from the shops of a Saturday. Him always on his own and them always on their own.

They'd walk up the hill or down the hill, her Mam and the man talking and Masie trying to hear what they said, until her Mam would say, "Goodbye Rabbie," and hold out her gloved hand. He'd take it and linger, looking so regretful. She'd give him a special smile—like she did now—just a wee smile, but it made her whole face glow.

Maisie loved to see her mother smile so. But then she felt her father stiffen beside her and heard the crick, crick, crick of him cracking his fingers.

· · · ● ● · ● ● ● · ·

In the last glimmerings of the day, Maisie sat at the table by the kitchen window, holding a glue bottle while her mother pieced together the bits of her broken figurine.

"If we can work out what goes where, we can stick it all together and you'd never know it's been broken." Flora turned two pieces of bright green and red china kilt until the edges matched. "Now put some glue just there," she said, and Maisie dabbed the glue bottle to the white edges of the china.

Simon brooded in his chair by the blackened cooking range, where a coal fire spat out red and orange flames. A pot stood on top; its smell filled the kitchen and teased Maisie's empty stomach, had done so since her mother put it on to boil after church. Her father turned the pages of his newspaper—he had a way of doing it, opening the paper, and folding it back so it cracked like a whip. Her mother jumped and the pieces of china fell from her hands.

"I dinnae ken why ye bother," Simon said.

"You gave it to me," Flora said, "that's why."

"It was a'ways an ugly thing."

Maisie watched her mother pick up the bits of china and press them together, wipe away a dribble of glue with the tip of her little finger and set the pieces down to dry, then sort through the other fragments on the kitchen table.

"Maybe that one?" Maisie pointed to a piece with red tartan on it.

"You're clever." Flora picked it up and held it against the rest of the china kilt drying on the table. "Have you all your things ready for school in the morning?"

"Aye." Maisie hoped maybe tomorrow would be better. Maybe it would be the start of things always being better. She thought of how that would be, to have everything better, always. "I'll call at Nancy's house on the way."

Crack. Her father turned another page of his newspaper and then took his pipe off the cooking range and reached into his pocket. "Dammit." He tugged on the pocket and there was the sound of tearing. Maisie looked at her mother, who was also watching Simon, her hands with the china fragments frozen.

He glared at them. "What're youse staring at?"

"Can I get you something, Da?"

"Where's my baccy?"

"It's on the shelf beside yer pension book," said Flora.

Maisie climbed onto her parents' bed, set against the kitchen wall. She stretched up and felt along the shelf till her hands reached the soft cover of the pension book her father took to the Post Office each week; next to it was the cold hardness of his tobacco tin.

He smiled when she handed him the tin. "You're a guid wee thing."

It made her happy that he approved. She gave him a kiss, there on the good side of his face—not the side where the firelight reflected off shiny red scar tissue that pulled his mouth up and his eye down until they nearly met. She tried not to look at that side. Simon laid his newspaper down on his knees, so close to the flames that she feared it would catch alight, then opened his tobacco tin and filled the pipe. He tore a piece off his newspaper, twisted it up and lit it from the fire, put it to the bowl of his pipe and sucked until the tobacco glowed as red as his scar. Then he held the burning splint of paper for her to blow out.

"For you." He smiled again.

The flame flared up, and the paper curled over, and she knew that when she blew, it would break, and the burning splint would fall onto the wooden floor. It scared her, but she blew to keep him happy. He picked up his newspaper and breathed out a cloud of choking tobacco smoke that drifted across the kitchen and hung over the table where Flora put fresh glue onto a piece of red china and stuck it into place on her broken figurine.

"There. You can hardly see the cracks."

"It's still ugly," said Simon.

"I'll fetch our tea now." Flora set out three bowls and spoons on the table. She edged past Simon, and he turned over another page of his newspaper. Crack. Flora flinched, then reached for the pot of soup. As she did so, he put a hand around her waist and pulled her to him, fondling her, smiling, his face so close to her body. Maisie dared not speak, hardly dared breathe, only watched her father kiss her mother's stomach and saw the panic in her mother's eyes as she stood there between Simon and the soup pot. Then she caressed him back and kissed his head and disentangled herself and Maisie could breathe again. Her eyes didn't miss a heartbeat of the interaction and she wondered if this was what love was when it wasn't fighting. Was this how love would be for her when she was grown up?

"Come and eat." Flora ladled brown liquid into the bowls and then fished out a gristly lump, grey from boiling. "Here Simon, I've kept the meat for you."

A peace settled over the room. Maisie slurped up her soup and wished she could have the meat. It seemed her Mam and Da were at ease with their soup and each other and with her, so she decided it was safe to ask the question that had been vexing her all day.

"What's a floozy?"

Chapter Two

April 1944

S he felt the plane's scream—it caught her heart, churned her gut, split her head—and then there was a splutter that stopped her breath until the screaming began again, so close the car shook. The driver slewed to a halt and Maisie jumped out, a teenager dressed in the light blue of an air force uniform, red curls tied back, turquoise eyes fixed on the plane flying in to crash at Sutton Heath.

There was scarcely a gnat's wing between the plane and the forest canopy over which it skimmed, spurting above the last line of trees, hurtling towards the yellow concrete of the runway, a mass of grinding, smoking, dying metal. Alongside Maisie, the plane blasted out a sideswipe of hot air that dowsed her in stinking fumes. At its nose there was a picture of a half-naked woman with the sun's rays shining from her head. Behind its wings was a white star, and above that a gaping hole. At its tail, a jagged piece of metal. And then the plane was past, disappearing in a roar of black smoke over the concrete horizon.

What a way to die. Maisie imagined the men inside the plane, the pilot flying them to oblivion. And the rest, how would they be—terrified into silence or calling for their mothers, girl-friends, gods, or whatever else they thought might save them?

Or did they, in that split second between life and death, open their mouths in a soul-shattering howl, drowning out the thunderous crash with a single animal scream?

Her scream.

Followed by sirens. And then silence.

Forest silence—leaves rustling, a twig snapping, birdsong—as unfamiliar to Maisie as the brightness of the sun, the hugeness of the sky, the flatness of this strange land.

Embarrassed silence.

Maisie shuffled.

"Your first time?" the driver asked. He'd climbed out of the car too, and stood beside her, smoking a cigarette with nonchalant ease.

She nodded. It had taken her two days to reach the airbase, shunted from Scotland on a crowded troop train, skirting around London, overnighting on a bench in a waiting room somewhere beyond the city, listening for air raid sirens, then next day lumbering east to Melton train station in Suffolk. There she'd been met by this man in his blue fatigues who did no more than nod to acknowledge her existence and drove, one lackadaisical hand on the steering wheel, the other dangling from the open window frame clutching a cigarette from which he took an occasional, deep drag. Meanwhile she, in her uniform and cap, nervous in the back seat, had tried to talk to him, but getting no response, had given up and gazed out at the newly-harvested fields they rattled by.

Round a dogleg bend they careered, a thatched pink cottage on the corner, and plunged into the forest, past a brick farmhouse, right and right again. Clickety-click the car bumped along a yellow concrete road, silver birches on one side, morose pine trees on the other, then whoosh, they were waved past the gatehouse and onto Sutton Heath airbase, where they now stood, awkward comrades-in-arms.

The driver threw his cigarette down and ground it into the dust.

"Prangodrome."

"Pardon?" she asked.

And then it started again. A red flare shot through the air, and another plane flew in, roaring low on the far side of the runway.

"Mercy me." Maisie caught her breath, hands tight across her chest to hold in the panic.

"You'll get used to it."

The driver slid back into his seat and Maisie, feeling foolishly naïve, clambered back into hers, and off they sped again along the service road that ran beside the runway. As the car crested the rise, Maisie saw the extent of the airbase; carved out of Rendlesham Forest in the final years of the war, built at the cost of a million trees to provide a place for damaged Allied planes to crash-land after bombing raids over Europe. There'd never been such an expanse of concrete. It had three parallel runways, two miles long and so wide that when Maisie looked across it, all she could see was yellow, until at the far horizon there was a green strip where the forest resumed. Halfway up this concrete ocean huddled a cluster of buildings, and at the front of them stood a dumpy grey control tower, where people were crowded on the rooftop watching the most recent drama.

A man wearing a white suit pumped foam over a smouldering heap on the nearest runway. Behind him a group of airmen, bulky in their flying suits, joked with each other, or so it seemed to Maisie, as they watched the destruction of their aircraft.

"How did they survive?" asked Maisie. "I thought the plane was set to crash. It was on fire, even."

"Flying fortress, tough buggers," said the driver.

One of the airmen detached himself from the group, took off his cap and ran his hand through a mass of black curly hair. He raised his face to the sun, as if, thought Maisie, he hadn't expected to feel it again. Someone on the control tower must have called out to him because he stretched out his arm and gave a thumbs up sign. And then he laughed.

"That man," said Maisie, "he must have flown all the way to Europe, dropped his bombs, got shot to pieces, flown back somehow and nearly crashed. And he's laughing about it. How can that be?"

"Yanks," said the driver.

It was hard to equate the insouciance of this young man with that other war hero, her father, with his glowering moods and fighting temper. Was he ever as happy and carefree in his war?

"He makes it look like it was nothing." She watched the young man out of the rear window, until the driver turned off the road onto a track towards a cluster of Nissen huts, her home, Maisie guessed, as long as the war lasted, or the air force decided to move her, whichever came first. The accumulated tiredness of the two days hit her; she was glad of the driver's silence.

The car pulled up outside a dun-coloured hut that would have blended into the landscape except that in front of it stood a young woman, poised, one hand on her hip, the other shielding her eyes. She overpowered her uniform, from the perfect victory roll of her hair to the glassy polish of her shoes. To Maisie's expert eyes, her jacket looked precision-tailored to fit her neat shoulders.

"There you are, Reggie. I thought you'd got lost. Stopped to watch the excitement I suppose. Be a dear and fetch her kitbag out of your boot, will you? No, don't dump it on the ground, leave it by the door—here—that's the job, and put it down gently, please." The young woman chivvied Reggie around, and, to Maisie's surprise, he let himself be chivvied, although with a dourness that said he wasn't happy.

"There's a good fellow." The young woman delivered a parting shot at Reggie, who ground his teeth, climbed back into his car and gunned his engine. Then Maisie felt herself become the object of attention from this glamorous person who rolled her eyes, opened the door to the Nissen hut, and with a mannered flourish of her elegant arm, swept her inside.

"Welcome to our luxury accommodation. My name's Constantia Beresford, but you can call me Connie if you prefer."

Maisie dragged her kitbag across the threshold. Inside its humped interior, the regulation drabness of the hut thrummed with the suppressed glee of young women. Clothes were artfully hung between iron beds to create an illusion of privacy. The shelves above were crowded with pictures of parents and sweethearts. An aroma of lavender battled with the smell of carbolic soap and won. In the centre of the floor a heating stove squatted beneath its chimney flue on which was stuck a poster of a lion on a red background with the words STAND FIRM. Above it was a picture of Princess Elizabeth, resolute in her army uniform against a sullen sky.

"It's grand." Maisie took off her hat and shook out her hair.

"Yours is the second bed along, the one with the mattress and bedding folded on it, and that's your shelf space. I'll be your neighbour for as long as you're here, so we'll have to be friends."

Connie extended a hand to Maisie, a casual gesture, as if she knew the person to whom she offered it would be grateful for the honour. At least, that was how it seemed to Maisie, who judged that this woman's accent and bearing marked her out as a member of what her father inveighed against as blithering idiot officer class. Maisie had always accepted his assessment until now, faced with the reality of this older, taller, altogether more exotic creature who was claiming her as a friend.

So she reached out and would have grasped the extended hand and shaken it—"Maisie Munro, pleased to meet you"—except that as soon as her sturdy fingers touched its white softness, the hand was withdrawn, as if the intention alone was sufficient, and all Maisie felt was a dab as light as a cat's paw before Connie was off, sashaying down the middle of the Nissen hut.

"Check the windows, which if you ever manage to open, you won't be able to close again to keep out the rain or the midges, so leave them shut. Especially in winter. Check the washstand at the rear. One for all of us, special concession. Don't hog it and make sure you refill the water jug. I'll show you where the latrines are later. Latrines? You know, pennyhouse, bog, yes?" Connie pivoted, retraced her tracks. "Check the fire. You'll be grateful for it when the cold weather comes, even if it nearly suffocates you."

But it was the iron bed that caught Maisie's attention. It was like the one at home and she looked through the metal slats to the space below and, for a moment, saw her younger self curled up. She'd promised herself on leaving home that she'd never hide there again. Kissing goodbye to her mother, she avoided her father's grasp, and discarded her pain, so she hoped, along with the stinky toilet in the dank stairwell.

"What's wrong?" Connie's insistent voice cut in. "Don't like the look of it? They're not so comfortable, but you'll get used to it. I managed."

"No, it's not that. It's just it makes me feel…" Maisie stopped. She didn't want to admit to this person, or anyone else for that matter, what it made her feel. That was her past. It was the reason she'd enlisted ahead of time and what she'd come all this way to leave behind. To give words to what she felt would allow the past into her present, and she didn't want that.

"Tired perhaps," Connie looked at her with apparent concern. "Let me help you with it." Saying which she pulled a sheet off the pile on the bed and shook it out.

Maisie unfolded the mattress, slammed it over the metal slats, and pulled the ends of the sheet across the bed.

"Hospital corners with the sheets, whatever did you learn at school? It's the only thing I remember apart from how to do spit and polish. Minimum effort, maximum effect, easy on the brain." Connie folded and tucked the sheet over a corner of the bed. "Is this your first posting?"

"It's my first time in England even."

"You're from abroad?"

"I'm from Scotland."

"Oh." Connie's discomfort was so brief that Maisie nearly missed it. "Silly me, I should have known. The accent. Well, never mind, you'll get used to us. We're not all savages, whatever impression the squadron leader may give."

"Is she fierce?"

"She's a pussycat underneath. Edie was at school with my mother. She's why I'm here. Packed off to this place in the middle of nowhere with one of Mumsy's old chums to keep an eye on me. What got you to join up? You look too young."

"My father was my inspiration." Even if it wasn't exactly the whole story, it fitted the occasion. Maisie guessed her new friend didn't have time or interest to listen to the more complicated version, about her desperation to escape the numbing violence at home and the grinding oppression of the factory work she'd been forced into. And there was some truth to her words. There had been a time when she'd been proud of her father. She pulled from her kitbag the photograph that her mother had pressed on her as she left. "So you don't forget us," she'd said, and Maisie had thought, if only.

Now she showed the picture to Connie. "That's him in his uniform."

"The Great War?"

"Yes. He fought at Gallipoli and the Somme."

"What a hero. He must have been quite a man to survive all that." Maisie caught an edge of envy in Connie's voice.

"For sure. He had a string of medals that he would wear on special occasions. He kept them in a tin trunk under the bed." For an instant Maisie felt its coldness against her back. But she shrugged it off; that was her old life and it wouldn't touch her again. "I signed up as soon as I could and he would allow." She put the photograph on the shelf above her bed. Her father the war hero, her mother the beauty. That's what they would be to anyone who asked her from now on.

· · · • • • • • · ·

They were walking over to the mess room for their tea, or dinner, as Connie called it, when she saw the American again, coming out of a hut near the control tower. He ducked with that instinctive awareness of height of a tall person. Without his padded suit he was slim—lanky, even—and younger, less certain. As he turned his face was caught in the light above the door, and she saw how sombre he looked, almost troubled. Perhaps it was the pallor of his skin and the blackness of his hair, or maybe it was just the distance or a trick of the light that made him appear so.

"He was on the plane that crashed this afternoon," she said.

"He was the pilot." Connie put her arm through Maisie's. "Roland Roseberry. Or more accurately," she affected a drawl,

"Roland Roseberry third at your service, ma'am. Southern gentleman. Old money. He did well today, although it's what this place is for, don't forget. You'll see a lot more like that. Most of them walk away from their planes in one piece like he did, but some aren't so lucky." She stopped and stared at Maisie. "Are you star-struck? You are, you little goose. I say Rollo," she called out, and he stopped in his tracks. "You've got a new admirer. Another one."

Maisie thought she would die, wanted the ground to split open and swallow her up. In future she'd be more cautious about exposing her feelings. As it was, she had nowhere to hide them. He'd been unwrapping a piece of gum and as Maisie felt his attention move from Connie to her, she saw him straighten up and smile and then she heard, "Roland Roseberry third, at your service, ma'am." He touched his cap and despite herself, Maisie struggled not to laugh.

"You were verra brave today." The words blurted out from her, and she thought how silly, how insignificant, she must appear.

He leaned forward. "Sorry I didn't quite catch what you said. All that noise today must have gotten to my ears."

Connie laughed. "Oh, do give over. She's Scottish."

Maisie felt a pulse of annoyance.

"I'm sorry," Roland said. "I didn't mean to be rude."

They were close enough to each other now that she could feel his scrutiny. It made her cheeks burn, but that didn't stop her examining his face, which was less arrogant, more vulnerable than she'd originally thought, darkened by the shadow of the day's events and beard growth. A curl of black hair stuck to the sweat on his forehead. He looked too unaware of himself to be a hero, more like a lad going home after a hard day's work.

She was about to tell him it was all right, she wasn't offended, she couldn't understand American either, when a jeep pulled up, marked with a single white star, and piled high at the back with young men. A door opened. "C'mon bud," someone shouted from inside and a hand stretched out and pulled him in.

He wound down the window and leaned out, chewing hard on his gum. As he saluted her, the jeep swung away. It did a tight turn around the two women and then for good measure, circled them again. The men on the back cheered. One of them gave a long wolf whistle.

"In your dreams," Connie shouted. The men on the back hollered, and the jeep roared away down the yellow concrete road off the base. Then she turned to Maisie and said, "You know what, by this time next year, unless those boys are very lucky, they'll all be dead."

Maisie saw the jeep stop at the gatehouse, caught the sound of male voices, then the barrier lifted, and the men and their laughter disappeared into the forest.

"How can you say that as if it doesnae matter? How can you be so calm about so much death?"

"To survive here, that's what you have to be."

"Not me," said Maisie. "Never me."

CHAPTER THREE

MAY 1944

M aisie wondered what pied piper she'd followed into this world of golden-stoned confidence.

Swallowing back the sickness that had come into her mouth for the umpteenth time during the journey along winding country lanes, she clambered out of the back seat of the Chevrolet into the courtyard of a Cambridge University college. Around her were glowing walls, dotted with doorways and mullioned windows, darkly anonymous against the brilliant sun. Above, the sky formed a startling blue canopy and the lawn in the centre of the quadrangle was as finely green as a carpet.

The trip had been Connie's idea, "to visit Cousin Jeremy, he's a student there." She'd invited Roland too. "Word is he's taken a shine to you and besides, the Americans have better cars and more petrol."

Roland had asked his navigator Eugene along to share the driving and then Guy Forrester from the control tower invited himself. "To chaperone you girls on your visit to my alma mater," he'd claimed.

"Cripes," Connie had said when the big green car with the white star rolled up outside the Nissen huts at Sutton Heath, with Eugene driving and Roland sitting alongside. She'd sandwiched Maisie into the middle of the back seat. "Guy fancies me, and I defo don't want to sit next to him and his wandering hands all the way to Cambridge."

And so it was that Maisie found herself floating down a river in a flat-bottomed punt as far removed as the moon from anything she'd ever known. It wasn't just the easy Englishness of the place, or even its wealth that marked out its separateness. She'd thought her friend Nancy rich, having a whole house to live in, but even she wasn't part of this world that was so deceptively simple, so understatedly self-assured. It reminded her of her first encounter with Connie, and how her friend's hand had slipped away before she had scarcely touched it. Perhaps it was how these people were, giving away so little and then eluding outsiders who got too close or found out more than it suited them to share.

Opposite her in the punt was Roland. He'd pushed past Jeremy to bag the place and stretched out his lanky frame, at complete ease, so it seemed, with himself and his surroundings, more at home than she felt although he was further from his country than she was. One of his legs had brushed against hers, accidentally she'd assumed; he'd apologised, she'd smiled, but then he'd left it there, pressed against hers, and she'd not moved hers either and since he didn't acknowledge it, neither did she. The heat it generated reached her cheeks.

He beamed. "You're glowing."

"I'm no' used to the sun."

Sitting next to him was the supposed reason for the visit. Cousin Jeremy. Maisie looked for a family resemblance. The elegance was the same, but their colouring was different. His hair was rust-coloured, so were his eyes, kind eyes in a soft oval face. Both were tall and slim. But where Connie used her height, he appeared embarrassed by his, scrunched awkwardly in his khaki uniform, with his cap clutched under one arm.

"Jeremy Stanhope. Delighted to make your acquaintance. I've heard so much about you."

Behind the shyness, Maisie could see curiosity, as if he was comparing his cousin's reports with the reality before him. "I hope I live up to expectations." She wondered what else they'd discussed and tried to shrug off her discomfort.

Connie, lounging beside Maisie, laughed.

Hovering over the two women, wielding the punt pole, stood the man who Maisie suspected was the real reason for the visit. He'd taken charge from their first arrival.

"Timotheus Granville, Tim to my friends," he'd said, caressing rather than shaking her hand with a seductiveness that she guessed was intended to make her feel singled out for his special attention, which she knew she was not. His clothes—white trousers, blindingly white shirt, striped blazer—seemed to Maisie to accentuate the calculated ease with which he intended to glide through the war. The effect was spoiled only by his shoes, which she noticed were dirty.

"What is it about those uniforms that makes you girls so damned attractive?" He held his punt pole balanced between his hands, as if considering his options.

"Perhaps because they mark us out as fighters?" Maisie parried.

"Touché." Jeremy's eyes sparkled. Roland laughed. Tim was silent. Maisie sensed his irritation.

The punt surged forward as he pushed his pole into the water and with barely perceptible effort, a flick of the wrist here, a slight shove there, propelled them all between the green-cushioned riverbanks. The languid heat, the calm of the river, the grace of the colleges floating by—Maisie was beguiled. She could live forever in this enchanted world and wondered what her Da would say at its so easy conquest of her.

"I'll give you Brits one thing, you know how to do splendour," Roland said. Maisie wished she could be as confident—or careless—as him.

"We've had a thousand years of practice. Bit of a head start on you chaps." Guy inserted himself into the conversation. He'd been consigned to sit at the front of the punt with Eugene who'd brought his camera for the occasion, and while Eugene clicked it at every passing building, Guy spent the time gazing with undisguised longing at Connie, whose skirt had ridden up her legs to reveal a hint of suspenders.

Roland had one arm over the side of the punt, trailing his hand in the water. The other was draped across Jeremy's shoulders. "You're in the Territorials?" Maisie wondered at his tone—was it condescension or possession?

Jeremy responded with the over-eagerness of a puppy. "Only for the time being. I go into active service next year."

"Not too active, we hope." Maisie had thought Connie asleep, but now she saw her friend was watching the scene through calculating eyes and she wondered whether it was Roland or Jeremy or herself who was the focus of her attention. She knew it wasn't the adoring Guy.

"This way—smile—gotcha!" Eugene turned his camera on them, and they were captured, three men, two women, an intricate web of arms and legs and interactions.

"Are you going to photograph everything?" Tim asked.

"Pretty much." Eugene refocused his camera. "This time, smile guys." And so they did, smiled like it was forever and there was no war, and Eugene snapped them. "When I get home, I want to be a photojournalist."

"How about you, Roland, what will you do afterwards?" asked Maisie.

"Finish law school. Practice in New York. Maybe I'll try for Congress later."

"I thought your family were plantation owners down south," said Guy.

"We left that behind long ago."

"They must have had slaves," Guy continued.

Connie tutted.

"Sure," said Roland. "You folks sold them to us."

"Steady on old chap," said Tim, the rhythm of his punting unbroken. "I say Connie, you've brought us a pair of American pinkos." Maisie guessed that Tim was at his most dangerous when he smiled.

Roland was unruffled. "We're the ones fighting for our freedom, remember," he said and patted Jeremy's back affably. "Looking forward to welcoming you into our ranks, comrade."

"It'll be over by the time he gets there," Guy said.

"Hopefully," said Connie. "We've already lost his brother."

Jeremy coloured up, though whether at the mention of his brother, or being the focus of a dispute or the centre of attention, Maisie couldn't tell. But she felt sorry enough for him to say, "If I lived anywhere half as beautiful as this, I'd have trouble tearing myself away too."

"Would you? Really?" Jeremy leaned forward, so only Maisie could see the intensity of the gratitude in his brown eyes. Or was it a neediness? It made her hesitate.

"Well, perhaps not exactly." When she saw his disappointment, she added, "It's just I've never seen anything like this before. My father's family were crofters in the highlands. He went to the city to make his fortune. Except he didn't. We lived on his war pension. And his stories."

"She's being modest. He was a hero, much-decorated, fought at Gallipoli and the Somme." Connie was watching again.

"How splendid." Jeremy's eyes glowed and Maisie realised that to have a conversation with this man, she had to look at his eyes to get a sense of his intentions, his words being too few and him deferring too easily to anyone who chose to cut in on him to be able to express a complete train of thought.

"What she's saying is that other people's memories aren't enough to live on," Roland told Jeremy in friendly fashion. "You'll be in the action soon enough and you can make your own."

"The main thing is to survive to have any," Tim said. "No point being a dead hero." He heaved on his pole and the punt lunged forward.

Something must have rippled the smooth surface of his consciousness and Maisie wondered whether it was Jeremy or Roland who'd annoyed him. "Is that what you're afraid of?" she asked.

"Me? Afraid? Never."

· · · · ·**·**· · · ·

Guy punted them back, with heavy guidance from Tim who sat next to Connie for the occasion. Maisie, not wanting to play gooseberry, took herself up front and sat cross-legged beside Eugene, who was still sprawled with his camera.

"Can I have a go?"

"Sure. I'll show you." Eugene knelt behind her and held the camera to her face. "You look through the viewfinder, there." Maisie saw ahead the river, a bridge, a couple leaning over it. "Then you press there." He put his hand over hers. His breath warmed her neck, his voice with its American accent was soft in her ear.

"Hey, what's going on up there?" Tim called out.

Roland turned around. "Take a picture of us."

Maisie swung the camera and through the viewfinder she saw Tim, with his arm around the shoulders of the reclining Connie. One of his legs was cocked up and his body bent towards hers, while she lifted her arm from the side of the punt and placed it on his stomach, looking at the camera with a teasing smile, as if daring Maisie to capture them just so. Above them hovered Guy, his punt pole held at an angle, dripping water into the river. Click, she had them.

"Let me focus it for you." Eugene stretched around her and fiddled with the camera. Roland came into focus, looking straight into the camera with an expression that made her feel weak inside. Love, she hoped. Next to him was Jeremy, glancing over one shoulder, his smile pulled lopsided with the awkward effort of it, so she wasn't certain if his admiration was directed at Roland or herself.

"That's amazing," Maisie said.

"What, me or him?" asked Roland.

"The camera, silly."

"Look at that, she rates a piece of metal above both of us." Roland gave Jeremy an affectionate cuff and Maisie hoped she'd caught the moment, the ease between them and the open admiration in the Englishman's face. She'd already stored an image of Roland in her heart.

"I'll let you have these pictures once I've developed them," said Eugene. "Now give me the camera and I'll take one of you."

So Maisie leaned back and Roland closed into the right of her, so near she could see the pulse in his forehead and the creases at the corners of his mouth which disappeared when he smiled. Up close she saw his dark brown eyes had a greenish tinge towards the centre. She wanted to kiss him, and perhaps she would have done, or he her, they were so close, and both of them, she sensed, so willing. But then she heard Jeremy's voice, "Cheese please," and his trusting, unlined face appeared at her left shoulder. His vulnerability had nothing to do with her, she told herself. If anything, he was Connie's responsibility.

"That's the one," said Eugene, and Roland put an arm around her and squeezed and their heads touched, his black curls against her red ones, at the exact moment the camera clicked. She wondered if it would catch the intimacy she felt between them, and whether he felt it too. But he had already moved on and was talking to Jeremy about everyone in America having cameras and how surprised he'd been at food rationing and how even the Pathé newsreels in the cinemas back home hadn't prepared him for the reality of bombed-out London.

"I've never been to London," she said.

"Haven't you?" Roland said, and then, "I'll take you one day." Jeremy and Eugene laughed at the surprise of it or maybe at the audacity of an American offering to show someone around their own capital city. Not that it was hers. She felt herself blush.

"Hey, cheapskate. Get him to take you to New York, now there's a city." Eugene packed away his camera, the end of their journey being in sight. Tim commandeered the punt pole from Guy and told everyone to stay seated while he brought the punt into the riverbank. But Guy refused to sit down and made the punt wobble so Connie cried out in only partly mock alarm. Jeremy laughed at her, a strange braying sound quite unlike anything to be expected from such a reserved man. Roland chuckled at the chaos while Maisie hoped no-one would notice her burning cheeks.

They lay on the grass beside the river, and then Tim took Guy off, reappearing with bottles and glasses. Maisie decided not to say she'd never drunk champagne as Guy shot the cork into the river with practised ease. Roland raised his glass to Maisie. She tried to stop herself reading too much into the gesture—everyone was toasting everyone—but she hoped it signified an intention. Then Connie announced she needed to find a WC and grabbed Tim by the arm, and they disappeared under an archway. When the champagne was finished, the men took themselves off across the river towards some bushes, and Maisie, finding herself alone, went to find Connie and the toilet. Through the archway and across the quadrangle was an open door. Inside, she heard Connie's voice come spiralling down a staircase. She followed it up, her shoes clunking on bare wooden steps, and knocked on the door.

"Come in." Tim's voice. They were standing self-consciously apart, Connie straightening her skirt and fiddling with her hair and Tim smoking. Her shoes were on the rug between them. As Maisie came in Tim blew a sliver of smoke into the air and then took a piece of tobacco from the tip of his tongue and flicked it into an overfull ashtray on a desk by the window.

"I suppose you want the toilet," he said. "It's across the landing. Excuse the mess. Damned scout hasn't done the room again. Or my shoes."

Maisie looked to Connie for an explanation, but she wasn't giving one, and by the time she came back into the room from the toilet, had already left. Maisie saw her from the window, running across the quadrangle, leaving her to walk over it with Tim.

"Terrific girl," he said.

"Yes. She's been very kind to me."

"How about Guy?"

Tim was smoking again, his cigarette in a short black holder, which he held to his mouth with a curious gesture, as if it was an object of great value and not just a way of keeping his teeth from being discoloured.

"He's a nice man."

"Don't fool with me, you know what I mean. How close are they?" Tim blew a stream of smoke above her head. "I'll bet those sharp eyes of yours don't miss a trick."

Maisie felt the harshness in his voice; he was someone who didn't take to challenge. "What his feelings might be, or Connie's, are not my business," she said. "I'm sure she'd tell you if you were to ask her."

"Hmm." Tim stopped and blew rings of cigarette smoke into the air, then pierced them with his holder. "That might not be such a clever idea."

· · ◆ ◆ · ● ◆ · · ·

"A last one for the record books." Eugene lined them up at the car, Connie, arm linked through Tim's with Guy standing possessively beside her. On his other side, Roland, peaked cap pushed back, leaning towards Maisie who inclined towards him, wishing that for this final photograph they could hold hands. Jeremy tagged on the end, his vulnerable face full of undirected hopefulness.

"Smile, like you mean it. Perfect. Posterity here we come." Eugene clicked. They all relaxed.

"Maisie, why don't you sit up front with me, that way you won't feel so sick," Roland said, himself climbing into the driver's seat for the journey back to their airbases.

Eugene clambered into the back, by the window so he could see the view. But then Connie said that Guy had to sit by a window, as he'd drunk too much and might be sick, and she needed to be next to a window for air. "I could pass out," she said. So

Eugene sat in the middle, leaning forward and staring out of the windscreen which, he remarked was covered with squashed insects. He'd just got out and was wiping away their smashed bodies, when there was a roar in the sky and a formation of planes flew overhead. He stopped and looked up and Roland got out to join him.

"Look at them." Jeremy shielded his eyes with his hands. "It's your chaps coming home, isn't it?"

"Yes, it's our chaps. But it's not home."

"They're splendid," Jeremy continued. Maisie remembered that he'd called her splendid too and wondered if it was his vocabulary or his feelings that were limited. Roland grimaced, as if what he felt couldn't be put into words, and Maisie wondered what it was and why he couldn't say it.

Guy broke the moment. "Come on, or we'll be late." Eugene climbed across him into the middle of the back seat. Roland slid behind the steering wheel, pulled out the choke and turned the key in the ignition. Jeremy saluted. Tim waved and just as the car disappeared through the archway at the front of the college, he blew a kiss to Connie, which Maisie—who'd turned around to see the last of the enchanted world—caught and said, "Look, Tim's saying goodbye to you." But Connie was busy arranging herself beside Eugene and by the time she'd turned around, they were out onto the cobbled streets of Cambridge.

· · • • • • • • · ·

They had to stop to refuel the car on the way back. Maisie held the funnel while Roland poured petrol out of a can from the boot. Guy went behind a tree, to relieve himself, he said, but they heard him being sick and he came back wiping his mouth and slumped into the car. Roland poured water over the windscreen and Maisie scraped off the dead insects with a sheet of newspaper. When they set off again, Connie fell asleep, and after a while, so did Eugene.

"Perhaps it's the smell of the petrol," said Maisie, so she and Roland opened the windows, and they bowled along with the cooling air blowing onto the three slumbering figures in the back seat.

"That was a grand day."

"Did you think so?" Roland said.

Maisie, challenged, had to admit that it was also unsettling. "It's a side of life I've no' seen before."

"Oh, I have. It was the same in the college I went to back home. A whole pile of people who can buy their way out of life's inconveniences, as they see the war."

"But you don't."

"No." Roland stared through the windscreen and Maisie supposed it was to concentrate on his driving. "My Dad brought us up with a very simple philosophy. The world's divided into good guys and bad guys. America may not be perfect—we may have been too slow to come into this war, we may segregate our forces, we may make mistakes—but basically, we're the good guys, and the good guys have to win, or the whole world's in trouble. That's why I'm fighting."

Maisie considered what she was fighting for. To honour her father's legacy, which was what she told people. Or because she would have to anyway once she was old enough to be called up. Or was it the other reason, the one she would scarcely admit to herself?

"I wanted something better," she said.

"A better world? We all want that."

"No. I mean something better for me. I wasn't brought up in the kind of world we saw today. My father was a hero, but when I said I grew up on his stories, that was it. We lived in two rooms, and the bathroom was along the landing. He used to sew kilts, he told me, but he never worked again after the war. He pretended he did, but his wounds were too bad. I left school…" She stopped, uncertain of how much to admit to this man who was, whatever her daydreams, still a stranger.

"Some of the things I've seen in England have been surprising," he said, "but it will change after the war. You'll see. And there's a lot that's good. Like your history and your culture."

"You've no' seen my culture."

"I'd like to."

"You'll be most welcome. You'll have to wear a kilt mind."

He laughed, a soft chuckle that she felt must surely denote an intimacy. "After we've been to London," he said.

"Yes."

"And before New York."

She liked the sound of that. As if he intended some permanence between them. So then she told him about leaving school at fourteen and the grinding job in the factory and how she'd worked the treadle machine till her legs ached and she'd finish the sewing until her fingers were pricked raw. She kept back the truth about her father for another day.

In return he told her about the futility of trying to study when the world was falling apart around him and how, when the crunch came at Pearl Harbour, his father had tried to stop him signing up. And then he'd met Eugene, who had family missing all over Europe, who'd given him a personal reason for bombing the hell out of Germany.

"Don't you ever get scared?"

He wrapped his arms around the top of the steering wheel, and puckered his mouth, and stared out through the windscreen crusted with a fresh layer of crushed insects. Maisie had given up expecting an answer, thought she must have offended him, before he replied.

"Scared? I'm not even sure I know what that means any longer. I've seen men blasted out of planes with nothing. I've seen 'chutes float past with body parts attached. Watched my own crew freeze to death, choke to death, bleed to death. The last time we got shot up by a German fighter, I saw the whites of the man's eyes as he flew past. And I thought, 'You've got it easy kiddo, you only have yourself to worry about. I have to bring my buddies home.' But scared, I don't know.

"I can tell you what spooks me though. It's when I get up next morning and see the empty beds in our hut, and then some new guys come to sleep in them, and we carry on. Sometimes I think about who will get my bed next."

"You mus'nae say tha'."

He laughed at that and teased her about her way of talking. He said it was quaint, which she said was impolite, and then they chatted about inconsequential things, and she thought she could listen to him all night. By the time they turned off the road into the forest and Roland stopped at her Nissen hut, and she jumped out and shook Connie awake and the two Americans dragged Guy along the path to his hut, she thought there was an understanding between them. When he got back into his car she heard Eugene say, "Couldn't you just have asked her for a date?" The car set off again, this time with Eugene driving, and Maisie's heart skipped a beat when Roland leaned out of the window and blew her a kiss.

CHAPTER FOUR

JUNE 1944

F ire leapt through the morning fog. Flames clawed at the dense air, threw incandescent curls of red and orange into the whiteness, roared into the heavy silence. A blistering, deafening inferno.

Black smoke followed, billowing towards Maisie as she walked from her Nissen hut. She put her hands over her face but the smell of it infiltrated her fingers, filled her nostrils, stuck in her throat. The cloying, giddy smell of burning petrol. Of planes crashing.

It had greeted her first arrival at Sutton Heath. It immobilised her now.

Then the black smoke rolled away, and a ghostly figure materialised out of the fog, a man on a bike pushing on his pedals with early morning weariness. He cycled alongside the flames, so close to them Maisie thought he must surely catch fire. Yet he seemed impervious, like someone from another world. He tipped his hat, "Mornin'," and disappeared into the whiteness, which then cleared to reveal the yellows and greens of Sutton Heath, the giant runway bordered with a line of fire, fed by jets of fuel from miles of piping engineered to burn off the fog.

Before Maisie could catch her breath, a plane appeared over the runway, shimmering in the fiery air like a mirage. Flames poured from one of its engines, fire landing in fire, until it seemed to Maisie the whole world was ablaze. And then another, and another, planes thundering into the relief of an unexpected landing.

The night bombers.

The British planes.

The American planes would be somewhere over Europe. The day bombers. She wondered if Roland's plane was among them and if so, where, and when it would return.

· · · · ●· ●· · · ·

She walked on towards the control tower to start her shift on the switchboard where she allowed herself to dream, to feel his hand under her elbow, see his smile, and how it smoothed away the worry lines in his forehead. She smelt his maleness and heard his American "Sure thing, buddy" drawl and pictured them together in London, as he'd promised, and then New York.

In the days since Cambridge, she'd joined her friends outside when the buildings at Sutton Heath emptied in the afternoons to watch the American bombers fly back from Europe, and held her breath at the ones that came in low over the forest for emergency landings. She'd searched among them for his plane, and when it wasn't there, she'd felt relief, then guilt at feeling relieved when others had died.

Then a sick panic had returned because the ones that survived to make emergency landings, however dangerous, were the lucky ones. The unlucky had already been obliterated somewhere over Europe, blown to smithereens in an explosion, or brought down by fighter pilots flying so close their grim faces were visible as they shot out the bombers' entrails. Or the crews had bailed out and floated down to raking gunfire from below. Or ended up as prisoners. Or worse.

And then she'd search again among the crippled planes grinding to audacious halts on the emergency runway for the one with the figure of the half-naked woman with the sun in her hair. Where was he?

"Get a grip, the board's gone bleeding mad," said Lily, sitting alongside her.

So Maisie put away her daydreams, adjusted her headphones, pulled out a line and plugged it into a socket on the switchboard whose lights were flashing "like Piccadilly Circus, except now even that's all blacked out," Lily said. "Bleeding Hitler." And when the board lit up again, she added, "Something's up. You wotcher, our Mr Churchill's got a trick up his sleeve." She worked the board with brisk efficiency, pausing only to mutter "Here comes the duchess," when Connie sauntered into the room.

"A letter for you." Connie waved an envelope in Maisie's face. "I predict it's from a young man." Maisie noted the small, neat handwriting and the Cambridge postmark, June 1944, and shoved the envelope into her pocket to open in her tea break.

When she got into the canteen and tore open the envelope and turned the letter over and saw the signature "Jeremy," her misery was complete. She crumpled the letter and smiled at Lily who was watching from across the mess room.

Connie sat down opposite her with a cup of tea. "Read it."

"Leave me alone."

"With that letter unread? I don't think so."

"It's none of your business."

"Oh, it is. You're my friend. And I suspect that young man who's just written to you in his ultra-tidy handwriting is my cousin."

Maisie sighed, smoothed out the letter, and then held it up and started reading.

"Out loud please," Connie said.

"No."

"Oh, be a dear. I'll end up reading it anyway, so you might as well get it over and done with. Go on."

Maisie reckoned there could be nothing in it worth keeping from her friend, nothing that the sender of this letter could have written that would touch her inner self. So she started again, this time loud enough for Connie to hear.

"'Dearest Maisie. I hope you don't mind my writing to you like this. But I just wanted to say what a splendid day it was when you came to visit with Constantia.'"

"Hmm." Connie sounded pleased.

"'I may have appeared somewhat reserved. It's a national characteristic which I'm afraid I possess in large measure. However, in addition to my natural reticence, I have to say I was completely bowled over. Constantia's descriptions did not do you justice and I'm afraid I found myself tongue-tied when presented with the reality.'

"What did you tell him about me?" Maisie asked.

"Just that you're a pretty Scottish girl."

"Don't believe you." Maisie read on. "'I had hoped that we might meet again soon. However, I am being deployed early and expect to leave Cambridge within days. I can't, of course, say for where I'm bound. However, I'm afraid you won't see from me the gallantry of our mutual friend, Roland. I fear I'm a lesser mortal.'"

Maisie felt herself struggle with the words and Connie chipped into her silence. "That's my cousin all over. So self-effacing when he's actually a clever, talented man. And nice with it."

But he was the wrong man, thought Maisie. The one she wanted was noble and heroic, had driven with her through the green countryside and talked to her as no-one had ever done before until she wanted to drive with him just so forever. And he'd promised to take her to London and New York. She thought her heart would break like she'd read in books because this man who'd written to her wasn't the one she wanted.

"He could have ducked military service, you know. Mumsy could have fixed it for him. Come on, read the rest." Connie nudged her.

"'I hope in some small way to play my part in our glorious victory, and once it is achieved, that we will be able to meet again, and I can persuade you I am not entirely an Englishman—' Oh, this bit's been blanked out." Maisie tried to decipher the words below the black line before reading on, "'—as our continental friends would say.'"

"Let me see." Connie held up the letter at an angle. "Must be something French. He likes his French, which is beyond me but evidently not the censors. And look at how he's signed himself, 'Yours affectionately.' How gentlemanly. That's Jeremy all over. What a nice letter."

"But..." Maisie felt herself dissolving into her disappointment.

Connie reached across the table and put her soft cat's-paw hand over Maisie's. "Look, I know you've got the hots for that American, and he has for you. Anyone except those themselves blinded by love can see that. But Jeremy's not to be sneezed at. He's a good man. I suppose I would say that wouldn't I, he is my favourite cousin. Besides which, he'll never be short of a few bob, so to speak."

Maisie looked at the letter. "Yours affectionately" not "Yours passionately" or "Yours sweeping you off your feet." She didn't recognise what Connie was saying or the sentiments behind it. Was this how her parents had felt when they had their picture taken, Mam in her finery, Da in his uniform—had they affectionately calculated each other was not to be sneezed at, or had they felt in that instant that their souls were locked together for all eternity, whatever had come of it afterwards?

"Oh, for goodness' sake." Connie squeezed Maisie's hand. "It's not the end of the world. He's not asking for anything, is he? Just saying he enjoyed the day and flagging up his interest for future reference. Come on, cheer up. Life's not so bad."

·············

That night Maisie woke in darkness to the roar of planes overhead. The air was cool, so she put her jacket over her shoulders and opened the door of the Nissen hut. The full moon shone down and by its cold light she saw that if it weren't for the planes, she'd have heard the wind in the trees, the full-leaved branches gyrating in a demonic dance while above passed wave after wave of bombers.

Stepping outside, she pulled the door closed and watched, arms folded against the chill as the bombers thundered overhead, silhouettes across the moon, shadows cast between the scudding clouds onto the runway before her. Behind her, the door to the Nissen hut opened and slammed shut and Connie appeared alongside.

"There's thousands of them," Maisie said.

Around the airbase doors opened and people tumbled out of their huts to watch. Dark figures appeared on the control tower. Maisie shivered for the magnificence of the machines, the courage of the men they carried, the relief that such a show of force could only mean that the war's end was in sight.

"It must be why Jeremy was mobilised early," said Connie. She watched the skies, open-mouthed, the only time Maisie had seen her over-awed. "I wonder where he is."

And where was Roland?

Maisie pictured him in one of the bombers overhead, sitting behind his controls, watching the night sky for danger, Eugene charting their course in the armada and photographing it out of the window, him piloting them to Berlin. And did he, in all the mind-blasting fury of it, have a thought for her?

"You're crying." She saw moonlight reflected on tears trickling down Connie's face.

"It's the hanging around I can't stand." Connie wiped her hands across her cheeks.

"You're a softie after all." Maisie had expected almost any response from her friend but this.

"This has to be the end. It has to. We can't go on with the not knowing, pretending it's all going to be happy ever after with bluebells and white cliffs when it can just as easily be jackboots and sauerkraut." Maisie slipped her arm around Connie's waist, but she twisted free. "Oh, bloody hell, don't set me off," and ran off in her bare feet to where Guy was standing with a gaggle of men by the runway.

"You're mad," Maisie shouted after her.

"Not me," Connie shouted back. "The rest of the world is, but not me. I'm completely sane." And Maisie saw the joy in Guy's face as he swung her around and wondered if it was at the prospect of the war ending, or the feel of Connie's body under her nightie.

There was no more sleep that night. By the time darkness had greyed to dawn, Maisie, sitting at the switchboard next to Lily, picked up fragments of conversation, "German radio... Invasion... Nothing from HQ."

"Told you so," said Lily.

They gathered around the radio in the mess room to hear the BBC's 8 am news announce a new phase in the Allied air offensive.

"What the hell does that mean, 'a new phase'?" asked Guy. "Why can't they just say we're driving the buggers all the way back to Berlin."

And then at midday. "Here is a special bulletin, read by John Snagge."

"Don't even start, Guy," said Connie. "We all want to hear this."

"D-Day has come." Nobody, not even Connie, could stop the cheering.

And then the one o'clock news announced the king would speak to the nation that evening. "What is demanded from us all is something more than courage and endurance," he said.

"Oh god, not more blood, sweat and tears," said Connie.

"Constantia, that's your king speaking," said Guy.

"I don't give a damn. I don't want to have to give a damn ever again."

And all the time, through the whooping joyousness of it, one question gnawed at Maisie's mind.

Where was he?

· · · ● · ● · · ·

It was a week before she found out, two weeks since the event itself because it turned out he hadn't made it to D-day after all.

"I'm sorry we couldn't let you know sooner." The American airman—Vince, he said his name was—twitched his leg up and down so that his foot jiggled on the floor of the little office at the airbase her friends had thoughtfully vacated for the occasion.

For a minute Maisie feared he might wet himself. He didn't want to be there, she could see from his fidgeting nervousness, the cap twisted between his hands, the sweat above his upper lip. At first, she didn't hear him. Then she saw his lips move, she heard sounds, but she couldn't put them together to decipher words.

When she did, and heard them string together into sentences, and it sunk in what he, this man Vince, was explaining, about the plane being hit by flak and spiralling down, no parachutes opening out below, before it exploded on the bombing run into Berlin, then she wished she hadn't heard, wished the words could be unsaid, that he hadn't told her, that he hadn't come. That events could be undone.

How could I have been so stupid? she asked herself. She should have sensed that some disaster must have stopped him from contacting her. It was her fault, if not that he had died, that she was alive and not known.

"Sometimes a piece of flak just has your name written on it." Vince looked miserable. "At least they all died together," he added, as if that made it better. "People think our planes are tough, but they're—"

"Like flying in tin cans," said Maisie.

"How did you know?"

"He told me."

Vince thrust out a package towards her. "When we were clearing out his locker, we found this, addressed to you, so I guess you'd better have it. Everything else is going to his folks back home, the citations and everything."

"Citations?"

"Didn't he tell you? His group got two distinguished service citations for bravery." Vince's words slipped out fluently. It was easier to say the good bits.

"A hero." Maisie thought of the other war hero, her father. The package she held was more bulky than a letter. She took a corner of the brown paper and tore.

"Look, um…" Vince squirmed, his foot tapping out a drum-beat on the floor, his cap scrunched in one hand, the other fumbling in his pocket.

"You want to go?" Maisie asked.

He held out a handkerchief. "You might need this."

It was only then Maisie realised there were tears running down her face, dropping off onto her jacket, big splodges that darkened the light blue. It was like she'd always remembered it, crying inside, she'd called it, so no-one could hear or notice her, so she could wrap up the hurt and bury it deep inside her and not feel it ever again. She turned and stumbled from the room.

She was sitting on her bed in the Nissen hut with an array of black and white photographs spread out in the front of her—the contents of the envelope.

Their day together. Their only day. All she would ever have of him.

"Knock, knock, anyone home?" Connie stood in the door-way.

"This one's for you." Maisie held up a photograph from the pile on the bed. "See how it catches Tim ogling you. I don't sup-pose either of you even knew you were being photographed."

Connie took the photograph. "I'm so sorry."

"I like this one the most." Maisie held up the picture of them all in the punt—Guy's face caught up front close to the camera, Roland and Jeremy turning in their seats, Jeremy doing a self-conscious thumbs up, she and Connie reclining at the rear with Tim hovering over them.

"It was such a happy day." She knew her cheeks were red, and she supposed her eyes were too, but she could hold fresh tears back, she told herself, just so long as—

"How about this one, it's lovely?" Connie, with her instinct for the jugular, had managed to winkle out the picture that hurt Maisie the most, the one that caught the moment she remembered best from that day. When Roland had pulled her to him and their heads had touched and she'd wished they could be like that forever, heads touching, living out the hope that she'd felt then. Looking at the photograph, she could see it burning in his face too, so brightly that she couldn't bear it. She turned away and rifled through the other photographs.

"You should send this one to Jeremy," Maisie gave Connie the picture of him shaking her hand, his hat pushed back, his vulnerable besottedness openly on display.

Connie twiddled the photograph in her hands. "It's all right to cry, you know."

"Have you got a thumb tack?"

Connie went to find one while Maisie collected up the photographs and put them back in their brown package. On the front of it was her name in his handwriting, his, she imagined, not Eugene's, a forward-leaning script with big loops and underscored with a strong line. As if he knew it was an ending.

She would pin up the picture that hurt the least, the one that showed them all lined up at the point of their departure, so the emotions were diluted, and she could see him, but not so close that she could see his feelings, or her own.

· · · · ● · ● · · · ·

She held herself together until she was in the forest. The wind was blowing, the east wind that they said tore in from Siberia across the North Sea, whipping over the tops of the trees that pitched and tossed and protested, but held firm. Walking beneath them, she could hear the wind, and if she looked up, she could see the turmoil it caused, but wasn't touched by it.

Once she started to cry, she couldn't stop. She sobbed, then howled, screaming louder than the noise of the gale blasting through the treetops, as if she could make it blast through her as well, blast out all her feelings so she didn't have to hurt any more, ever again. Not like this.

She remembered how it had felt to be close to Roland on the boat in Cambridge, the quiver of his body. And how he'd shared intimacies with her on the drive back to the airbase, bared his inner self, so she'd felt it to be at the time. And she'd done the same, gone deep into herself and found feelings she never knew she had. Or else had buried long ago in a tin trunk in her soul.

And then she pictured the words he'd written on the front of the package: "For Maisie" not "For my one love" not even "For dearest Maisie" and wondered if she'd misunderstood, if her fantasies had been just that, idle imaginings on a hot day. That thought was so bad she blocked it out and then she cried for the betrayal of her dreams as well as the destruction of her love. New wounds over the scars of her childhood.

The wind subsided, and a fog settled on the forest. As she walked back through its blankness, tendrils of black smoke wound between the trees.

When she reached the airbase, flames from the pipelines along the runway were burning off the fog. A plane flew in, a day bomber: an American plane. But not his, thought Maisie, never his, ever again.

Wound up in her own grief, she was about to walk on when she saw the plane had no undercarriage. It would land on its belly, on the gun turret slung underneath, crushing, unless he was lucky, the gunner trapped inside. Maisie had heard people talk of these crashes, of the pilots who killed one of their crew to save the rest. Maisie imagined them now, skimming in behind the veil of fire. The gunner's screams, the pilot's guilt.

And then she thought, enough, I can't live feeling all these tragedies.

She was exhausted. Her tears were finished. She promised herself that, whatever life brought, she'd never allow herself to be hurt so much ever again.

Chapter Five

March 1945

"Jeremy's coming to Ipswich." Connie set down her breakfast tray opposite Maisie in the fug of the airbase canteen. Her newly bleached hair was pinned back from her face and crimped into perfect curls that just cleared the collar of her jacket. She swung her hips around and lowered herself onto a chair with the easy confidence of knowing that most, if not all, the men in the canteen were watching her.

Maisie cradled her mug of tea. *"Next stop Berlin,"* promised the crumpled newspaper lying on the table in front of her, heavily thumbed pages spattered with tea stains and bacon fat.

Outside, a cold March wind cut across clear skies and buffeted the greening trees in the forest. Inside a determined chatter rumbled around the breakfast tables. For the first time she could remember, there was the prospect of a life that did not involve war. But in the nine months since D-Day, Maisie had learned that in an unpredictable world, clouds didn't always bring rain, or blue skies heat, any more than a lack of tears meant she'd stopped hurting for a dead love.

"He wants to see you," said Connie.

"How do you know?"

"He told me so. We had a long phone conversation. It appears he's smitten."

"I'm no' ready."

If Maisie had looked more closely, she would have seen that whatever show Connie was putting on for the canteen, tilting her head to eat her toast, cocking her little finger to drink her tea, there was calculation in her eyes. "You can't let a single day last year determine your entire life."

Maisie sipped her tea. She'd learned to hide her grief, but not to forget it. After the heady summer that had followed D-day, she still felt as bleak as the winter that then descended. At her insistence, Connie had cropped off her hair, and although her friend had objected, "It's too curly, you'll look like a red poodle," for once she'd obeyed. So now Maisie sat in the mess room, tight curls around a pensive face, and considered whether to make Jeremy's visit another rite of passage.

"What do you have to lose?" Connie prodded her. "He's a good man. He's done his bit and survived it. That says something."

"That he's been lucky."

"No. That he was sensible enough to realise that life would go on afterwards and that he wanted to be part of it. Like Tim. Like me. And you if you'd admit it."

Connie leaned across the table till her face was almost touching Maisie's. "Listen, I know how much you loved your American, but let's face it, half the girls around here are in love with any American who'll promise them Hershey bars and nylons, or the world in an oyster or—if they're very lucky—a one-way ticket to New York in return for a grope or more. Especially if it's free. Not to say that yours was like that, of course," she added hastily, "but you must know the reality of it by now. I mean did he ever even kiss you?"

"Kind of." Maisie didn't add, one kiss, tossed out of a car window.

"Did he tell you he loved you?"

"He didn't have to."

Connie propped her elbows on the table. "Mmm. You're a hard case."

"What did he put in his letter with those pictures?"

Maisie felt a stab of anger. "You looked."

Connie laughed. "I've no idea what you're talking about. I only know you're staring a gift horse in the mouth. Jeremy's young, he's rich, he's my cousin. There's plenty to like about him, even if you don't want to love."

· · · ● · ● · ● · · ·

So, Saturday morning found Maisie at Ipswich station where she learned that Jeremy's train had been delayed.

"Best wait there." The man in the ticket office, greasy jacket cuffs, cigarette wedged behind his left ear, lifted a stubby pencil and pointed across the road. "You'll see the train—if it comes."

Maisie crossed from the station yard to where a hotel stood, a long, thin, heavily timbered building, unscathed among the scarred docks and factories beyond. Outside a newsstand billboard blared the previous night's disaster: "Bomb kills nine." She gave the news boy a sixpence, folded the newspaper under her arm and went inside.

Sawdust covered the floorboards; the ceiling was black with age and tobacco smoke. Along the back ran the bar, beer pumps arrayed along the centre, glass mugs hung overhead. Maisie let her eyes adjust to the gloom and took in the lunchtime crowd, mostly men, mostly in uniform, then edged her way between them to the bar and bought a half pint of cider. "Long glass, please." She pushed away from the bar, then noticed someone sitting at a table in the far corner from the door. He didn't look old enough to be in uniform, scarcely into his teens, sitting all alone drinking a pint of beer. His figure was familiar, dumpy with sloping shoulders, round head set squatly, mousey hair plastered flat on top. When she went closer to get a better look, he put down his beer mug and smiled, a squidgy smile in a face not used to happiness.

"Wee Jimmy." She put her drink on his table and sat down before her trembling legs gave way. The rank sourness of urine and boiled cabbage that had smelt out the stone stairwell filled her nose. Wee Jimmy with his hopeless eyes and grey face that she'd always had fixed in her mind at age five. "You're too young."

He snickered, picked up his pint of beer and took a swig. "So were you." He wiped his sleeve across the top of his lip.

"I was seventeen, old enough that my father could sign for me. You aren't even that old."

His whole body subsided. "Are you cross with me?" She imagined the misery seeping out of him, the dank wretchedness of their childhoods, like the greyness that trickled down the stairwell of their tenement block. She saw it collecting in a pool under the table—there was so much misery she might drown in it, like she'd nearly done before. It wasn't anger she felt at the sight of him across the pub table.

"No." She shook her head. "I'm no' cross with you, Wee Jimmy."

His face brightened. "I'm glad." He clenched his shoulders as if he was hugging some secret to himself and Maisie wondered if she should ask him what it was, or if it was better not to know. "I only did it for you." She felt the grey mire on the floor rise up and wash over her, as if it could reclaim her for itself.

Wee Jimmy clutched the handle of his beer mug, rounded fist, plump fingers, his face unlined and expressionless as a balloon. As he drank a trickle of beer overflowed and slid down his chin.

He put down his mug and wiped his mouth again and smiled across the table at her. "So's I could be your hero."

Maisie was aware of the surrounding noise in the pub, boots clattering on wood, voices, male voices, laughter. Someone bumped the back of her chair and a man asked, "Okay, love?" She raised a hand to stop the interruption to her train of thought as she tried to work out what she might ever have done that could have triggered such a response in the impenetrable figure sitting in front of her.

"Oh Jimmy."

"A war hero. Like your Da." Wee Jimmy's smile disappeared, and his round face assumed such a blandness that Maisie wondered if a person with such a face could feel anything at all, and then thought that perhaps this was how she appeared to the world too, as someone who couldn't feel. And then she wished she couldn't.

"Not that he's much of a hero as I could see. Thump, thump, crash, scream, 'No Simon, no.'" Wee Jimmy's voice went up to a falsetto, and he wiggled in his chair. "And then yer Mam would scuttle down the stairwell with her coat and hat always on, even in the middle of summer, as if she could cover up the bruises and no-one would know what'd happened. But I knew. I always knew everything. He called me a daftie, but I were always a canny eejit."

He clenched his beer mug until his knuckles went white with the effort and his face changed from bland to angry to knowing. He swigged his beer and then mopped a puddle of it off the table with the sleeve of his jacket and put his mug down with precision.

"Not that he didn't have some reason for it what with her goings-on as he called them with that Robert Macpherson."

It all came back, the beatings, the screams, the shouts of "Floozy" that she heard as she lay curled up under her bed. She took a gulp of cider. "Did you ever see Mr Macpherson come to our door?"

Wee Jimmy lifted his head and rolled his eyes and Maisie watched him consider.

"No." He shook his head, "No-one came after you left, not that I saw, not unless it was the minister. He might have come."

Now she thought about it, Maisie couldn't remember when anyone had ever come while she was at home. "And did you ever see my mother step out dressed up for any goings-on?"

"She never went out on her own at all after you left."

"What, never?" Maisie thought of the letters from her mother, talking about her father and church and how Nancy's house looked when they walked up the hill on Sundays, now that Nancy's parents had moved out to the country for safety. But she hadn't understood from what her mother had written how much her world had shrunk.

Wee Jimmy pursed his lips till they were a tight dot in the softness of his face. "Not as I recall. He wouldn't let her. He would go to the shops with her, and they went out together to the kirk of a Sunday. I don't remember that she ever went out on her own. Not once you'd gone."

Thinking back, Maisie realised her mother had rarely gone out before without either herself or her father. On the occasions that "Rabbie" as her mother called him, had bumped into them walking home from school or the shops and walked with them up or down the hill to the corner of their street, she'd always been there to see that, whatever the warmth in his eyes and the joy in her mother's, there'd never been anything more than a handshake before he turned away. Then she and her mother would hurry along to the entrance of their tenement block, where her mother would always say, "Best not mention this to Da, eh?"

She buried the memory deep down where it belonged, like it was an unexploded bomb, and then she put all the sandbags of her life since on top of it and resolved never to go near it again.

"Why did you come here?"

"To find you." He relaxed, pleased with himself now, sitting drinking his beer as if everything was all right after all, no matter what horrors he'd left behind at home or encountered since. "You know I've always watched out fer you."

Maisie felt a coldness in her stomach. There was so much she hadn't understood. She thought of the little white face that would peer through the railings of the stairwell whenever she left her flat, and of how Flora would give the forlorn boy their scraps and how he'd sit on the stairs and lick every last morsel off his fingers. When they were older, she'd spot his figure at the street corner, or hanging around the school playground not far from her. "There's Wee Jimmy," Nancy would say when he padded behind them with his lopsided walk and his flat feet, and Maisie would toss her head and refuse to look back or wink, as she knew Nancy would be doing.

And now here he was, the dank greyness of the tenement block, with its stench of piss and poverty, sitting across the table from her. The misery of that world swirled around her. No, it wasn't anger she felt when she looked at him.

"Jimmy, do you really want to be my hero?"

A glow crept over Wee Jimmy's face. Maisie tried to remember another time she'd seen him happy.

He nodded.

"Then watch over my mother."

"Until you come home?"

She knew even as she said "Yes," that she wouldn't go back, that there were too many layers of deliberate forgetting laid over her memories, and she wasn't going to risk uncovering them. Wee Jimmy, meanwhile, was sitting so still, transfixed, that she wasn't sure if he'd heard, or perhaps the import of her words hadn't sunk in. "Please," she added. "Watch out fer her. For my sake."

He didn't move, gazed at her, round eyes in his round face, his mouth opened into a little "o".

"D'you hear me, Wee Jimmy?"

He nodded. "I do."

She felt the past recede and decided to move before it had a chance to return.

"I've got to go, so I'll be saying goodbye the now." She took her coat off the back of her chair.

"You've no' finished your drink."

"I have to meet someone." She fumbled to get her arms into her coat, until an American airman pulled it over her shoulders, and then squeezed her, his beery face too close to hers. She pulled away, pushing her chair, making it grate among the sawdust on the wooden floor.

"Kiss me." It was Wee Jimmy. "Please." She had to go, should have left already. If she delayed, caught between the American and Wee Jimmy, the moment would pass, and she would be lost. She saw the face that had peered at her through the metal bannisters, unchanged, still her father's daftie, only larger, but surely still as innocent as a child.

"I've never been kissed before."

"And then you'll watch over my mother?"

"Yes."

He couldn't hurt her. She wasn't going back; she'd never have to see him again. She bent and kissed his cheek, felt the clamminess of it, smelt the stale sweatiness. He didn't move. She pushed past the American. At the door she turned around. Her newspaper was still lying where she'd left it on the table. Wee Jimmy's eyes were closed. His hand was on his cheek where her lips had been.

· · · · ●· ● · · · ·

It didn't matter where she walked so long as it was away. She crossed the bridge over the mud-banks of the river, past a street of rubble, buildings flattened or teetering, a woman in a flimsy dress clutching a child's jacket, pushing away the tin-hatted warden at the cordon, picking her way across a pile of bricks, "It was mine, mine," and disappearing through the gaping front of a house with no roof and all the windows blown out.

It was enough, Maisie thought. There was only so much a person could take and then you had to grab hold of life, whatever the consequences.

She doubled back towards the station, where the London train must have arrived at last, because people were hurrying from the hotel. Wee Jimmy was among them, clutching her newspaper under one arm, scuttling along with his lopsided gait in all the khaki-coloured anonymity.

A neat figure stood at the edge of the crowd, distanced from its chaos, tapping a cigarette on a silver cigarette case, checking his watch, putting the cigarette into his mouth, cupping his hand around the lighter, then slipping the silver case into his pocket. Pressed trousers, fitted jacket, peaked cap.

"Jeremy." He was different, of course. The vulnerability was still there, that warning that if she got too close, she risked becoming the guardian of it. She realised, now she looked at his face, that it was handsome and, when he saw her and his anxiety disappeared, as open and friendly as she remembered. But there was a shadow overlaid. The bright innocence had gone. It's what the war did to people, she supposed.

"You've not changed a bit." He threw down his cigarette, took off his hat, grabbed her hand and shook it as if his life depended on it.

"My hair's away," Maisie extricated her hand from his. "Did you no' notice?"

She guessed it must have been the first time he'd laughed for a while, the way he threw his head back and gave that braying laugh she remembered from last summer, like she imagined a donkey might sound. An unexpected exuberance from a cautious man.

"It suits you," he said finally. "Your personality. Irrepressible."

"Shall we go somewhere?" Maisie asked. "Away from the station, I mean."

She linked her arm through his and started walking, hoping that Wee Jimmy wasn't watching her, peering between the iron railings of the platform, or peeking out of the train that was sitting in the station. She shivered.

"Cold?"

"No, just thinking." She pushed Wee Jimmy out of her mind and back into the past that couldn't hurt her. "Have you had a good war?"

"I've survived."

"Connie says that's the main thing."

"It's not enough though, is it?" he said. "You've done much more than that, so my cousin tells me."

Maisie wondered what her friend had been saying about her and why, and whether there was something more she should know about this man who was content to let her steer him up the hill, her hand tucked into his arm. Even his walk was gentle, his body moving beside her in seductive fashion, like a cat, sexy. Perhaps she might have noticed it before, if only it hadn't been for...

She didn't want to go there. She found something to say. "Why are you here?"

"Can't say, hush, hush. I'll have a car coming to the station for me after luncheon. It's not long, I know, but I wanted to see you again, however briefly. Connie told me that our friend Roland was lost. I was so sorry to hear about it. I imagine it must have been quite a blow for you."

That didn't begin to touch how she felt. He spoke as if it was just something else that had happened and would heal over, a calibrated pain, like a pilot trimming the settings on his plane.

"Maisie?" Jeremy was bending forward, his worried face in hers.

"Let's not talk about it." There would be no remembrances of Cambridge or punting on the river, no longings for a pilot who wondered which newcomer would sleep in his bed next. There would be only the here and now, walking with a catlike man through a town of shattered buildings and cratered roads.

"What will you do afterwards?" she asked.

"Crikey, that's a big question. Go home, find a job, I suppose. It's hard to say. I'm not looking forward to it very much. Oh gosh, that sounds awful doesn't it?" He rubbed her hand where it rested on his arm. "I don't mean about the war ending. It's just that I'll be going home with nothing to show for it. You know. I can't say I've been an ace pilot or landed on the beaches of Normandy or marched on Berlin. I can't really say I've seen any action."

"But you've survived."

"Yes. I've been lucky."

They found a hotel in the town centre. "It's expensive," said Maisie. She didn't say it was more expensive than anywhere she'd ever eaten in before. But Jeremy didn't notice, or if he did, it didn't show, and when they'd sat down and been served their soup, and then their chicken stew, and she'd watched to see which knife and fork he used, she thought perhaps it was a stroke of good fortune she'd met Wee Jimmy after all. Because before she might have told him that she too would go back home, to Scotland, once the war was over. But now when he asked her what she would do afterwards, she said, "Well, one thing's for certain, I won't go home."

He didn't ask why not—perhaps Connie had warned him off, or perhaps he didn't care. But he seemed pleased and smiled and reached for her hand across the table until the waitress came with their pudding. He only ate a spoonful and then pushed his bowl away because, he said, queen of puddings was too sweet for him, and patted his mouth with his napkin, and Maisie was torn between finishing the sweetest thing she'd ever eaten or appearing impolite.

Outside the station he took both her hands in his. "Dear Maisie. It would be lovely to see you again, and perhaps even, when all this is over, you might like to come home and meet my parents."

His brown eyes were softer than ever, and she whispered, "Yes," and closed her eyes and waited to feel his lips. On her hands at least. And waited.

But all that kissed her face was the afternoon sun and when she opened her eyes, he was gazing at her with fondness, tinged with apprehension. He pulled away, perhaps it was the car arriving for him, she told herself as the driver opened the rear door for him and he climbed in.

She waved as the car drew away, but couldn't see any sign of him waving back, and then a bicycle cycled too close, and she had to jump out of the road.

· · · · ●· ●· · · ·

The Nissen hut was empty when she got back. She looked at the picture over her bed, the one with them all together on that day she needed to forget. She opened her big envelope of pictures and rifled through them. There, the one she wanted, with her head so close to Roland's and on her other side, a bit apart, Jeremy. She rummaged through the box on Connie's shelf and took her scissors and cut out the picture of Jeremy. He was in his uniform, with his hat on, looking straight into the camera—a handsome army officer. She took down the picture pinned to the shelf, extracted the thumb tack, and stuck it into the picture of Jeremy which she put in its place.

CHAPTER SIX

APRIL 1950

Maisie was laughing, walking beside Jeremy down the country lane to St Mary's Church for the christening of their daughter.

Julia, born four years after they wed in Ipswich Registry office in the dog days between war and demobilisation, Jeremy in his army uniform, she in the white dress she'd styled, to the envy of Lily on the switchboard, from a parachute.

He'd assured her then it was the happiest day of his life. But to Maisie he seemed happier now, and more confident, holding Julia aloft like a trophy, the astonished child clutching her father's jacket and watching his lips move as he sang. "The bells are ringing for me and my gal!" He shaped his lips around the "my gal" and directed the words with such pride at the child, that if she hadn't been the mother, Maisie might have felt jealous.

The baby looked like him, with her pale face and tufts of brownish hair and her eyes at nine months turning from blue innocence to cautious hazel. Normally father and daughter shared the same expression of placid imperturbability. Julia stretched out a finger and stuck it in his mouth as he sang, "They're congregating, for me and my gal."

Putting the seal on Maisie's happiness was Flora, who'd travelled south for the occasion. Maisie had worried how her mother would cope with the heat, the reserve, the Englishness of it. Needlessly it turned out. Flora in her coat and cloche hat, was smaller, greyer but happier than Maisie could remember. She and her mother had worked together on Julia's christening robe, stitching together with it the pieces of the missing years since Maisie had left home. When they'd tried out the dress on Julia, pushing the baby's plump arms through the delicate lace, Flora had beamed. Maisie saw how the warmth of her regard included Jeremy, and was glad.

St Mary's Church nestled in the heart of Goddington on the outer fringes of London. Jeremy had bought them a house nearby, close enough to the station for his commute into the capital to work. The salary for his first civvy street job as an official in the Home Office wouldn't stretch that far. "One day though," he promised her. Meanwhile the house was bought courtesy of his father. "It's small change for him," Jeremy assured her. Maisie was uneasy, but acquiesced. There were other priorities. Like the christening, to which Jeremy's song pulled her back.

"The parson's waiting, for me and my gal." And he did a shoe shuffle which made Flora exclaim, "Mercy me." Maisie's heart missed a beat—she grabbed her baby from him just before he slipped. But even the near death of her daughter, as she saw it, or a bit of a blip, as he put it, couldn't dampen their spirits.

Down Goddington High Street in the spring sunshine they bowled, Jeremy with his catlike gait, Flora struggling to keep up, between stone houses and neat shops redolent with the assurance of centuries. They turned into the shaded lane that led to the churchyard. Here ancient graves, elaborate monuments for the wealthy, plain slabs for the rest, were equally weathered into anonymity and overhung by malodorous yew trees.

When Jeremy had first brought Maisie to the church, she'd felt intimidated by its brooding solemnity, the frocked otherness of the choirboys, the incomprehensibility of the service, some of which was in Latin. Jeremy had managed it with the easy nonchalance of someone who belonged, who knew when to sit and stand and kneel, who could wrap around his shoulders the mantle of grace invoked by the mellifluous vicar, and just as easily shrug it off in the church porch as they left.

Today as they approached its flint walls, the sound of applause ruffled the disapproving yew trees and sent a group of sparrows scudding into the air. Connie was clapping, hands stretched past the big belly of her pregnancy and Tim, exuding masculinity beside her, slapped his hands together, then cupped one around his mouth and let out a "Whup, whup." Maisie noted how seamlessly he'd eased his way from university to army to property development, taking in marriage to Connie as part of what life owed him.

Jeremy's mother, Leonora, failed in her best efforts to keep her composure and with an elegant pattering of her hands and a "Bless her," scuttled—if anything Leonora did could be as unrefined as scuttling—to Julia and kissed her on a surprised cheek. Dickie, the baby's grandfather, stood to attention, then chucked her under the chin and said to his son, "Pretty little thing, what? A boy next time perhaps, eh?"

And Jeremy, whom Maisie had known to wither under his father's disapproval, laughed in the old man's face. "You actually laughed," she would tell him later. "You should do it more often."

As Maisie held Julia, she felt she was vindicated—that she and Jeremy had demonstrated the seriousness of their intent, that in marrying they'd been more than another hasty pairing of young people looking for something to cling to in the wreckage of war.

With her mother there to prove that however much poorer her upbringing had been than Jeremy's, there'd at least been beauty and grace in it, even if Flora, unlike herself, had been unable to escape the shadow of her father.

"He was so sorry he could nae come," said Flora. "His health. You know, he was injured..." She didn't have to complete her sentence.

"Poor chap." Dickie thrust his hands in his pocket and Maisie heard coins jingle. "Gallipoli and the Somme, I gather. Brave blighters, those Scots."

"You must be delighted with how well your daughter's done," said Leonora. "And now a baby, the image of our young Alfred. You know we lost a son in the war." She extended a hand for Flora to shake.

Leonora was Connie's aunt, her mother's sister, and Maisie noticed a family likeness in the condescension. Connie, her couture dress straining over her bump, whispered something to Tim. He nodded and chuckled at some private joke, and then shouted to a man wheezing his way towards them through the churchyard, flushed face, coat open and flapping over the beginnings of a paunch.

"Guy Forrester. On my life. Late again. Come on, godfather, you nearly missed the show."

Guy stopped, flustered, tucked in his tie, did up his coat buttons. Tim opened his mouth, ready no doubt, thought Maisie, to press home his advantage. But then a rattly-engined black cab bumped along the walkway and stopped at the entrance to the graveyard. The door opened and Tim's mouth fell slack.

"Nancy, I'm so glad you could make it," was all Maisie could manage.

Her school friend had become Betty Grable. The brown eyes still danced, the smile still turned to dimples in her cheeks. But her hair was no longer plain brown and wavy. It was blond and fixed into elaborate curls at the front and topped at the back with a neat hat. Her breasts filled her jacket which flared over a skirt that may have been too tight for comfort on her hips but that won undisguisable admiration from Tim.

Flora filled the vacuum. "Mercy me, how fashionable you look."

"London suits me." Nancy bent down from her peep-toe high heels and kissed Flora. "It's so nice to see you again, Mrs Munro. And is this my wee goddaughter?" Nancy minced—there was no word for it—past Tim, past Guy, past Dickie, probably past every man she met these days, thought Maisie.

"Julia, meet your Aunt Nancy," she said to her daughter.

"Aunt Nancy. Tsk. That makes me sound like some old boot-face. It's good to see you looking so well, Maisie. And you must be Jeremy."

They eyed each other. Jeremy seemed to be the only man who saw past the teasing exuberance to the woman Maisie knew. Nancy Gillies was the one friend from her childhood who she dared to allow to be part of her present, who understood how far Maisie had travelled and what she'd left behind. Jeremy stretched out a hand in his uncomplicated way and said, "How lovely to meet you." And Nancy leaned forward, and her flirty dimple disappeared as she said, "Mind you look after her."

And then Jeremy put his arm around Maisie, and she felt the warmth of his body and caught his look of what was it, love, pride, boasting, 'Look at the man I am with my wife and my child.'

Connie interrupted the moment. "I'll take the baby, Maisie. The godparents are supposed to carry her."

"In your condition?" Nancy scooped Julia out of Maisie's arms. "Let me," and led the little procession into church. Julia peered over Nancy's shoulder and blinked at the collection of people following behind. Nancy looked over her shoulder too.

And then she winked.

Maisie remembered how Nancy had always winked over her shoulder. At Maisie going up the hill to church. At Wee Jimmy padding behind them both on the way to school. Now it was at Tim following her into the christening. Who was to know this was just what Nancy did? Not Tim. He gawked. Connie scowled.

Maisie didn't care. Let them fight it out between them. It was only a wink.

· · · ● · ● · · ·

"You don't have to go back you know," said Maisie.

She and Flora were alone in the garden. Her mother had carried a blanket out through the French windows and spread it out on the lawn which reached down past a rose garden to a wilderness area that backed onto woodland. Maisie smoothed out the blanket and placed Julia in the middle, the placid baby content to roll around in the sunshine and let her grandmother tickle her toes.

Flora wore a cotton voile dress that she'd adapted from one of Maisie's, the softness of the fabric and the lightness of its pattern gave Flora a young, carefree air, or perhaps it was the weeks of peace that had relaxed the lines on her face. Whatever, now Maisie saw her mother as she remembered her from earliest childhood, the smiling face in the mirror, the pretty blushes in church, and got a glimpse of the woman her mother might have been if she hadn't spent her adult life at the receiving end of violence.

"You could stay here. We've plenty of space." Too much, Maisie could have added. Jeremy assured her she'd get used to it, but she felt they rattled around in the house with more space, it seemed, than all the tenements of her old home put together.

"Your father will be expecting me."

"You could say you need more time."

"It was good of him to let me come at all."

"Good of him? To let you see your granddaughter?"

"He'll be angry if I stay longer."

"What right's he got?"

"He can't manage on his own."

"He should have thought about that before..." She stopped short. Even now, there were too many scars.

Flora picked at the blanket. "He never meant you any harm." A shadow fell over her face.

Maisie knew where that came from, inside where the pain was. She carried the same shadow over her own life and nothing, not her marriage, her home, not the baby even, had dispelled it.

"Why do you make excuses for him?"

"It was the war. He was hurt."

"So were you." And now Maisie allowed herself to start remembering, she couldn't stop. "I spent so many nights under that bed listening to him hurt you. And then that wasn't enough for him—he hurt me, too." She felt the panic, the tightness in her chest. "I thought I was going to die. I was only eight years old Mam, only eight."

She could hear it again, his soup dish crashing against the wall, and him shouting and her Mam shouting. and then someone screaming, screaming, and it's her screaming. And all she can see is a dark shape that blocks out the light and it's his foot and it kicks and kicks until she doesn't know what happens next. And the agony of his boots against her body matches the hurt she feels inside.

"He nearly killed me, Mam." Maisie put her head in her hands as if that would obliterate the memories.

"He nearly killed me. And all because I asked him, 'What's a floozy?'" She felt herself a child again, curled up under the bed, behind the tin trunk, felt the fear that she'd so carefully buried erupt through the layers of failed forgetting, burst out and chill the day. She was as alone as ever, just her and the terror that she'd never shared.

She felt a hand on her arm, then around her shoulders, and she turned and hid her head in her mother's neck, breathed in the comforting smell of her, felt the warmth of her mother's arms around her, the tears on her mother's face, and tried, oh how she tried, to feel safe.

"I'm so sorry. I should have protected you from him." It was the first time Maisie could remember her mother addressing their suffering and the cause of it. Oh, she'd alluded before to the violence. "A bit of a disturbance," she'd call it or said her father had suffered "One of his funny turns," and had inflicted "just a wee hurt." The anguish in Flora's voice made Maisie feel even worse.

"It's no' your fault," she said.

"I should have done better."

"You should have left." Maisie didn't know who to feel angry with, her father for what he'd done, or her mother for putting up with it.

"I'd promised him. As long as we both lived." Flora kissed Maisie's head. "And there was you to think about."

"Not now. Not any longer. There's only yourself now. You can leave. You can stay here. You can be free."

"I couldn't abandon him. He needs me."

"He needs a punchbag. He'll go on hitting you as long as you're there. You told me once he was sick and that may be the truth, only it's a sickness that will kill you, not him. Don't go back, Mam. Please." Maisie took her mother's face in her hands and cradled it, kissed it, stroked her hair. "Please."

But she could see she was losing her. Flora was pulling away, straightening the dress across her shoulders, reaching out for Julia who was grizzling gently on the blanket.

"It's my choice. I made it a long time ago. One day you might understand."

Maisie felt a veil come down between herself and her mother, like the strip of net curtain across the window of the room in the tenement. Through which she saw only the filtered emotions of her mother's inner life—it wasn't hers.

"I won't return, not while he's there. You do realise that don't you? You won't see me again unless you come down here." She had no idea how her words would land with her mother, or how much they might hurt her. Or whether they might at last make her mother choose her over her father.

"You thought the world of him once." Flora picked up Julia and cradled her in her arms. The baby reached out and grabbed at her grandmother's hair.

"Not after that."

"Have you told Jeremy?" Flora was disentangling her hair from Julia's fingers, distracted, tickling the baby under her dribbly chin.

"No," said Maisie.

"You should. What your father did left its scars on you too. Your husband needs to know."

"I don't know how he'd react."

"He's a good man, Maisie. He loves you and Julia dearly. He'd never do anything to hurt either of you. I can tell."

· · · · · · · · · · ·

Flora knelt on the floor in the back bedroom, pulling the thread that ran from the needle in her hand to the hem of Maisie's dress. "There," she said. "It's finished."

They'd worked on the dress together—tight-sleeved, shaped bodice, waist-hugging, with pleats down the left side of the skirt that fell to Maisie's slim mid-calf. The deep green silk fired her red hair which she had fixed back to look like Bette Davis.

"It's beautiful, Mam." Maisie regarded herself in the long mirror.

Flora pulled the thread taut. "My wee girl."

Maisie heard a regret in her mother's voice, as if, after the war, the marriage, the child, this was the more significant point of departure. Their time together was slipping away when they had only just scraped the surface of what was between them. "I'll always be that," she said and wished she could make her words convey her intention. And then she felt a tug and heard a snip and sensed the release as Flora cut the thread and the dress settled around her.

"You look grand," said Flora. "I don't mean grand, grand. I mean just grand."

She wore the dress the day Flora went home. Connie dropped by as they were preparing to leave, parked her car next to theirs in the driveway, sidled around Flora's suitcase pre-positioned on the doorstep, peered upstairs to where Jeremy and Flora were checking there was nothing left behind, and then settled herself on the sofa in the sitting room. Maisie tried not to show her dismay.

Connie slipped off her shoes. "Bloody feet swollen up. Oh, I say, what a nice frock."

"My mother made it."

"I wish she'd make one for me." Connie pulled her maternity dress over her pregnant stomach. "I'm fed up with feeling like Humpty Dumpty in a smock."

"She's leaving today."

"Oh, what a shame, I've left it too late." Connie winced and rubbed her bump. "I hope the little bastard's not as vicious when it's born. The thing is, Tim won't even look at me in this state."

"Jeremy said I was beautiful when I was pregnant."

"Well Tim's not Jeremy. Apart from my stomach proving his virility, I think he'd rather I disappeared from sight for the duration."

For the first time, Maisie detected a vulnerability in her friend. "I could make a dress for you," she said.

"Oh would you?" Connie brightened. "Something seductive. I've got competition. Not that I haven't always. Anything drifting by that takes Tim's fancy, and he's off. Normally I can rein him in, but like this I'm not in such a strong position. It doesn't help that you got pregnant first, when everyone knows that Jeremy..." She stopped.

"Let me carry it for you, Mumsy." Jeremy's voice in the hall.

"Mumsy?" Connie's eyebrows arched. "Where did that come from? But then he always was the accepting type."

Perhaps if Maisie's emotions hadn't been so invested in Flora's departure, she would have questioned her friend on what everyone knew about Jeremy, or what it was about her mother that had to be accepted. Or she would have paid more attention when Connie asked her about "that woman's" circumstances.

"What woman?"

"The other godmother."

Instead, Maisie shrugged her off with, "Nancy Gillies? Career girl," and went out to help Flora on with her coat and watch as she settled her hat on her head and secured it with a hatpin. Jeremy pattered down the stairs carrying Julia in one arm and Flora's bag in the other, agile as a cat, but it still made Maisie's heart stop that he was so casual about their daughter's safety. So she ran to take the baby and organised her husband to put Flora's luggage in the car and set Julia on her grandmother's lap in the back seat.

"I can see you're busy." Connie levered herself off the sofa and waddled out the front door. "I'll leave you to sort out your mother."

Maisie was distracted, telling Jeremy to turn the car around in the driveway without bumping into the camellias or scratching against the privet hedge, all the while wondering how her childhood wounds would ever get to heal without Flora's emotional sticking plaster. So she barely heard Connie mutter, "Tell your friend to watch out, though. I won't let Tim go without a fight." And she was locking the front door when she heard an engine roar and turned to see Connie reversing at speed up the drive and out onto the road.

CHAPTER SEVEN

JUNE 1954

Maisie had never bought a dozen eggs before. She'd saved up her food coupons for weeks and counted them out now onto the counter of the grocer's shop in Sewell, the small town closest to her village.

"Just think, Mrs Stanhope, soon you'll be able to buy whatever you like again." The grocer's blunt fingers fastened the lids of the grey egg cartons on the marble counter beside salty-smelling joints of bacon and dried out slabs of cheese. He looked at her through the condescension of his half-moon glasses and smiled at Julia, grown from placid baby into contented child, gazing awestruck beside her.

Maisie didn't like to admit that even before the war had brought food rationing, she'd never known anyone buy so many eggs, not in her tenement at least. If she did confess, it would be one more story for him to circulate about the Scottish woman who the butcher said bought bits of meat that no-one else would touch. So Maisie bit her tongue, buried her guilt at the extravagance, and carried on.

"A pound of flour please."

Mr George stepped heavily up his ladder and surveyed the shelves that lined the gloomy back wall of his shop. "Plain or self-raising?" A split-second pause and she felt his cunning eyes gleam before he asked, "What's it for?"

"My birthday cake." Julia jumped up and down with dutiful excitement "I'll be five." She held up the fingers of one hand and beamed.

"That's nice, isn't it? Happy birthday Julia. Such a good girl. What kind of cake?"

"Angel food." As soon as she said the words, Maisie regretted her mistake. "It's American."

"Oh." He made it sound like an accusation. "Most people like a Victoria sponge."

"I had American friends during the war," Maisie said.

"Of course, I didn't mean anything by it. Better make it self-raising." Mr George hurried down his step ladder and put the packet of flour on the counter, pushed his glasses up his nose, and stuck his thumbs into the waistband of his expansive stripy apron.

She finished her list, her shopping lined up on the marble counter, and Mr George rang up the prices, Julia singing, "Ping, ping, ping," along with the cash register.

"Cheerful, just like Mr Stanhope," Mr George said.

It sounded like another accusation to Maisie, one she knew to be true. Her daughter had inherited Jeremy's equable temperament as well as his mellow looks. She handed over her pound note and put the groceries into her string bag, all except the eggs which Julia carried stretched out in front of her like an offering. Mr George ran round and opened the shop door with its jangly bell, but didn't bow to her like he did to her mother-in-law.

"I want to sit in front with you," said Julia.

But Maisie refused her. "Daddy says it isn't safe."

So the little girl climbed into the rear of the car parked at the kerb right outside the shop on Sewell High Street and sat with the eggs on her knees while Maisie drove to their village, crunched up the gravel drive and let them both in through the front door of the house. Where on the hall mat they found an envelope addressed to Miss Julia Stanhope, with a birthday card and a pound note inside and the words, *"Sorry I can't be with you tomorrow. Please get yourself something nice. Your loving godmother, Nancy."*

"That's good of your aunty to remember. She has such a busy life. I'll put the money in the post office for when you're older."

To herself she wondered why Nancy had sent money as a present. It was the kind of thing Jeremy did. "Buy yourself a new frock," he'd say and tuck a few extra pounds into the housekeeping, himself not having the time or interest to go shopping with her, and she not having any money outside what he provided, however generously. Sometimes she wished she could be like Nancy, and have more to fill her days than making angel food cake; something of her own beyond nurturing her husband and child. Something that told the world, and herself, that she amounted to more than Mrs Jeremy Stanhope.

But she was happy, she told herself as she unpacked the string bag, put the milk in the new fridge, the butter on the cold slab in the larder, the flour and sugar on the shelves above. She no longer felt intimidated by the house. They'd grown into it. They'd built a garage at the front and turned the fourth bedroom into a sewing room where Maisie's latest creation hung from the picture rail, a birthday dress for Julia, with a billowy full skirt and a wide bouncy sash.

It was only when she opened the front door to travelling salesmen and they asked to speak to "the lady of the house," that she realised that her accent wasn't English enough, her bearing wasn't grand enough and the scarf she wrapped around her head to do her housework wasn't posh enough for her to be accepted.

She pushed the thought down as she cooked Julia's cake, separated the eggs, beat up the whites, added the sugar, sifted in the flour, put it in her new electric oven, then waited in nail-biting anticipation for it to transform into the airy sweetness that would be the envy of her daughter's little friends.

··•••••••··

"Look, it's perfect," she said to Jeremy when he came in from work with a newspaper under his arm and a bunch of flowers as an apology for being late home. "Angel food cake."

"Clever girl." He brushed past her and stood at the kitchen sink, staring out of the window at the darkening garden and washing his hands. Not speaking. She retrieved his dinner which had dried out in the oven.

"Is something wrong?"

Usually he kissed her. Tonight, he opened a kitchen drawer and took out his napkin in its silver ring inscribed with his initials, sat down, and draped the cloth over his knees. When Maisie set down the plate of shrivelled lamb chops in front of him, he gave them a desultory poke.

"What's this?" he asked.

Normally he'd joke over culinary disasters, sing "Animal crackpots in my soup," at the very least. Tonight, he pushed the plate away. The cutlery clattered.

"It's not like you." She tried to soothe him, made him a cup of tea and tipped his spoiled dinner into the bin. Then she heard sounds that echoed from her childhood: him rustling open his newspaper, rifling through the pages, folding them over. Crack. She jumped. "Did something happen?"

"This." He slammed the paper down and pointed to an article circled in black ink.

Maisie picked up the newspaper and read out loud, "'In the death of Dr Alan Turing, mathematics and science have lost a great original thinker.'" She stopped, not knowing what to make of it and his face giving no clues. "I'm so sorry. Did you know him?"

Jeremy nodded. Maisie read the name again. It meant nothing to her and as the article was so short and so far back in the newspaper, she wondered how important the man could have been.

Finally, Jeremy spoke. "I worked with him during the war."

"I've never heard of him."

"That's because you never take any notice of anything around you, other than this bloody house and the bloody garden and, and... your bloody angel food cake."

Maisie stepped back against the cooker. She felt her heart pound and a cold sweat break out on her face. She didn't dare look at him. Julia was upstairs in bed, and she was only three steps from the back door. Which wasn't locked. And besides, this was Jeremy, not her father. It wasn't the same. It couldn't be.

His chair grated on the floor. She braced herself, closed her eyes, smelt her own fear. And then she heard him sigh and say, "I'm sorry." She opened her eyes: she was dizzy with relief. "That was uncalled for," he said. "There was no excuse for speaking to you like that."

Would this be the end of it? She fiddled with the newspaper, re-read the article. Waited.

He still wouldn't look at her. "He killed himself. Cyanide. There was an inquest. The department was involved."

Someone had drawn a big black asterisk at the bottom of the newspaper and beside it she read, "'The Coroner Mr JAK Ferns remarked that he was forced to the conclusion that it was a deliberate act for, with a man of that type, one would never know what his mental processes were going to do next. He might easily become unbalanced and unstable, and the coroner thought his mind had become unstable when he decided to end his days.'

"Mercy me. Whatever does that mean, 'A man of that type?'"

Jeremy worked his jaw so hard the veins on his temples stood out till she thought they'd burst. "The type of man who's so bloody brilliant he practically won the whole bloody war single-handed. A complete bloody hero. That type of man."

She heard his footsteps on the stairs long after she'd gone to bed. She waited for him to come into their bedroom, but he went on by. She didn't call out to him, didn't know what words would bridge the gulf, and wasn't sure enough of her own feelings, or if he touched her, how she would respond. Then she heard the door to the spare room shut. In the morning she heard her daughter's voice, "What are you doing in here, Daddy?" and she took him a cup of tea. He'd recovered himself enough to sing happy birthday to Julia over breakfast and make her laugh with his silly versions of the song. His feelings about the suicide can't have run so deep after all, she thought, to have been so quickly forgotten or easily buried.

· · · ● · ● · ● · ·

To Maisie's directions Jeremy pushed back furniture, rolled up carpets, blew up balloons and draped paper chains looping from the front hall to the dining room. There she set plates of dainty sandwiches filled with cheese and tomato and chicken paste, and chocolate biscuits and fresh scones topped with cream and strawberry jam. When Julia and her little friends gathered around the tea table, hair brushed, shoes polished, frilly dresses starched to attention, to Maisie's embarrassment Jeremy sang, "Have you heard, I married an angel," and kissed her. The twelve little girls covered their faces with their hands and giggled "Ugh" and then sighed, "Oooh" as she brought out the angel food cake.

"That looks nice." Connie stood behind her daughter's chair. She was the only mother at the party, Calypso being a year younger than Julia, and much less compliant, requiring a firm hand, so Connie said, to stop her from wrecking the entire event.

"Have some." Maisie held out a plate, but Connie shook her head and touched her stomach.

"Watching my weight again. I just hope it's a boy this time, then I can stop. Our marriage wouldn't survive another one."

Maisie looked across the tea table at Jeremy, paper hat on his head, blowing on a hooter, rolling his eyes, making the little girls laugh, popping a balloon, making them scream, party dresses wilting in the summer heat. He'd started spending the occasional night at his club in town, "as chaps do." Maisie told herself that the unease she felt about it was down to her lack of familiarity with the world of chaps and clubs.

On those nights Julia would climb into the big double bed in her parents' room, with the picture of Jeremy in his army uniform on the bedside table and cuddle up to Maisie who would tell her about Scotland and Julia would fall asleep sucking her thumb. Then Maisie would turn over, wrap her arms around herself and wonder if this was all there would ever be between herself and Jeremy. But if she sometimes regretted his reserve, she knew, watching him lead Julia and her friends in a conga out into the garden, that there was nothing he would do to threaten their marriage.

Connie stayed behind after the party. "I'll help you to clear up," she said. Then, shooing Calypso and Julia out into the garden to play, she sat down in the kitchen with her feet up on a chair while Maisie washed up the dishes and Jeremy ferried a child home.

"At least you don't have to worry about him that way," said Connie, with an emphasis on "that" as if Maisie should understand everything involved in her choice of words.

"I don't worry about him at all." Maisie piled the left-over sandwiches on a plate and put them into the fridge. When she turned around, she found Connie seemed unaware she'd even spoken.

"The thing about Tim is he enjoys the chase. Normally I make sure it's just a chase, but now I've blown up like a barrage balloon it's a bit iffy. I'm going to need some more of those nice dresses you make. Sexier this time if we're to survive."

"But he's devoted to you. He told me so that day in Cambridge."

"That was ten years ago," said Connie. "And back then, of course, he needed my father's money. At least you don't have that problem with Jeremy."

Maisie felt her cheeks burn. She washed the tea plates and stacked them on the draining board. When she turned to get more off the table, she saw her friend shift in her chair, wincing as much, it seemed, from doubt as discomfort.

"It's serious this time." Connie uncrossed and re-crossed her feet on the kitchen chair. "He's been after the same woman for quite a while."

"Do you know who she is?" The plates hardly needed washing. Maisie dipped them in the water and stacked them to drain.

"As a matter of fact, I do." Connie picked an imagined cake crumb off her dress. "I hate to say it, but it's that friend of yours. Nancy. Sod's law that we're inextricably bound together because of Julia."

Nancy. She of the winks over the shoulder and the blooming hips. Maisie never thought her childhood friend had meant anything by it. She took a plate off the draining board and started rubbing it down with a sodden tea towel.

"The trouble is..." Connie's voice wobbled, her lower lip quivered. She was closer to tears than Maisie could have thought. "I do actually love him. Oh, I know everyone thinks it's a marriage of convenience, his mother's breeding, my father's money, and perhaps it is for him. But I love the bastard, I really do. And I don't want to lose him, especially not to a floozy like that. Don't look so bloody shocked. It's what she is." Connie fumbled in her handbag, pulled out a cigarette and lit it. She sat back and blew out a stream of smoke. "You're lucky with Jeremy. I know he's not the sparkliest, but he's a good man."

Maisie washed and dried the dishes and put the party rubbish out in the dustbin. Yes, Jeremy was a good man, though she tried to remember when they'd last shared the passion on show between Tim and Connie. But she was happy, she reminded herself as she and Jeremy tucked Julia into bed and their daughter kissed them, "Goodnight, Mummy, Goodnight, Daddy," as their heads touched over hers.

• • • • • • • • • •

The heat of the day continued after dark and later in their bedroom, even with the curtains drawn back and the big bay window full open, there was an oppressive airlessness. However long she lived here, Maisie felt she'd never get used to this cloying southern stickiness. She lay beside Jeremy with only a sheet over their bare bodies. Outside an owl hooted. There was a brutal scream and Maisie flinched. Jeremy laughed.

"It's only a vixen. Silly girl."

"Tim's having an affair with Nancy." Maisie rolled over and propped herself up on an elbow. Jeremy was on his back, gazing up at the ceiling. His eyes flickered in the moonlight. He was awake, but not talking, which annoyed her. "I said Tim's having an affair."

"I heard you."

"Can you believe it?"

"Of Tim, yes."

"But he and Connie have always been such a couple. That whole palaver about the trip to Cambridge. It was all about her getting to see Tim. It had nothing to do with you. They'd been bonking in his room when I went in."

Jeremy chuckled. "You're a goose. Of course they had. It was the war. Everyone was bonking everyone as if their lives depended on it." He leaned towards her, and she felt his hand run over her face, then onto her shoulder and down her arm.

"You weren't."

His hand reached her hip and stopped. "No."

She wished she could see his expression. She wished his hand would go on down her body. It didn't. The moment passed. She sensed it was her fault it was spoilt and felt regret.

"D'you think I should speak to Nancy?"

"Definitely not."

"But I introduced them. It was my fault."

"If it hadn't been Nancy, it would only have been someone else. That's the way Tim is. They'll sort themselves out one way or another. Come on, let's go to sleep." And he took his hand off her hip and turned over.

Maisie sat up in bed. The moon peered in the bay window, its light harsher than the gaslight of her childhood. It silvered the contours of her husband's back, touched the veneered sets of his and hers bedroom furniture, and picked out the soft chairs where their clothes lay folded together.

"But he loves Connie really."

Jeremy's reply was muffled.

"I can't hear you."

He turned onto his back. "I said it's possible to love more than one person at a time."

"Not like that."

"Even like that."

"You wouldn't do that, would you?"

"What?" In the moonlight his face was like ice.

"Love another woman?"

The ice cracked. He smiled.

"No, I'll never do that. You're the only woman I'll ever want."

She lay against his back, put her arm around his body, felt the warmth of his stomach and then reached her hand down to his flaccid cock. Another time, she thought. After all, she was happy. She blamed the unsettling moon for her sleepless night.

· · · · ●·●· · · ·

Jeremy was right. Connie and Tim sorted themselves out. The baby was born that Christmas. "A boy, Tim's ecstatic, the floozy's in retreat," Connie enthused as she squeezed her post-natal bulges into a girdle and sheathed it in the slinky gown that Maisie had run up for her to wear to a New Year party in Chelsea. She gave Maisie an envelope—"For you, for the dress"—and when Maisie opened it, she found a cheque made out to her and signed with her friend's name at the bottom. It was the first money she'd earned since the war and she felt it light a small flame of independence inside her.

When the child was christened that wet spring, Connie was triumphant. "The floozy's defeated," she whispered as she walked arm in arm with Tim who carried their son Frederick Christopher Beaufort into church.

And then in the summer's heatwave, when Connie brought little Freddie with Calypso to Julia's sixth birthday party, she announced, "The floozy's been ditched. Good riddance."

At Julia's insistence there was angel food cake, and a conga, eventually, right at the end, when Jeremy appeared, having stayed over at his club the night before, arriving just in time to be mobbed by the crowd of little girls from Julia's Church of England school.

Connie jiggled Freddie on her hip and sighed as Jeremy led the little girls dancing around the garden. "He's such a good father."

"Yes, but..." He hadn't kissed her, barely looked at her when he came in. Sometimes she felt like a bystander in his life, while her own, as she headed for her thirties, was slipping by.

"But nothing. Look how he is with Julia. Oh do stop whining Freddie. Here you hold him." Connie passed the baby to Maisie who stroked his head while he put a hand into his mouth and started to cry in earnest. "And at least you don't have to have another sproglet just to keep him. I knew I should have brought nanny."

A few days later a birthday card arrived for Julia with money inside. Again. Maisie was irritated, it was as if her friend judged her time to be too important to spend it buying a birthday present for her goddaughter. Then she read the note in her friend's floral handwriting. *"I'm moving back to Scotland to be near my parents. Please get something nice for Julia. Love Nancy."*

"She couldn't take the competition," said Connie when Maisie phoned to tell her about her rival's departure. "It must have been those clothes you made for me, ha, ha. You should go into business."

"You were right about Tim and Connie," Maisie told Jeremy when he came home from work that evening, late again.

He poured them each a gin and tonic and held up his glass. "Told you. Chin, chin," he said. "To their happiness."

"And to ours." Maisie clinked her glass to his, but she wondered if they still had the same understanding of happiness. Baking cakes in an empty house wasn't going to be enough.

CHAPTER EIGHT

FEBRUARY 1958

I t was easy to pick out the house in the barefaced brick terrace down the backstreet.

Neat rows of green shoots poked through the brown earth of the garden behind the chain-link fence. There was no sign of life inside the house and Maisie checked the number against the address she'd copied off the postcard— "skilled seamstress looking for work"—in the window of Goddington Post Office. But as she clattered up the garden path, Maisie had a sense of being watched. On the doorstep, she rang the bell and then scanned the windows. Net curtains covered the one downstairs, upstairs both were shut tight. All were in darkness. A mellow "tonkle, tonkle" sounded to her left. She turned and saw bamboo chimes blowing in the wind under a rowan tree by the front door.

She rang the bell again and was about to give up when the door opened, and a man appeared. He was a good deal younger than Maisie, a little taller than her, and she guessed that under his heavy black overcoat, he was thin. Bare feet poked out below black trousers that ended just above his ankles. His jet-black hair was plastered around his pale, oval face.

"Mrs Stanhope," Maisie said. "I've come to speak to Mrs Ling."

The young man's expression remained impassive. "Ah yes," he said. "I'll call her."

Maisie expected to be asked in, and stepped forward. but to her surprise, the young man closed the front door, and she was left on the doorstep. She put her head to the door and heard voices, and somewhere inside the house a door banged. Then nothing. Then suddenly the front door opened again, and she found herself face to face with a young woman, her black hair cut in a fierce chin-length bob and piercing eyes set above high cheekbones. She was wearing a coat, like the young man who hovered behind her.

"Mrs Ling?" said Maisie.

The woman turned to the young man and spoke to him, urgent words, ending with a kindly nod and a smile at Maisie. The young man translated. "She says you are very welcome. And she says to tell you her name is Tseng Hsiao Ling. You should call her Hsiao Ling. She says you can come in."

A corridor ran from the front door to the back of the house from where, through a curtain of trailing beads, came wisps of steam, the smell of fish cooking and a clanging of pans and loud voices. Light spilled along the drab linoleum floor and the walls were heavy with condensation. The young man opened a door into a room at the front of the house.

It exploded with colour. Red banners with gold lettering hung above the fireplace. A red lantern was suspended from the central light, another stood on an elaborately carved low table in the middle of the room. A red, green and gold dragon's head glared at Maisie from the opposite corner. Alongside her was a small shrine with a white statue of a woman on it, sitting with one leg folded under her and the other raised in front and bent at the knee. One of her arms was stretched out, the hand facing downwards in a gesture of sultry forgiveness. In front of the statue were three satsumas and a bunch of red and gold chrysanthemums, and beside her three joss sticks smouldered in a bottle, threads of sweet-scented smoke winding above her head.

But Maisie saw past the decorations to the hallmarks of her childhood poverty: the bare floorboards, the two battered chairs, the cold hearth, and pushed against the wall, a bed. Not even its bright red cover could hide the fact that this was a best room where people slept.

"Where shall I...?" Maisie felt awkward.

The young man pulled forward one of the chairs, "Please sit, please sit." He knelt down by the fireplace and turned on the gas and lit a match and crack, pop, the fire burst into flame. Hsiao Ling meanwhile picked up a plate of white cakes from the table and held them out towards Maisie and smiled encouragingly.

"Sticky rice cakes," said the young man. "They're for our new year." He smiled at Maisie's questioning face. "The lunar new year."

She took a cake and put it on her lap. "I came about the sewing...." she started.

By the time she'd finished, her head was thumping with pain. It had taken twice as long as she'd expected to negotiate with Hsiao Ling. The young man translated, following them from the heat of the gas fire downstairs to a cold room upstairs. "Hsiao Ling's workroom," he said. A thin young woman in a brown overcoat sitting at a treadle sewing machine barely paused as she looked up and smiled while her feet jigged on the treadle and the needle of the machine jagged up and down. Beside her was a pile of fabric and behind her a curtain screened off a double bed, with three pillows along the top.

Then Maisie was taken downstairs through the bead curtain to a lean-to at the rear of the house where orchid plants hung on pieces of bark suspended in the humid air. There she was introduced to an older man—"My brother, Hsiao Ling's husband"—who was frying fish in a deep pan over the stove, sprinkling it with spices from an aluminium shaker. He smiled and nodded and spoke to his wife in a guttural tone. A much older man sat on an upturned tub in the corner of the room, peeling potatoes and tossing them into a bucket. "Our father," said the young man. And then he pointed to a tiny woman swathed in a bright green shawl sitting in an easy chair in the corner. "Our mother," he said.

Finally, in the front room, by now stifling hot, she'd listened to endless conversations as Hsiao Ling debated with her brother-in-law and then her husband, who left his cooking to join in, whatever Maisie said about the timing and pricing of her sewing.

But her persistence paid off. When she stood up to leave, explaining she had to collect her daughter from school, she knew she'd got herself a seamstress for her dressmaking business, one who would work from home while she, Maisie, set up a boutique, that would sell to young women their bridal dreams, and in between times, provide their mothers with outfits that would make them feel young again.

At the front door, under the tonkle of the bamboo wind chimes, she turned to shake hands with Hsiao Ling. "Thank you."

Hsiao Ling held out a red packet and nodded to her guest to take it. Maisie wasn't sure what to do, not wanting to offend, but not knowing what was in the package, or what kind of transaction it might imply. She looked to the young man for an explanation.

"My sister says it's for your daughter. It's a gift. She says to tell her happy new year."

"That's so kind of you." Maisie felt the package. It seemed there was money inside and it was on the tip of her tongue to say she didn't approve of giving money as gifts. It was bad enough that Nancy did it and these people were strangers. Flora would have said it smacked of charity, a sign they couldn't cope. But that was a different time and place. Maisie put the packet in her bag, next to the rice cake that she'd secreted there, that was now congealed into a sticky mess.

Hsiao Ling and her brother-in-law smiled on the doorstep and then went back inside their house and shut the door, leaving Maisie to retrace her steps down the garden path.

· · · · ● · ● · · · ·

"It's a sixpence." Julia prised open the red packet that evening. Pink-skinned and smelling of lemon soap after her bath, she was wearing a tartan dressing gown, and her hair, brushed by Maisie till it shone in the firelight, was held back by a plastic hair clasp in the shape of a butterfly. Maisie said it was too childish for a nine-year-old, but Julia insisted she liked her butterfly clasps and would wear them regardless of what anyone said.

"Fancy giving a sixpence and it's ages past new year."

Jeremy looked at her over his newspaper. "It's a lucky six-pence."

Julia turned the sixpence over in her plump hands. "It looks like an ordinary sixpence to me. How do you know it's lucky?"

"I don't know, do I?" Jeremy sat back in his easy chair, stretched out his legs, crossed his slippered feet over each other, and waited for whatever drollness his daughter came up with next.

"Then why do you say something if you don't know it's true?"

"If we could only say things that we knew to be true, we'd not say much at all." Jeremy laughed, and when Julia looked perplexed, he laughed even more.

"You are silly, Daddy." Julia put the sixpence back in its red packet. "But I'll keep this sixpence, and when I'm grown up and you're very old, we'll see who was right."

Jeremy appeared settled these days, thought Maisie, enjoying their daughter's growing independence, relaxed about her plans for what he called her ladies' emporium. "You need some pin money," he'd said originally, but as the reality grew closer, she'd felt him draw away. Now, as she talked about her encounter with Hsiao Ling, he took refuge in his newspaper.

"Working wife. A pioneer. That's my girl."

· · · ● · ● · · · ·

By the time that year's cricket season started, Maisie's dream was taking noisy shape. She signed the lease on Mr George's old grocer's shop, which had been defeated by the new self-service supermarket up the road.

A bemused Jeremy was dragged in to envision how the out-dated counter and drab shelving would make way for the light décor and soft furnishings of Sewell's first bridal boutique. He'd made the transfers into the bank account she'd opened so she could pay the bills herself, his money joining the housekeeping she'd saved up over the years. Connie chipped in with a con-tribution, "Though in return I want control over the interior design and first dibs at your frocks," she said. And then the builders had moved in with their hammers and drills and saws, shaking their heads over the cost of the marble shipped in from Italy and the plush carpeting that Maisie, at Connie's insistence, had ordered from Belgium.

The cricket season was in full swing when Jeremy's parents, arriving for Sunday lunch, announced they were flying to Naples on holiday. Dickie was dressed in his cricket whites to take his son to watch the match on the green that afternoon. Leonora wore a floral print, her powdered face and permed hair concealing—as Maisie had learned—a sharp mind.

"I want to see Pompeii." Dickie watched with disapproving eyes as Jeremy sliced into the Sunday roast.

"Father, I can carve, you know." Jeremy fumbled with the long knife and then cut into the rib of beef which spilled its red juices onto the carving platter. "It's perfectly cooked, Maisie, you've done us proud." He laid a slice on his father's plate. "It'll be too hot for you in Pompeii."

Dickie picked up his wine glass. "It should be cool by October."

"We're taking a villa in Naples." Leonora spooned boiled cabbage and potatoes onto her husband's plate. "Is there horse radish, Maisie? No? Never mind dear, we'll manage. I want to see the museums. They've been much-restored I'm told. No fat on mine please, Jeremy. You're sitting very quietly, Julia. What a good girl you are."

Julia swung her legs. Maisie knew that now she'd been praised for sitting in silence, she'd hardly say a word for the rest of the meal.

"Why don't you go by train?" Maisie asked. "It must be a lovely journey through the Alps."

"Never been on a plane. Want to do it before I pop my old clogs."

"It's no' safe," said Maisie.

"Nonsense, dear. Everyone flies these days. It's quite the thing." Leonora spooned vegetables onto Jeremy's plate.

"That still doesnae make it safe." Maisie watched the red blood from the joint spill over the edge of the carving platter and stain the tablecloth. She didn't notice Jeremy catch his mother's eye and put an anxious finger to his lips, or his father shake his head and roll his eyes, or Julia look around the table in solemn silence at the discomfort of the adults.

"You haven't seen how easy it is for a plane to crash." She felt palpitations in her chest. "It only takes a screw to come loose or someone to flip the wrong switch. Or they can run out of fuel, or be hit by a bit of flak, or run into a mountain." She knew she was talking herself into a panic, but she couldn't stop.

"Well, that's not going to happen nowadays, is it darling?"

Maisie looked from her husband to her father-in-law to her mother-in-law. The assured incomprehension in their faces made it worse. "You haven't seen it, like I have."

"Steady on, old girl." Even Jeremy seemed annoyed.

There was a squeaking sound; Julia was folding her knife and fork together on her obediently clean plate. Jeremy said to her "Why don't you go outside and play, poppet, and I'll come and get you for pudding?" Julia patted her mouth with her serviette and then rolled it up and put it beside her plate. She kissed Maisie. "Don't be sad, Mummy," words which landed like darts, before she ran out.

Jeremy stretched across the table and took Maisie's hand. "The war's been over a long time, darling." His hairline was receding which made his face more exposed, more vulnerable.

"But planes still crash."

"It can't have been that dreadful. We did win, after all." Leonora positioned her knife and fork together with restrained precision.

"You don't understand." None of them did. Not even Jeremy. None of them sitting around the table had seen the planes that thundered out, sputtered back. They hadn't heard the silences or the screaming madness of young men who'd seen too much. "The first plane I ever saw crashed. A flying fortress. So-called. It came in so low over the forest, I thought it was going to land on me. It was as if it was in slow motion, coming out of the sky, falling, falling, until—"

Maisie brought a hand down, gliding over the table and then banged it down so the wine glasses tinkled, and Leonora started back in her chair. "After that it was every day until by the time D-day arrived, we had one hundred planes landing a day, crashes, engines on fire, undercarriages retracted, ambulances, fire engines. You probably think those bombers were big powerful aeroplanes, I suppose that's what they told you on Pathé News. But they weren't. They were like,"—Maisie searched around for words that surfaced out of painful memories—"glorified tin cans."

Dickie quaffed at his wine glass. "They've improved aviation safety since then."

Maisie turned on him. "You didn't see those boys come back shot to pieces, with frostbite, blue sometimes from lack of oxygen."

"At least they came back." Dickie shifted in his chair. "Unlike our young Alfred."

"Don't, Dickie, please don't." Leonora's make-up couldn't conceal the emotion in her face. She stood up and started clattering the plates, stacking them up, clinking the cutlery, banging the lids onto the serving dishes. Jeremy tried to intervene. "Someone has to do it, and I can't sit and listen to this any longer." When he wrestled the stack of plates from her hands, she sat down as heavily as such an elegant person could and gazed bleakly at her husband.

Maisie put her hands under the table and clasped them together, wrung them around where no-one could see her shaking turmoil. She tried to feel sympathy for her in-laws and their loss. But all she could feel was the sweaty terror of war through the hazy peace of their Sunday afternoon. She stood up and picked up the carving platter. Its weight steadied her hands, but when she put it down on the kitchen table and saw the congealed mess of meat, she thought she'd be sick.

"It's over Maisie, it's all gone, it's past." Jeremy rinsed the plates and stacked them in the kitchen sink.

"I was only seventeen, Jeremy."

"I know, I know."

"You get on with your life, and then just when you think everything's all right, boom, it jumps up and hits you. Like it's been there, the bogeyman sitting in the corner all that time, waiting to pull you down again." She pressed her fingers on her eyes as if she could block out the sights. "But don't worry, I'll be all right."

"That's my girl." The worried frown on Jeremy's face disappeared. He wiped his hands on a tea towel and twisted his fingers through her curls. "See if you can patch things up with my parents. They don't always show it, but they do miss my brother."

"I will. But I still don't think they should fly to Italy."

"And perhaps don't mention the shop." He kissed her head. "It might be a step too far for them today."

When they went back into the dining room together, Julia was sitting at the table, hands folded neatly on her lap, listening wide-eyed to her grandparents talk about Naples.

"Can we go there too?" she asked her parents.

"One day maybe," said Jeremy.

"Can we fly?"

Chapter Nine

October 1958

J eremy took the day off work to drive his parents to Heathrow. Maisie was in her dressing gown making breakfast when he came downstairs in a pair of dark trousers and a yellow jacket.

"You'll be noticed," she teased him.

"You never know who you'll bump into at the airport."

It was still dark outside. Crisp, autumnal, pre-dawn quiet. His parents had been right, Maisie thought. Now that October had arrived, it should be cool in Naples.

"Tell your parents I hope they enjoy their flight." She stood on the doorstep and held out a cheek for him to kiss, which he did, and then crunched across the gravel to the garage. "And you be careful driving."

He turned and smiled at her, nodded, then reversed the car out of the garage, turned it around, and drove off, the car a black shadow on the driveway, him invisible inside.

She went about her day, walked Julia to school, then, since Jeremy had taken the car, took a taxi to Sewell to her bridal boutique. She'd pushed the builders over the refurbishments, they'd sucked their teeth and warned of delays, she'd insisted it must be open for the start of the new school year. She'd prevailed, and now she sat on the Louis Quinze chair Connie had chosen, as if

Chippendale wasn't good enough, her mother-in-law had said. Julia was at school, her husband on his way to Heathrow and she looked at the idle rolls of fabric and rows of hopeful dresses, waiting for the tinkle of the door that announced a customer.

At lunchtime she locked the shop, hung up the elegant "Closed" sign and went home, listening to her transistor radio in the kitchen while poaching a solitary egg.

Jeremy should be back soon, should have been back already. He'd probably stayed to watch his parents' plane take off. She hoped he hadn't had an accident; he could be absent-minded with his driving. She'd stay in to meet him and they could spend the afternoon together. The shop wouldn't suffer. The news came on and she lent it half an ear. Jeremy was always urging her to take more interest. The first women peers were taking their seats in the House of Lords, MPs would attend Parliament next day after their summer recess. The Government was doing something or other. It rumbled on.

And then she heard the words, "A flight to Italy has been reported missing."

So few words, so much significance.

Maisie turned up the radio, but the news had already rolled on. She wondered if she'd misheard and whether Jeremy had heard at all. She switched the transistor over. Light music. She switched back again. Perhaps he'd caught the news on the car radio, or at a pub if he'd stopped for a drink, and then turned back to the airport. Or perhaps he'd been too shocked to drive at all. But then surely, he'd have found a phone box and called her. She went into the breakfast room and checked that the handset of the phone was on its cradle, which it was. If he'd phoned, she'd have heard.

She took the radio into the breakfast room and phoned Heathrow and then the Foreign Office and then Heathrow again, listening to phones ring out and fiddling with the radio to catch news bulletins until it was time to collect Julia from school.

"What's wrong Mummy?" The child wasn't usually so perceptive.

"Something's happened." Then Maisie realised she didn't know what she could tell her daughter, or how Julia might react and whether she could deal with that and the uncertainty. "Go to your bedroom and read a book until teatime."

"But Mummy—"

Maisie buried her head in her hands and wished she knew where Jeremy was. "Do as you're told." And then she felt even worse. She hadn't meant to shout.

Her daughter turned her back and thumped up the stairs, pulling on the bannister, dragging her satchel behind her.

The afternoon news brought confirmation of a type. A British European Airways plane had crashed in Italy. Dickie had insisted on taking a British flight. Maisie went into the breakfast room and dialled the Foreign Office again and held on while the phone rang out in an empty office somewhere in Whitehall. She was holding on for Heathrow when she heard a car in the drive.

Jeremy came in through the French windows, a blaze of glory in his yellow jacket, carrying a bunch of red and orange chrysanthemums and wearing sunglasses, smiling. He was unusually rosy, he must have had a good day. She tried to work out how to tell him, tried to form her mouth around the right words.

His face fell. "Something's happened." He pulled off his glasses.

"There's been a plane crash in Italy." She felt like an assassin. "A British plane." She pulled out a chair, and he sat down with a whumph, as if all the air had gone out of him. She took the flowers from his slack hands. They were rolled in a piece of brown paper that was wet. She put them on the draining board and searched for words that might make things better. "I'm so sorry."

"It can't be true."

She put her arms around his shoulders and rested her cheek on his head.

He pushed her away and held his arms across his body and rocked like it was a physical pain. "Perhaps it's not—"

"Theirs? Perhaps—"

"How did I not know?"

"It's only just been on the news. I suppose there's a chance—"

Julia ran into the kitchen. "Daddy, Daddy, guess what..." and fell silent. She stroked her father's knee, and he clutched her like she was a life raft on the flood tide of his grief. Maisie wondered why she hadn't been able to provide the same degree of comfort. She made her daughter a sandwich and sent her back upstairs.

Jeremy locked himself in his study and she heard him on the phone, alternately talking and crying. She wondered who was at the other end—Connie, perhaps—she was after all his cousin, although she wondered why it wasn't herself to whom he turned.

At six o'clock he joined her to watch the news on television, squatting grim-faced in front of the set as if it would bring him closer to his parents. A mid-air collision with an Italian military jet, it said. The Italian pilot parachuted to safety shortly before his plane exploded and was picked up by a fishing boat in the Mediterranean. All thirty-one people on board the British plane died, among them Sharon Cartwell, a 25-year-old model from London.

"We saw her being photographed at the airport," said Jeremy. "Father was most impressed." And then he started to cry.

Maisie phoned Heathrow for more information, then tried the Foreign Office. Afterwards she found Jeremy huddled in one of the deep chairs at the fireside, his right hand across his eyes, his left hand hanging over the chair's arm. So helpless, she thought. Her compassion was tinged with irritation at that hand, dangling.

After Julia was asleep and Jeremy sent upstairs with a glass of whisky and two aspirins, Maisie went back into the kitchen to clear away the remnants of the day. Jeremy's newspaper was crumpled on the table. His sunglasses lay in pieces on the floor. The chrysanthemums burned their bright colours on the draining board.

Usually Jeremy only bought her flowers on special occasions, special to him at least. She wondered what had been on his mind this time.

· · · ● ·● · ● · ·

Jeremy disintegrated, leaving Maisie to deal with the repatriation of his parents' bodies, to put notices into The Times and organise the funeral. She sent out a flood of elegant cards to her in-laws extended network of family and friends, saying, "Jeremy Stanhope Esq regrets to announce..."

"What do you want to put on it?" she'd asked him.

Jeremy was on the phone in the breakfast room. When she knocked and went in to ask him about the cards, he put his hand over the mouthpiece and muttered at her over his shoulder. "It doesn't really matter."

"They say you should put something that sums up their lives, like a family motto or a favourite saying."

"Whatever you think best."

So, at the bottom of the cards in italic letters she had printed, "They touched the face of God." Julia took one to school to show to her teacher. "Miss said it was very appropriate," Julia reported back, sombre-faced.

Maisie hoped the funeral would give them a route back to normalcy, but when she looked across the double grave in the October drizzle, she saw that her husband's face was still closed to her.

Jeremy had walked out of the church beside Connie, who put her arm around his waist and whispered to him, and Maisie had to remind herself that the two of them were cousins. Tim stood by his wife and then a fourth figure joined them—late—Connie's fervent admirer and Julia's lacklustre godfather, Guy Forrester. He'd tidied himself up, Maisie noticed although he still hadn't managed to arrive at the church on time. His hair was brushed, though, and his coat was buttoned up. He didn't have a black tie on. It looked like he wore his school tie, or perhaps his Cambridge college tie, as if he'd never got past those days.

She sensed their otherness, their entitlement, her exclusion. She'd thought things had moved beyond that, but now she saw how easily they'd retreated into their own world, drawn the drawbridge, shuttered up their faces, and shut her out. They stood lined up across the grave in the autumnal gloom, as distant from her in their thirties as they'd been on that bright day in Cambridge. Guy took off his glasses and rubbed them, then put them back on again and smiled wanly at her.

She wondered if they still thought all it took to get by was a bit of what they called breeding and a splash of money, and whether that was, in fact, still the case.

"Oh Mummy." Julia was dressed in a black fitted coat and a matching hat as Leonora would have wanted. She clutched Maisie's hand and started to cry as the cold earth thudded into her grandparents' grave. It must have landed hard on something inside Jeremy because after the funeral he withdrew further into himself, leaving Maisie to sort out the practicalities of winding up his parents' estate.

· · · · ● · ● · · · ·

Dickie Stanhope would never allow anyone into his study. When Maisie let herself into it, she could see why. The room in-side her in-laws' echoingly empty house, was imposing enough. Wood panelling, an expansive oak desk, a leather sofa. Spread across everything were piles of unopened letters, bills that she couldn't tell whether they'd ever been paid, bank statements that screamed red. She spent a week searching before she found documents transferring the Stanhopes' house and a farm in Dorset, she'd never heard about a farm, to Jeremy's brother Alfred. But she couldn't find a will.

"It's such a mess, and seeing their property made over to Al-fred like that will upset Jeremy even more," Maisie told Connie over the phone.

"Go and see Guy Forrester. He'll know what to do." Connie was brisk. "He sorts out all kinds of messes. He's cleared up a few for me over the years." Maisie could hear Connie inspect her nails and knew not to ask what messes. "You'll find his number in the book."

She did as she was told and arranged to visit him, taking a suitcase crammed with papers salvaged from Dickie's study, lugging it past Guy's immaculate receptionist and depositing it on the coffee table in his well-ordered office. Guy had lost weight and his new tie looked as if it had been chosen by a woman.

"Verra nice," said Maisie.

"Shantung silk, only the best." He smiled and smoothed it down but didn't volunteer any more information.

He undid the catches on the suitcase. It sprang open and a slew of papers slid onto the carpet.

"Lordy, what a mess."

"They always seemed so sure of things." Maisie collected up the papers and piled them back into the suitcase and hoped the despair she felt didn't show in her face.

"I'll have to speak to Jeremy at some stage, you understand. It's his family's affairs after all." There was a sharpness in Guy's voice that caught the raw edge of Maisie's nerves. "There must be some explanation."

"Of course. You'll need to be careful with him though, he's still a bit..." Maisie's mouth worked, but she couldn't find the right words.

"What?" His eyes were sharp too.

"Fragile. Struggling. He's finding it hard to deal with the reality of things." She folded her hands in her lap and wondered why she hadn't worn gloves like her mother would have done.

"Mmm. He's not the most practical, is our Jeremy. But he's a good man, Maisie. One of the best. You need to look after him."

At Christmas Jeremy bought a tree and set it up in the sitting room and then watched Julia decorate it. He drifted out of the room before she'd finished. When Maisie went to get him to switch the lights on, she found him standing at the French windows in the breakfast room. She called him and when he turned around, she wondered for a moment whether he recognised her, or if he knew where he was.

In early February Guy phoned to say he'd worked his way through the papers and needed a meeting with both of them. "Jeremy has some tough decisions to take."

"Just as he's starting to find himself again."

"Sooner rather than later."

"Oh Guy, that doesn't sound so good."

"Could you pop in first thing tomorrow for a chat?"

That evening, looking across the fireside at Jeremy laughing at what he said was Julia's execrable French accent as she sang Frère Jacques, she feared what the next day would bring. Despite the warm humour of her husband and the misplaced confidence of her daughter, she felt a twist of fear. She thought of the bitter firesides of her childhood and how much had changed since then. How much she had to lose.

"You haven't forgotten, have you?" she asked Jeremy when she put his tea and toast on the breakfast table next morning. "We're seeing Guy Forrester first thing."

"I had, but now you've reminded me, I've had to remember. Unfortunately."

Once she'd leaned on him. Now he was like a child who needed looking after. Yes, that was how she'd deal with him for the duration. She got him his coat, gave him his gloves, put his scarf around his neck.

· · · · ●·●· · · ·

When she opened the front door, there was a murkiness outside, a fog was gathering, and it muffled the crunch of their feet on the gravel, and Julia's chattering behind them.

"You can drive." Jeremy let Julia into the back of the car and climbed into the passenger seat. After they dropped Julia off at school, he turned on the radio.

"On the second day of his ten-day visit to the USSR—the first by a British Prime Minister since Sir Winston Churchill's during the war—Mr Harold Macmillan will go to the Moscow Kremlin for talks with the Soviet Union's Communist leader

Mr Nikita Khrushchev. They are expected to discuss cultural matters of interest between the two countries..."

"Well, that will ruffle the old codgers in the department."

Maisie's heart sank when she saw the tea and biscuits set on Guy's desk. Opposite him were two hard-backed chairs and a discreet box of tissues sat on a small table between them. Guy stood up and shook their hands, keeping the desk as a barrier between them—protection, thought Maisie, against any emotional involvement in what was to come.

"So sorry for your loss, Jeremy." Maisie noted the guarded formality of Guy's greeting.

"Thank you." Jeremy undid his jacket and sat down, fiddled with his tie and smoothed down his hair, although it was always tidy. If he had any inkling of what was coming, he didn't show it.

"Maisie." Guy nodded to her and poured three cups of tea. "Milk? Help yourself to sugar." He handed her a teacup, set one down next to Jeremy and then reached into his top drawer, took out a plastic container of sweeteners and clicked one into his cup. "Got to watch myself, you know." He took a sip of tea. His cup rattled against its saucer as he set it down, and Maisie wondered if it was nerves that made his hands shake or if he still had difficulties with alcohol.

"Were you aware of your parents' financial affairs?" Guy picked up a wodge of paper stapled together at one corner.

"Only very generally." Jeremy picked up his cup and saucer. Maisie wished she'd told him about what she'd found in Dickie's study. "They'd transferred the bulk of their estate to my brother, their eldest, to avoid death duties. When he was killed in the war, I suppose it reverted back to them, as the rules applied at the time."

"And then?"

"I've no idea. My father never discussed it with me. We weren't exactly, how can I put it?" Jeremy crossed his legs and balanced his cup and saucer on his knee. "He didn't have the confidence in me that he had in my brother. He didn't approve of my"—Jeremy shot a look at Maisie—"lifestyle."

Maisie's cheeks burned. She knew she was the cause of her father-in-law's disapproval, but she wished Jeremy hadn't spelt it out. Her teacup was empty. She put it back on the tray on Guy's desk.

"Ah." Guy made an elaborate display of putting on a pair of gold-rimmed glasses and picking up the thickest of the documents on his desk, and paging through it and then looking at Jeremy and then her. Half-moon glasses, noted Maisie, and felt herself being condescended to again.

"Is there a problem?" she asked.

Guy licked his thumb and turned over another page. Outside a phone rang briefly and a woman's voice said, "Good morning, Mr Forrester's office."

"Because it seems, from what I've been able to discover," Guy continued as if she hadn't spoken, as if nothing mattered but the document in his hands, "that he didn't do anything. At all. Did he ever talk to you about money?"

Guy looked at Jeremy over his glasses. Maisie saw the shrewd lawyer inside her husband's bumbling friend. Her heart sank further.

"No." Jeremy seemed oblivious. He finished drinking his tea. "It wasn't the kind of thing he did. My parents lived the way they always had. They couldn't get the servants after the war, of course, but apart from that, their life went on regardless."

"Except,"—Guy paged through the papers—"year by year they ran up debts, some secured, some not, that ballooned out of all proportion. They have assets, of course, which will all have to be realised. But even so, what with debts and death duties, the estate is likely to be as near as dammit bankrupt."

"You mean they failed?" Maisie asked. It was the word her mother would have used.

Guy scowled.

Jeremy winced. "That's a tad cruel, darling." He squeezed her hand, and then, with what seemed to Maisie to be an unbearable calm, asked Guy. "Is that it?"

"Unfortunately, not," Guy continued. "Were you aware that your house formed part of their estate?"

"You told me it was ours." Maisie couldn't stop herself rounding on Jeremy.

"It was. Is. My father bought it for us when we were married. He told me so."

"But it wasn't registered to you. He kept it as part of his estate." Guy made a show of paging through his document, reorganising the papers on his desk, adjusting his glasses—anything, Maisie guessed, rather than face up to the implications of what he was saying.

"He never trusted me." Jeremy jumped up and walked around the office, stopped at the far wall, in front of a print of Van Gogh's sunflowers, and thrust his hands into his pockets. "It was always Alfred this, Alfred that. Alfred's in the rugby first, Alfred's earned his rowing blues, Alfred's got his commission. He was never able to see beyond my brother. And this is the consequence."

"Do you mean we could lose our home?" Maisie asked Guy.

He looked at her over his glasses. There was nothing wrong with his eyesight that needed glasses, she realised. He could see right through her brave face to her despair.

"Let's not jump to conclusions just yet. Nil desperandum as we classicists say, eh Jeremy?"

Jeremy didn't turn around. He tilted his head and put a hand around the back of his neck, and strained to breaking, and then burst out again. "They carried on after the war as if nothing had changed, but the whole world had changed, had no place for them and their kind and they couldn't recognise the enormity of it all. I sometimes wondered, if it hadn't been for my brother dying, they'd have ignored that the war had ever happened."

"There are things we'd all like to forget," Maisie said. "This is too much for us, Guy. We'll have to get back to you." He sat behind his desk, engrossed in his papers. "Guy? Are you listening to me?"

Guy took off his glasses. "Yes of course. Tricky situation all round."

"I suppose we should say thank you." She held out her hand to him over the cold dregs of the teacups, held it until he stood up and shook it in his own, plumply perspiring. There was an awkwardness to the way he patted Jeremy's shoulder and "old-chapped" him on their way out. Maisie wondered what it must be like to upend a friend's life.

She drove Jeremy to the station, leaning over the steering wheel, her head close to the windscreen to peer through the thickening fog. Forget Dickie and Leonora and Alfred. She was tempted even to think forget Jeremy. Although her husband was in the car, she felt completely alone. Fortune had been as insubstantial as the silky pat of a cat's paw, withdrawn before it could be caught. Jeremy disappeared into the station without looking back.

That night he didn't return home. "Pea-souper," he said on the phone. "Best stay in town." When he came back the following night, he brought a bunch of flowers and kissed her.

"You won't lose your home," he said. "I promise you it won't come to that."

She didn't demur. She humoured him. She knew that whatever happened to their home wouldn't be down to him. The bright hope they'd shared at the start of their marriage had guttered. What came next would be down to her.

CHAPTER TEN

AUGUST 1964

"I want to look like me." The girl in Maisie's shop was on the cusp of serious beauty, with thick blonde hair cut into a sharp geometric shape around a face of fine pallor and enchanting features. She stood with long thin arms akimbo, and one leg stretched out in a posture that should have spelt rebellion, but actually, thought Maisie, mentally measuring her up for size, and noticing that she didn't yet have much in the way of breasts or hips, was rather sweet.

"You must have something that suits the occasion,"—Connie, reclining on one of the velvet cushioned chairs, shook her head in exasperation—"which is not about you. And don't you dare light up in here, you'll stink out the clothes. Come to think of it, open the door, we could do with a breeze, it's so hot."

Maisie waited. Other mothers and daughters had done battle over their conflicting dreams in the rarified whites and pastels of her shop. They'd fought over the fabrics and designs, then haggled over the prices of their visions of perfection. But this was Connie and the teenaged Calypso, whose networks had delivered success for her bridal business.

"We can do anything you want." Maisie, in her mid-thirties, had perfected an elegant work style, a cowl-necked cream silk blouse and a grey pencil skirt with her red hair swept into a twist. It exuded the assured professionalism on which she'd built her reputation—that and her revered canny discretion about mother-daughter conflicts. The tape measure hanging around Maisie's neck was for effect. It was true she did some measuring, but the cutting and stitching together of her customers' fantasies was all done by Hsiao Ling.

"You could have a nice dress like the one Princess Margaret wore when she met the Beatles," was Connie's conciliatory gesture to her daughter.

"I don't suppose they fancied her."

"Oh God."

"I want something sexy."

"If only your father hadn't named you after the biggest tart in history."

"Mummy!"

Maisie wondered if the tantrum would end in tears.

"It's true." Connie turned from her daughter to her friend. "You're so lucky with Julia. She's so sensible, tucked safely away at that school in Switzerland."

"Perhaps we could try this," Maisie fetched a roll of sky-blue satin and draped it over the girl's petulant shoulder.

"Calypso," said Connie. "Don't be rude. Tell Mrs Stanhope what you think."

Which she did, so Maisie got another roll of fabric, and then another, and another. And then they flicked through the magazines spread out on the glass coffee table, and Maisie sketched out designs from the pictures Calypso picked out, with the modifications Connie demanded, until the thick pearly carpet was even thicker with discarded drawings. Too long, still too long, too short, but with expensive fabric, lacy sleeves, pearl-coloured tights, perhaps? Maisie was refereeing between mother and daughter when the phone went.

"Excuse me a minute." Maisie was glad of the interruption. She slid past the racks of ready-mades to the back of her shop where a replica antique phone stood on a marble table beside a mirrored dressing room. "Good afternoon, Sewell Bridal Boutique. How can I help?"

"Hello, Maisie?" A warm Scottish accent came down the line.

"Is that you?" Maisie turned to where Connie and Calypso were leafing through a fashion magazine. Two women bickering, one on the brink of life, the other in her prime, both determined in their pursuit of happiness. And beyond them, the luxuriously gowned mannequins that looked out of the shop window onto the street with its niche shops basking in the afternoon sun. It was a tableau from some other life, not hers. The mother and daughter were squabbling, beyond them cars were moving along the road.

But all she could hear was a man shouting, "You're my wife" and the slapping of flesh, the slamming of a door, the pounding of leather on stone steps. All she could see was scar tissue flickering in firelight, and the starry darkness of eyes clenched under the bed. Nancy had been part of that life, her friend from a childhood she'd tried to forget. It washed over her; the years and distance between didn't matter.

"Maisie, Maisie." She wasn't certain if the sound came from the phone or from Connie who was smiling and pointing at the magazine in her hands. She turned her back and cupped her hand around the elegant phone.

"Can I call you back later? I'm with a customer."

"Of course, you're busy." There was a new tone in Nancy's voice. It was apologetic, Nancy was excusing herself for being so bold as to make a demand of her. "Have you got something to write with? Here's my number."

When Maisie returned, Connie's attention was momentarily distracted from the magazine lying open on her lap. She said, "I say, are you all right? You've gone quite pale."

Calypso snatched up the magazine, thrust it under Maisie's nose, and jabbed at a photograph. "Mummy's agreed to that one."

Maisie tried to focus. Twiggy. Of course. Predictable after all.

"Not bad news, I hope." Connie's shrewd eyes had always been able to strip away the peripherals and get to the heart of things.

Inwardly Maisie said, not this time, you can't know about this. Outwardly she made do with, "Everything's fine, no worries at all." She forced what she hoped would pass for a smile for Connie and to Calypso she said. "That's a grand choice. It will be a new addition to my collection. We've not done a couture mini-dress before."

· · · · ● ● ● · · · ·

When the two had left, with the design settled, the fabric ordered and a date set for the first fitting, Maisie turned the lights off in her boutique, hung up the tasteful "Closed" sign and locked the front door. She drove home, seeing in her mind's eye a street where cream stone houses were bordered by grey stone walls with blousy roses tumbling over. She wondered if Nancy still winked over her shoulder or whether life had beaten that out of her. She parked in the garage and let herself in through the back door.

The house was silent. Julia was finishing her education in Switzerland trying to learn French. Jeremy was not yet home from work. Maisie made herself a cup of tea and took it into what used to be the breakfast room, now her study.

On her desk was a picture of the three of them, she and Jeremy and Julia on holiday in Torquay the previous summer, all of them slightly awkward with each other, not agreed on what they wanted out of life, and not talking about it, but all very fond of each other in that understated English way. A bond she'd fought to rebuild since his parents' death and so precious she didn't want it spoiled by any incursions from her past, as threatened now. This call, she knew, could only be about her own parents. She pulled the piece of paper with Nancy's number on it out of her handbag and dialed.

"Hello."

"Maisie? I'm so glad you called back; I was worried you might not."

"Which of them is it?"

"Wait a minute, I cannae hear you." A shuffling noise came down the phone and Maisie felt her heart pound. She listened hard and heard voices, a door shut, and then the footsteps returned. "I've turned the wireless off. Oh Maisie, I'm afraid your father's had an accident."

Maisie felt a great whoosh as the tightness in her chest eased. She sat back in her chair and closed her eyes in relief. She listened to her breathing, in, out, steady now and felt her head clear. She fought back the impulse to say, "Thank goodness."

Nancy was still speaking. "I'm so sorry." She must have said something else, from her tone it must have been serious because at the end she gave what sounded like a sob. Perhaps she thought she had to let Maisie gently into the reality of what had happened, because it took another few sentences for her to introduce the word "death."

Maisie tried to find sorrow for him but couldn't. Instead, there was a fresh anxiety. "Is my Mam all right?"

"That's just it Maisie. She's at home now. I'll fetch her over tomorrow so you can talk to her on the telephone. The doctor's been out to her, and she's resting now. When I left, she was sleeping in yon bed in the sitting room. The thing is we don't know for sure what happened."

"I thought you said there was an accident."

"Well, they went out for a walk together, but she came back alone." Now Nancy had moved on from the basics to the detail, Maisie could hear an edge of excitement in her voice. "Mrs Mawhinney up the road, you know, the one who always twitches her curtains, she said your mother was in a terrible state, running down the road with her hat off and her hair askew, which isn't like your mother. And then she only sent for an ambulance hours after. They found your father fallen down a bank up by the woods."

"I know the place. He used to go up there to throw the rubbish out. He'd take me with him when I was a child." Maisie could picture the bundle that her mother would have given her father, the refuse wrapped in a piece of newspaper that unravelled as it rolled down the bank and all the ruins of their life together would tumble out.

"That's what your mother said. I suppose he was throwing the rubbish down and slipped. They think it was a heart attack, but they're holding an autopsy just to be sure ye ken. The police spent a long time with your mother. No-one understands why she waited for so long to get help for him after she got back."

Maisie could imagine Mrs Mawhinney's curtains twitching as the police cars came and went. "My poor Mam."

"She's bearing up, all things considered."

Yes, thought Maisie, she'll be bearing up if she's allowed, what with the curtain twitchers and the gossips and the police jumping to conclusions about any sign of her being less than a grieving widow. Even now she probably won't tell the whole story.

"Um, I don't like to be so morbid about it, but they won't release your father's body for a while."

She wondered if Nancy thought her a less than grieving daughter. She tried to make amends. "Oh dear. I'm sorry. This is all such a shock." Outside, the sun came slanting in across the garden and lit up the fruit trees along the east wall. The apples were swelling into red ripeness. It would be a good crop this year. She tried to conjure up the feelings that should lie behind such words.

"So, you've got plenty of time, you know, to sort things out."

The clock in the kitchen struck five and its little door sprang open, and the cuckoo popped out. Jeremy had bought the clock when they'd gone to Switzerland to take Julia to her school. They'd all laughed over it in the shop and Jeremy had said, "It'll remind us of you, always popping out to tell us what to do." It still managed to catch Maisie by surprise.

"Oh," she said.

"It must be so hard for you. Take your time to work things through. Will you be needing anything the now?"

"Tell Mam I love her."

The words hung between them. There was so much unsaid. Maisie gathered herself. "And how about you, Nancy? it's been such a long time. How are you?"

She could hear the relief in Nancy's voice that her friend hadn't forgotten, that she still cared. "I'm a'right." Her voice relaxed. "I've got a wee job in a solicitor's office. Just typing the now, but he says quite soon, next year mebbe I can take on a bit more. I've got a wee house of my own too, not so far from my parents, and the laddie's doing fine."

Now there was a surprise. Maisie was about to ask his name and how old he was, but before she could, Nancy had finished the conversation and said goodbye and hung up, leaving Maisie wondering why her friend hadn't mentioned the boy's father.

She phoned Jeremy but his secretary must have left because it rang out at the other end, which, she thought as she put the phone back in its cradle, was just as well because it meant she could sort out her feelings before she exposed them to him. The tea in her cup had a cold scum on it, so she went into the kitchen to make a fresh one, but then changed her mind, poured out a jug of water, took a bottle of scotch and a tumbler from the drinks' cabinet in the dining room and went out into the garden.

· · · · ● · ● · · ·

Since Julia had grown up, they'd changed the garden around, she and Jeremy. It had gone some way to closing the chasm that had opened between them over his parents' death, him clearing the ground, her planting, both agreeing that, since there was no need to dig for victory, they would dig for beauty instead.

At the far end, where the garden merged into the managed wilderness of the Green Belt, Jeremy built a trellis which Maisie covered with a white clematis, and then planted an apple tree beside it. "So, it becomes the Garden of the Hesperides," he teased her. And she, not wanting to ask, "Where's that?" pursed her mouth and directed the delivery men to place the elaborate garden seat just so. Julia had insisted that her swing should not be moved, so it continued to rust beyond the rose garden at the far side of the lawn.

Maisie sat down with her scotch, put the bottle and jug of water on the grass and kicked off her high-heeled shoes. The fine stubble of the mowed lawn poked through her stockings. She stripped them off and curled her bare toes through the grass, sipped her scotch and stretched out on the seat. She shut her eyes. Emptied her mind. There was birdsong in the wilderness behind her. Children's voices sounded from the next-door garden but one. A wasp buzzed around. She held her breath, and the sound trailed away. She took another sip from the tumbler and the whisky fumes mixed with the chocolaty scent of the clematis flowers that hung over her.

Was it the alcohol or the sun that made her feel so flushed? She bent an arm behind her head and wiggled herself into a comfortable position on the bench.

When she and Jeremy had first moved in, the stuccoed grandeur of their house had overpowered her. Today, as she looked across the garden at it, she felt the house and she were equals, partners even. Its solid walls reflected the lowering sun, cast a glow that touched the rusting swing, caught the lush colours of drowsy roses and coddled her reclining self. The alcohol burnt an inside track. She searched for the name of this unfamiliar emotion.

Throughout her whole life, as long as she could remember, she'd felt fear, carried it inside her like an incubus. Lived with it until it had become part of her. She'd learned, in every interaction, to keep a bit of herself separate, listening for the tightening voice, watching for the clenching fist, bracing herself for what came next.

And now the cause of it was gone. What she felt was safe.

She took another sip of whisky and tried to evoke happier memories of her father. That might reassure her that there had been some kind of affection. The medals, the coat with woven seams, the respect of the church elders, his voice—"My bonny lass"—the handhold as they walked up the hill to throw the rubbish out. No, she couldn't go there. Not yet.

And then she realised that however hard she might try to feel how other people did when their fathers died, like Jeremy had done when his father did, she couldn't. She felt glad her father was dead. The admission of that shocked her, and she wondered whether it made her complicit in his death, and whether she should feel guilt.

Except she didn't. What she felt was the muzzy happiness of whisky and late afternoon sunshine, the soporific perfume from the clematis flowers, the sweetness of the birds in the woodlands behind her, until she wasn't sure whether her headiness was due to her senses, or the alcohol, or her own released emotions.

She heard a car at the front of the house. It crunched on the gravel driveway, stopped, the engine ticked noisily over, then revved up again and puttered away. Jeremy must have got a taxi from the station. She turned her head as he appeared at the French windows.

His tie was undone and dangled around his neck, his jacket slung over one shoulder, light summer trousers moving with that catlike walk that had attracted her at their first meeting. His eyes were hidden by sunglasses. But his lips were smiling, that warm, genuine smile she'd always known. Forget his eyes, she thought, it's his smile that's the window to his soul.

They'd had their difficulties, she thought, like after his parents were killed and when they'd fallen out over Julia's schooling. But he'd never threatened her, never raised a hand, scarcely raised his voice, never made her feel anything less than loved and supported. She'd never quite been able to believe it, until now, and at last, she felt safe. She put a hand over her eyes to shade them against the sun and watched him walk across the lawn towards her.

She wondered what their life might have been like if it hadn't been for her father, and the fear instilled in her, and whether she should have told her husband. He'd deserved to know the truth. It had all been so destructive, she could see that now. She wondered if there was a way to repair the damaged time.

"How's my goddess?" He stood over her, silhouetted against the light. "And what's this?" He inspected the whisky bottle, held it up to his eyes and peered down it like it was a spyglass. "Are you drunk?"

She giggled and squinted at him. He stood between her and the sun, a dark shape against the light. She wondered for a moment, in his shadow, if she could have seen his face, what his expression might be. "Here," she held up her tumbler to him. And then he threw his jacket across the back of the bench, sat down beside her, and took off his glasses.

"What's up?" His hazel eyes matched his hair that had receded, leaving a tidemark of his age, a shining whiteness, tinged pink in the sun. His vulnerability was what had originally struck her, and still did. But now she knew what lay behind it, she knew the core of him, she'd been there. She put her arms around him and kissed him. She'd have kissed him on the mouth, but he turned his face away and she, caught off balance, kissed his ear instead.

"I really love you." She nuzzled his earlobes. They were long, a sign of long life she always said, and sensitive.

He took the whisky tumbler from her and gulped from it. "You mean you've finally decided?"

She kissed him again, on the lips this time, and leaned against his body. It was still slim and supple. Young enough. There was still time for them. She undid the buttons on his shirt and felt the smooth skin of his chest, smelled the whisky on his breath, mixed with tobacco smoke and something fresh, his aftershave perhaps. She felt him hesitate, pull away. He took another gulp of whisky.

"Please," she said. She took the glass from him and emptied it, then turned it upside down. "See, finished." She dropped it on the lawn.

He put an arm around her and pulled her to him, brushed a hand against her knee, pushed up her skirt.

"No stockings."

She kissed him again, longer this time, and he opened his mouth, and she was in. He put his hands behind her back and grappled with her skirt, then pulled. "Bloody buttons," he said. She heard a tear, and the skirt came loose. She giggled again.

"You are drunk. I've never made love to you drunk before."

"Or on the lawn."

She put a hand on his crotch and felt it rise. He was breathing hard now, his head back against the garden seat, eyes shut, the sun on his back. Then he sat up, threw his jacket on the ground and pulled her down, so her head rested on it, and she stretched out under him on the soft warm grass. She smelt his sweat now and felt her own wetness, lifted her legs and then he was in and moving, moving.

"Well," he said afterwards. "That was a surprise."

He sounded pleased. He had a contented smile on his face, smug almost. She felt muzzy from the sex, the drink, the heat. They lay side by side and listened to the birdsong, and the woman two gardens away nagging her children to come in. Maisie could have lain just so all night to avoid spoiling the feeling between them. He seemed content too, putting a hand inside her sweaty blouse and fondling her breasts. And then the sun dipped down, and they were left in shade.

"We should go inside," he said.

"Not yet." She kissed him again, pressed herself against the length of him and wished she could capture the moment, distil the essence of it so that whatever came later she could always say, this is what we had, this was us. But he was determined, already standing up, brushing the grass off his trousers, rubbing his knee where the fabric had stained green, shaking out his jacket. So she got to her feet, pulling her bra into place, holding her broken skirt, giving him the jug, drained of its water, the empty whisky bottle, and retrieving the tumbler from under the bench. He put one arm around her, and they walked in through the French windows.

"It's too late for the news," he said.

She wanted to tell him her feelings, her sense of what their life together might have been and could yet be. They were still young enough. She wanted to say she was sorry. He deserved that at least. But then she'd have to explain why, and she didn't want the past to come between them now.

So she made him a sandwich and a cup of tea which he put on their bedside table and then lifted the sheet for her to get in beside him. He leaned over her, and they made love again. It was slower this time, less passionate, but, she thought, more expressive of what existed between them. Afterwards he drank his tea while she disentangled her emotions. This evening was theirs. She wouldn't let her father spoil their happiness.

CHAPTER ELEVEN

AUGUST 1964

I t felt the same. Daylight filtered through the strip of net curtain tacked across the closed window. From outside came the laughter of children playing in the street below. The sound—but not the sense of it—carried through the thin glass panes. Her father might have gone but his spirit lingered; Maisie could feel it hovering in the room.

In the corner by the kitchen, the three-legged table was missing its lacy cover. Its bare legs were exposed. Somehow the china figurine had survived; the web of repair lines across the kilted man and his adoring dog told the story of the years she'd been gone. Next to it the photograph in its linen frame had dimmed into a sepia haze.

The two best chairs still sat in the middle of the room. They were faded, but on a bigger piece of carpet that stretched all the way from her feet to a brown-painted cabinet in the far corner. That was new, or at least new since she'd left. She didn't suppose it was new from a shop. Next to it was the fireplace which had an electric heater in it. The mirror above it was split from top to bottom.

Then there was the bed. With a shape in it, a small, neat shape under a grey blanket. It could have been herself; it was her bed once. Maisie caught her breath. She bit her lower lip but couldn't keep in the sob.

"It's a'right hen." Nancy's voice was a whisper. "She's peaceful now. The doctor gave her something this morning, and she's been sleeping since."

· · · · · · · · · ·

As Maisie stepped had out of the black cab at the entrance to the tenement block, fresh off the evening train from Waverley Station, the curtain in the downstairs window twitched. Along the street old Ellen Ferguson, or was it her daughter, stopped, leaning on her trolley bag, to watch the arrival. When Maisie paid off the taxi driver, she looked up and saw a light on behind the nets in her mother's kitchen window and the shadow of a figure. The clatter of her high heels echoed up the stairwell and then, in the greyness, the door on the landing opened and Nancy appeared above the bannister railing.

"I'm so sorry for ye." Nancy's face, mellowed into the round-cheeked comfortableness of a premature middle age, was smothered with sympathy. When Nancy folded her arms around her, Maisie felt the comfort radiate from her friend's body.

"Come away in." Nancy took Maisie's little suitcase and led her into the room. "You sit with her. I'll fetch you some tea."

Nancy opened the door to the kitchen and Maisie saw the old range below the chimney. On its black-leaded top a tin of Crawford's shortbread stood beside a folded newspaper and a shiny metal electric kettle. To one side was an armchair. The back was hollowed where he'd sat, and the upholstered arms were dark with grease. Her father's imprint. She thought she saw him turn his scarred face to her, saw firelight flicker on the red veneer of his scar tissue, inhaled the acrid tobacco smoke that knotted itself in her gut, and felt herself choking. Then Nancy appeared in the doorway with a cup of tea.

"Here y'are."

"I don't know what I'd have done without you."

"You would have managed. You and your Mam always did." Nancy put the cup in Maisie's hands.

Maisie tiptoed across the room and perched herself on the edge of the bed. Flora was lying curled on her side with a grey blanket drawn up around her chin. Her body was so still and silent that Maisie lent over to check she was still breathing. Her mother's skin was china-white over fine bones, her cheeks tinged pink, and her silvered hair was braided and whorled over her ears. She looked more peaceful than Maisie could ever remember.

She sat on the bed and drank her tea. She could still smell the fear. The grey blanket covering her mother was thick with its sourness. She put her teacup under the bed and went to the window, lifted the net curtain. It came away in her hands, so brittle where it was nailed into the window frame. She wrenched at the handle and pushed on the frame until it burst open. Outside, women were calling their children in off the streets. She could hear them clearly now, sharp sounds that ricocheted around the tenements. The lowering sun soothed her face. She filled her lungs with fresh air and went back to the bed.

The movement must have disturbed Flora because her eyes sprang open. For a moment they registered fear, then confusion, before Maisie saw them focus on herself.

"You've come home."

Flora pushed herself up in the bed. She adjusted her blouse, so it sat straight on her shoulders, patted her hair into place, and then tilted her head and smiled at her daughter.

"You still look beautiful, Mam." Maisie wrapped her arms around her mother and the two of them clung to each other, survivors of their secret Armageddon. Maisie was afraid she'd crush her mother, she held her so tight and felt how thin, how fragile she'd become. As if it was only her mother's burning will that had carried her through these final years.

"It's over, Mam. It's done."

"So it is."

"Are you all right? You're no' hurt?"

"No, I'm no' hurt." Flora pulled herself away from Maisie. Her uncertain eyes cast around the room, and then fixed back on her daughter. "But I dinnae know if I'm a' right. It'll take a while before I know that."

"I'm not sorry." Maisie took her mother's hand, saw how hard and cracked the skin on her palm had become. "I know it's evil to say so, but I'm not sorry he's gone. I'm sorry for the manner of it and that it had to be so hard on you." She didn't trust herself to look at her mother's face now she was awake.

"It's no' easy to know what to make of it."

Oh, but it is, thought Maisie, he was a brute who beat you and now he's gone—you're free to be the woman you were always meant to be. She took her hands and kissed them, as if she could will it for her.

"I'll more than miss him. We were together for so long. It's fifty years ago that I promised myself to him before he went off to war. I told him I'd wait for him, however long."

"You kept yer promise, Mam."

"So I did."

At what price, thought Maisie. She kissed her mother, there on her forehead where there was the mark he'd left that night. She felt the bald spot at the back from where he'd pulled out the clump of her hair. Those were on the surface. She wondered whether her mother's inner scars went as deep as her own. The difference was she'd have longer to live with hers.

"Is his tin trunk still under the bed?"

Flora nodded.

"Are his medals still in it?"

"I'll give them to Wee Jimmy. He's no' got any of his own. It's fitting he should have them. I don't suppose you want them."

Maisie shook her head.

"I did love your father, mind. He was handsome and brave before..." Flora fell silent, twisted the wedding ring around the finger on her left hand. "It wasn't his fault what happened." Outside a car backfired, a dog barked. "He loved you from the moment you were born."

"He hurt us awful bad."

"We'd best forget that."

Maisie wondered how much Flora had to forget. Nancy had said there were questions about the accident and why Flora had come running home alone. But she wasn't going to ask now, perhaps never. She didn't care to know the answer. Her father was dead, that was enough. And if there was more to be told, she hoped it could be buried with him, so that no-one would ever have to find out.

"I never want to remember ever again."

"Come under the blanket." Flora lifted it up and Maisie slipped off her shoes, laid out her jacket and climbed underneath. Then the two women held each other close and whispered about how their lives had been, and how they would be yet. The last of the sun cast its light across the floor. The air cooled. The street fell as silent as the room.

The day's business was finished.

"YOU"

1965 - 2008

Chapter Twelve

July 1965

Y ou arrived early, for the only time in your life. Isla Leonora
Stanhope.

At first it wasn't obvious what was happening. You took
centre stage, one noisy baby intent on making an impression.
The rest of us were all tied up with our own separate struggles
to adjust. It could have been as simple as that: normality with a
new baby. Except it wasn't.

You were screaming the place down when I got home from
school in Switzerland. Father was walking around the house
jiggling you in his arms and singing "Rock-a-by-baby," with a
silly smile on his face as if that would placate you. Mother was
crashed out in bed.

Meanwhile I, your sulky 16-year-old sister Julia, shut myself
in my bedroom, turned up the sound on my record player,
opened the windows so the neighbours could hear my rebellion, and wondered what to do with my life. I was qualified for
nothing, hadn't even managed to learn French. And now I'd
been displaced. Yes, I was jealous. In those first months of our
life together, I wished someone would notice me.

Mother didn't pick up on my drifting around and Father
drifting away. Perhaps between having you and worrying about
her business she didn't have the headspace.

After my grandparents' will debacle, Mother had taken over responsibility for the family finances. Father took to spending more nights at his club in town and by the time you were walking, he was only coming home at weekends. He'd hold out his arms and call, "Isla!" and you would toddle towards him with your arms out and his face would light up. A fly on the wall might have said, "these saccharine suburbanites." But then there was me, following behind you, pestering Father about how long he'd stay, and there was Mother disappearing out the door to the latest wedding. You were too little to notice the undercurrents, much less to understand them.

The year Sergeant Pepper came out was the year Father finally disappeared. There was no sudden walk-out, he wasn't one for dramatics, but somewhere between my singing along to "She's leaving home"—as if I could—and realising I loved you and didn't want to run anywhere, I noticed he'd faded out.

One evening at the start of that last summer Mother came home from work and shut herself in the breakfast room. We hadn't seen Father for over a week and I was starting to feel we'd been abandoned by both our parents. You'd just worked out how to open doors and were standing outside the breakfast room with your little fingers on the door handle, laughing at the naughtiness of it. As I picked you up, I heard Mother's voice on the phone inside saying, "No, Jeremy." I put a hand over your mouth and pressed an ear to the door. There was a brief silence, and then I heard Mother say, "Ye cannae do this to us," after which her voice tailed away.

You were wriggling to get free, and I took you upstairs and put you into your cot. You stood up and shook the railings and screamed. Even then you were allergic to being cooped up. When I got back down to the sitting room, Mother was hunched up on the sofa watching television. Her eyes were red, there were tears in them. When I asked her why she was crying, she said it was just the film she was watching about a homeless woman whose family broke up.

"It reminded me of things."

"But you've never been homeless," I said.

"Not as such."

"Well then."

"Life's not always so straightforward, Julia."

Father scaled back on weekends with us until one day I realised I couldn't remember when he'd last visited. I collared Mother about it one evening when she came into the bathroom while I was giving you your bath. You were two by then, pink-skinned with big blue eyes and a headful of fine red hair. Trust Mother to have such a beautiful child. Your little face would beam whenever you saw me, as if your happiness depended on me. You made me feel needed. Sometimes I imagined you were mine.

That night you held onto the side of the bath and jumped up and down in your funny bow-legged way and laughed when you saw Mother. She didn't seem to notice.

"I've got to do a fitting tonight, so I'm going to be late. You'll be fine looking after Isla, won't you?"

"D'you think Father might come this weekend?"

She stopped, halfway out of the door, as if she wanted to hide behind it. "Why d'you ask?"

"Just wondering. Are we going to see him sometime soon?"

You were holding one of your little hands out to Mother and calling, "Ma, ma." It made me want to cry that Mother just stood by the door and watched. She didn't even smile at you that I could see.

"I don't think we'll be seeing your father again."

You laughed and bounced up and down in the bath and squealed, "Ma, ma."

"Why's that?" I made my voice as neutral as possible to hide my shock. I didn't want to know the whole story, just whether in the general scheme of things I would be able to factor in my father.

"Circumstances change, things happen. Ye cannae always control events."

She appeared composed, but her accent told me she wasn't. It always went Scottishy when she was stressed.

"Did you have a fight?"

"Yer father's no' the fighting type." Her face grew sad, and she turned away and then I heard her run down the stairs and slam the front door. I wondered if it was because I looked so much like Father, and she didn't like to be reminded of what she'd lost. If I'd known that last time we'd gone out—he'd taken me to the cinema to try to make me feel better about not having a boyfriend, not that I was bothered—but if I'd known it really was going to be the last time, perhaps I'd have said something meaningful. As it was all I did was tell him not to be so silly for throwing peanuts into the air and trying to catch them in his mouth and laughing that hee-haw donkey laugh of his that made people turn around and stare. I'd acted as if he was nothing to do with me.

And then without my realising, he was gone. The Lonely Hearts Club Band played on through that summer while I took you toddling around the garden. It was your talking that finally hooked me. Your eyes didn't change colour like mine had done, and you would fix me with their baby blueness, and hold out a daisy or a rose petal you'd picked up off the lawn and make babbly noises and then you'd scream with frustration when I couldn't understand. Until one day when you were babbling away you suddenly came out with "Ju, Ju." It made me stop. You were so pleased with yourself, you said it again. "Ju-ju."

Unconditional love is cataclysmic, so I discovered that day. When you held me with your baby blue eyes and said my name, it triggered something deep inside me. Perhaps it's what a mother feels when she holds her baby for the first time. Perhaps it's what Mother felt for me once. Or maybe it's what a lover feels, someone who's going to follow you to the end of the earth. Like Omar Sharif trudging through the snowstorm in Dr Zhivago to find his beloved Lara. Perhaps someone might feel like that about me one day. But meanwhile I knew for certain I didn't want to leave home. My love for you was unconditional, and whatever life threw at you, I wanted to be there to help you catch it.

"Ju-ju."

Everything about that moment stuck.

• • • • • • • • • •

Mother's boutique took off. She'd done a mini-dress creation for a wedding some years previously and she put a replica of it in the smaller shop window on the right side of the door. In the big window on the left she put a Priscilla Presley meringue-type creation as worn by the latest royal bride. As our customers came in, I'd put bets on whether they were a mini or a meringue. Mother said I had a calming effect, especially when things got hysterical. She said she could rely on me. "Your father's lost his job. The business is all we've got now." She sucked me in. When she said, "And there's Isla to think about," she knew I couldn't refuse.

Hsiao Ling replaced the lean-to behind her house with a proper extension which became the workroom for her team of seamstresses, and her husband moved his catering business to a pint-sized takeaway by the railway station. Mother said the upstairs of the bridal boutique could be used for the dress-making, but Hsiao Ling said it suited her to work from home. She was younger than Mother and her little Rose was born the same year as you. Most days I'd drop you off at Hsiao Ling's mid-morning on my way into the shop and pick you up in the afternoon. You'd come marching out of Hsiao Ling's house clutching something you'd made, a squashed-up paper dragon or a misshapen sticky bun or something, with Rose hanging onto your arm and crying for you to stay. It was always that way round. You never cried.

One particularly fine spring afternoon I took you from Hsiao Ling's to the shop. Which was in meltdown. Aunt Connie was there with her daughter Calypso, she of the original mini-dress wedding outfit. Now she was getting married, a teenage bride, but not shotgun, Aunt Connie said she had to have a proper gown, by which she meant full meringue. Calypso was throwing an epic strop. Mother was standing just inside the door to block Calypso's escape route and I had to squeeze in around her, dragging you behind me. Your eyes were out on stalks.

"I want something like Sharon Tate wore." For a beautiful girl, Calypso had a voice like a cheese-grater.

"Your father won't pay for anything like that." It was at times like this I thought of my godmother Connie as Constantia. She sat on the pink velvet upholstered occasional chair that she'd chosen for the latest revamp of the boutique, and spoke to her daughter with such froideur the temperature in the shop went down a few degrees.

"I'll run away to a registry office."

"You'd get no attention. You would have to actually be Sharon Tate to do something like that and get noticed."

"What do you think, Ju-ju?" Mother tossed the grenade in my direction. Trust her. Although I was only a year older than Calypso, it felt like we were from different generations.

The three of them turned on me. Mother had on her work uniform, a genteel grey skirt, silky blouse, tape measure around her neck, hair swept up, still resolutely red, courtesy of a good colourist. My aunt had on a pale lemon suit which showed off her pencil-slim figure to perfection, even sitting down. But she couldn't compete with her daughter in the beauty stakes. Calypso would be the most beautiful bride we'd ever dressed—if she didn't bolt.

"Well at least I'll have the cutest flower girl, hey Isla."

You'd let go of my hand and waltzed up to Calypso, holding out the fan you'd made at Hsiao Ling's—half a paper plate from the takeaway—painted bright pink and green with an ice lolly stick for a handle. You put on your sweetest smile for her and held out the fan. Even at that age you knew a kindred spirit.

I sensed my opening. "Mini-dresses are a bit passé."

"So you did learn French after all." Aunt Connie affected surprise.

But this was my chance to shine, and I wasn't going to let her put me off. "We could do you something more of the moment, you know, fine tulle or a chiffon if you prefer—more fitted, or transparent, exotic beadwork, lace, mystical, fabulous of course. Have a look at this." I picked out the most voguish of our magazines and leafed through it to the summer fashion pages, pointing out the picture of the new girl singer, Joni Mitchell, "See, that's so you."

Calypso looked at the floaty dresses and went quiet. They were very romantic. Mother held her breath. Aunt Connie feigned indifference. You chose that moment to throw up on the pastel carpet. Mother got cross. Aunt Connie laughed. Calypso wasn't bothered—she'd got what she wanted, which was all that mattered.

The wedding was picture perfect. Mother went as a friend of the bride, you went as the flower girl, and I went to manage the dresses which everyone said were spectacular. Calypso's was copied from a classical painting of her namesake, a vampy Greek goddess confection reinterpreted à la flower power. You were dressed as a little nymphette loaded with flowers and ribbons and walked behind Calypso with a metaphorical "Look at me" sign above your head. You already had that funny lilting gait that added to your joyousness and you basked in the attention. A lesser bride would have been outshone.

· · · · ·●·● · · ·

A couple of weeks afterwards Uncle Tim came into the shop as I was cashing up for the day. His son sauntered in behind him. Freddie had been at the wedding, of course, in his top hat and tails. Now he was wearing flared jeans and a dark shirt, and with his thick black hair down past his ears, he was the swoon-inducing image of George Harrison. He didn't notice me, but loitered by the display racks poking moodily at the rolls of fabric. A few years younger than me, he seemed older, perhaps because he was more sophisticated.

"Julia, isn't it?" Uncle Tim asked. "You look just like your father."

I tried not to think about Father too much. It had been tough getting used to the idea that he'd abandoned us. "Have you seen him recently?" I'd never associated Uncle Tim with Father. He was a sleek man with a wolfish air, as if he was always on the prowl, either for women or business victims. He'd done well from redeveloping old bomb sites. Although his dark hair was thinning, and he had the beginnings of a paunch, his glad eye still followed any passing mini skirt. So Mother said, and I felt his attention alight on me for a millisecond. "How is he?" I asked.

"He's fine." I thought he might say more. Instead, he held out an envelope to me. "This is for your mother. I thought I might see her here."

"She's been in town all day." Inside the envelope I found a card, a cream-coloured notelet with a big "Thank you" in Aunt Connie's swirly handwriting. Folded inside that was a cheque, Coutts of course, signed 'Timotheus Granville Esq' in his blunt black ink. "You could have posted it."

"She's a shrewd little businesswoman, your mother. I've heard you take after her." He lingered as if he had something else to say.

Freddie sauntered up. He was out of my league as well as being younger. But I didn't want to be completely forgettable, so I gave him what I hoped was an alluring look. "Come on Pater," he said. "I'm on a promise."

"Okay, okay." Uncle Tim tossed me a smile.

I felt a pulse of lust, but not for him. I wondered how he would cope with the competition.

· · · · ●·●· · ·

Things got easier when you started school. Mother and I took you for your first day at the Goddington Church of England primary. It was my old school, a bog standard, red brick building surrounded by grey tarmac with iron railings that had somehow managed to survive the war. The disgusting toilets still hadn't been replaced and were in a block at the bottom of the playground. Rose started the same day. We drove from the posh end of the village, Hsiao Ling walked from her house in the terrace down the back street and we lined up outside the railings and waved as the two of you disappeared through the swing doors at the school entrance hand in hand. From behind you were indistinguishable in your grey mackintoshes and red berets except that Rose's black bob sat neatly below her hat, while your carrot-coloured bunches clashed horribly with yours. You both seemed cheerfully confident. You turned just before you went in and waved. Mother was checking her watch at the time so didn't see. I waved and blew kisses. Rose turned around too, and Hsiao Ling shouted intense encouragement to her.

· · · · ● · ● · · · ·

When Freddie next came into the shop some years later, it was as a prospective bridegroom. Handsome had turned into drop-dead gorgeous. He and his Anna-Beth stood side by side holding hands, both just down from Oxford, him from doing classics like his father, her from reading history, saying they wanted something modern, they weren't ones for convention. Mother went into a terrible spin. The bride was the grand-daughter of a peer, a government grandee to boot. Big in prop-erty with Tim. And on the strength of Connie's recommenda-tions, the mother of the bride, the Hon Mrs Beauchamp, had commandeered the new chaise longue, now covered in an oyster brocade from where she said, "Now let's see what you can do for us. Off you go Freddie, this is my department."

Cue the unrolling of fabrics, the leafing through of design books, the rummaging in the bride's handbag for photographs torn out of magazines. I tried to catch Freddie's eye on his way out, but he blanked me.

As I was carrying in the second round of teas, the phone went on its little marble stand.

I held the receiver out to Mother. "It's the school, for you."

She winced and took it and started talking but kept her eyes on the Hon Mrs B, who took a sip of tea, and rearranged her handbag on the chaise longue, and then, as Mother continued on the phone said in her piercing voice, "Of course, if it's inconvenient…"

"Och no, it's no problem at all, Mrs Beauchamp." Mother looked panicky and held the receiver out to me. "It's about Isla. Can you sort things out please Ju-ju?"

It didn't take long. When the headteacher's secretary said you were in trouble and I was to come immediately, I grabbed my keys and let myself out the back into the carpark and drove off before Mother had even noticed.

Children in messy PE kit were running around the play-ground under the direction of a frazzled-looking teacher when I parked outside the school gate. Inside the junior school entrance, I turned left down the corridor that led to the head-teacher's study. The walk of shame for naughty children. I'd never had to do it. Now my adult shoes clattered on the stone floor and echoed off the green tiled walls. From the hall I heard a piano strike a chord and the piping voices of young children. "Bobby Shafto's gone to sea…"

Around another corner in the holding area outside the head-teacher's room, you were standing against the grease-shiny wall with Rose. At age ten you were still best friends, two skinny schoolgirls dressed in your school uniforms. But that's where the similarities ended. Rose had her head down. You scowled defiance and what with that and your red hair, I didn't think this was going to go well. Sitting opposite on a brown canvas stacking chair was a furious-looking Hsiao Ling.

The headteacher's secretary stuck her head around the door. "Mrs Woods will see you now."

As I walked into that study, and saw the grey filing cabinets, the shelves weighed down with worn textbooks and the wooden desk with the framed slogan "Sufficient to the day," I felt the years fall away. Mrs Woods waved at two chairs set to one side, but didn't look up from the papers she was reading. Hsiao Ling and I sat down. You two girls stood facing the headteacher across her desk.

"By all the very reliable accounts I've received, your girls' behaviour was disgusting." Mrs Woods' mousey hair was held in the iron grip of a tight perm and heavy lines stretched from her nose down to her mouth. Her glasses had extravagant wings on them; she took them off now and held them in one hand while she inspected the girls, and then us.

Hsiao Ling folded her arms.

"What are they supposed to have done?" I asked.

"You must be Isla's mother," Mrs Woods said.

"I'm her sister."

"Hmm. Of course," Mrs Woods returned to Hsiao Ling. "And you must be Rose's...?"

"I'm Rose's mother."

"Well, the girls were caught misbehaving in the toilets. In fact, it's fair to say they instigated something of a riot."

Those toilets. I remembered freezing my bum off in winter, and feeling sick from the stink in summer. We girls had to queue up on our side, while the boys whipped in and out of theirs, or sometimes just went in the bushes around the back. The dividing wall between the two didn't go to the ceiling.

"It appears," Mrs Wood put her glasses back on and read from the piece of paper in her hand, "that your girls shouted rude words from their side of the toilets and then proceeded to throw objects over the wall at the boys, one of whom complained of being hurt. My deputy had to sort out the fracas." She whipped off her glasses. "Well girls, do you have anything to say?" Click, click click. She tapped one of the arms of her glasses against her clenched teeth and let us all stew in her displeasure.

Rose bent over and buried her face in the sleeve of her jumper. You stood ramrod straight, your hands curled up at your sides to hide your bitten fingernails.

"Are you sorry?" The glasses went back on her nose. Mrs Woods waited for the apologies.

"No," you said.

"What did you say?"

"I said no." Your hair blazed. "I'm not sorry. The boys started it."

Hsiao Ling saved things. She launched a stream of words at Rose, alternately angry and pleading. Rose nodded, occasionally sobbed, finally, straightened up, rubbed her hands across her eyes and pushed back her hair. She put an arm around your shoulders and whispered into your ear. You nodded. Then Rose took a step forward, reached up her hands and put them on the headteacher's desk.

"We're very sorry, Mrs Woods. Please forgive us for being such naughty girls. We will never behave so badly, ever again. We promise."

Mrs Woods studied Rose. Next, she scrutinised us adults: I hoped my face was suitably contrite. Finally, she turned to you.

"We includes you does it, Isla?"

A snowflake would have shattered the silence that followed. You and Mrs Woods eyeballed each other. Rose interlaced her fingers and wound them around to breaking point. My head throbbed.

Finally, you spoke. "Yes."

"What did you say?"

"I said yes." You scowled.

"Yes what?" Mrs Woods didn't need thumbscrews.

"Yes. It. Does."

That was enough. Mrs Woods folded her arms and rested them on her desk. The glasses went on again and she almost smiled. "Well, since you've both apologised and given an undertaking regarding future behaviour, I won't take this matter to the governing body. This time. There mustn't be a next time. You're both clever girls. You should use your brains to achieve your goals."

Hsiao Ling said thank you as we left the office, which I thought was a step too far.

Mother came up trumps—perhaps it was because she was buoyed up by the success of the Beauchamp meeting. She was sitting in the breakfast room with the French windows open, drinking a glass of wine when we arrived home. You threw your schoolbag on the table and sat down and glowered while I reported on events in the headteacher's study. Mother laughed, a tinkly, fragile sound that we didn't hear so often.

"It was so unfair." You stomped off to your room.

Mother got me a glass, and we finished off the bottle of wine. As the evening wore on, she told me stories from her schooldays, the leatherings in the classroom, the pitched battles in the playground, the food stolen from other children or from shops on the way home. She spoke as if it was all completely normal. Mother had always seemed so proper that I had to rethink some of my assumptions. It had been a long time since I'd felt so close to her. And then she suddenly came out with, "We're going to have our hands full with Isla."

Even with my tiddly brain, I thought, where did that come from? You were growing up, but what you needed was your mother, not a sister with a limited emotional range. Somehow

I'd become part of her "we" without knowing it. I wasn't sure I was ready for the responsibility.

· · · ● ● · ● ● · · ·

Something Mrs Woods said must have stuck, because there were no repeats of the toilet scene, which was as well because we were snowed under with Freddie's wedding. Not that the bride was a problem; Anna-Beth turned out to be everyone's sweetie, which was as well, given her dragon of a mother.

"Freddie's organised for us to go to Tahiti for our honeymoon," she whispered. After months of chopping and changing, we were nearly there, in the silky cocoon of the dressing room in our boutique, curtains drawn. She stepped into the frothy extravaganza her mother had insisted on, and I wished I could find fault with the girl who'd bagged Freddie. The angled mirrors reflected images of Anna-Beth and her dress into an eternity of white perfection.

"Freddie adores Gaugin," she said. "He's a brilliant artist, he'd make it his life if he could. I told him I wouldn't mind love in a garret with him in Montmartre or something, but Mr Granville insists he goes into the family business. I suppose he has to start somewhere. And Grandpa will help him, of course. Contracts, you know."

"It looks as if it needs a bit of a nip in here." I tugged at her dress. "You brides are always losing weight."

She put a hand on her waist and twisted around and a zillion reflections of her lovely face inspected the detail of her back. "I don't mind. I just want all this to be over. It's gone on so long and it's not really me, you know."

"Then why are you doing it?" Normally I avoided prying into our brides' feelings or motives—it wasn't in our business interests to unsettle them—but her groom was the only man I'd ever lusted after.

"Mummy, of course. It's her day really. She needs it even more now that Grandpa's been knocked off his perch."

That hadn't helped La Beauchamp's temper. There'd been a General Election which had resulted in a change of government and Le Beauchamp senior, the grandee, losing his government job. Mother and I weren't political, but we were pleased to see the Beauchamp nose put so out of joint.

"And now we've got that dreadful little man and his pipe running the country again. I thought we'd seen the back of him." Mrs Beauchamp gave us the benefit of her opinion.

"My father smoked a pipe." Mother didn't usually let her feelings show with customers.

"Hmm. Says it all. Oh, how lovely you look darling." The sight of Anna-Beth floating out of the changing room on her chiffon cloud stopped her mother in her tracks.

When it got lighter in the new year, you insisted you could find your own way home after school which was a relief when we were so busy. Sometimes you'd go to Hsiao Ling's for tea. Other days you'd bring Rose to our house after school, and you'd raid the fridge for something to eat. More than once, you raided my make-up.

I and my unconditional love should have been there for you after school, but we were still under the cosh at the boutique. If I felt guilty about your coming home to an empty house, I told myself a few more weeks of fending for yourself would do you no harm. I asked you for a raincheck till after Freddie's wedding.

"What's that?" Your ears always pricked up at anything that sounded like money.

"It's an Americanism," Mother said.

It was my turn to be surprised. "How do you know?"

"I had American friends in the war."

"I meant what's unconditional love," you said, and then when I looked hurt you added, "Jo-oke," and rolled your eyes.

The Thursday before Freddie's wedding, Mother and I got all the dresses from Hsiao Ling's and arranged them in the upstairs room at the boutique. It was like dying and going to a heaven full of floaty white beings with human shapes but no faces. When I said as much to Mother, she asked if I was feeling all right; I wasn't usually sentimental.

We loaded everything into the delivery van to take to the Beauchamp's estate near where my grandparents used to live. Kevin, our driver, had been with us for six years, but Mother still didn't trust him to handle the dresses. A wiry man, with a lean face and combed-back thin hair, he followed the styles of the latest pop groups, which that spring meant tartan trousers cutaway above the ankles. You liked it, though it grated with Mother.

Kevin drove out under the archway first and waited at the main road until Mother caught up in her nifty sports car. She insisted on having it as a company car to impress our younger generation of customers. I stood on the pavement and Kevin saluted me—bossette he always called me—before they disappeared off down the A3 into the countryside. Both drove too fast. The leaves on the plane tree were that brilliant green of early summer. The evening was mild, and the forecast was good. The dresses were fabulous. Everything was set for a triumph of a wedding.

Night had fallen by the time I'd finished clearing up the shop, picked up the last snippet of fabric and strand of thread, refolded the last sheet of tissue paper. Even then I had to drive the long way home to fill up my car with petrol. When I finally arrived, I found Mother's car parked in the driveway. A light was on upstairs, but the rest of the house was in darkness. My tired brain chuntered into alarm mode. As I got to the door, you opened it and looked at me with eyes that told me you'd had to be the adult in whatever was unfolding inside.

"Oh Ju-ju. Granny's died."

CHAPTER THIRTEEN

JUNE 1975

You stood in the doorway with your little-girl solemn face. And I, who should have been there to pick up the pieces for you, had to listen to you explaining: "Aunty Nancy phoned. Mummy said she went in and found Granny dead in bed. Mummy said they didn't know how long she'd been there. Just imagine being dead in bed and no-one knowing. Mummy's very upset."

"Oh Isla." I couldn't find the words for my sense of failure.

You led me through the house. It wasn't a gloomy place, but tonight I wished Mother had kept some of father's chintzy cheerfulness. The lilt in your walk choked me up. You weren't made to mop up adult grief, and it was that rather than sadness for my grandmother that got to me.

Light spilled from the breakfast room. The sound of crying stopped when we went in. You walked over to Mother and tried to comfort her, stroking her hair with your little hands, and kissing her face.

"Please Mummy, don't be sad." You put your arms around Mother and rocked her as if you were trying to soothe a child, resting your head on her shoulder, and patting her back. But there was fear in your face that Mother couldn't see. I nearly missed it, too. You were such a free spirit, I hadn't understood how dependent you were on her. And however much I loved you, she was your mother. It was her grief, rather than our grandmother's death, which shook your world.

Mother pulled a hankie out the sleeve of her blouse and wiped her eyes. "It must have happened in her sleep."

"At least she didn't suffer. That must be some comfort."

"Honestly Ju-ju. Is that all you can say?" You screwed your face up. "Mummy's just lost her mother. D'you have to be so... so hard-boiled about it?"

"I didn't mean to be. I'm really sorry." I didn't know what to feel. The last time our grandmother had been to stay must have been when you were a baby and I was away in Switzerland. Other than that, it was photographs, birthday cards, parcels at Christmas for us and the occasional trip home for Mother. Now it was too late. Perhaps it was the lack of memories that was so sad.

"Can I come to Scotland with you, Mummy?" you asked.

"I'm not so sure. It might be best if you stayed here." Mother was usually so decisive. Now she was flattened.

Next morning, for the first time I could remember, Mother didn't go to work. She already had the coffee machine going when I came down and poured us each a cup and then announced she'd get a lunchtime flight to Scotland. It took a few minutes for the significance of that to sink in.

First, she was going to fly, something she'd always point blank refused to do.

Second, she was going to miss the Beauchamp wedding.

"Freddie and Anna-Beth will be happy regardless of whether I'm there." Her face was drawn and blotchy. The skin around her eyes was puffy. As she lifted the bottle to pour milk into my coffee, her hand shook and the milk sloshed into the saucer. "You and Hsiao Ling can take care of things."

Then you came downstairs dressed for school. "You didn't come to bed last night, Mummy."

Mother didn't reply. She looked old.

"I waited for you in your bed so you wouldn't be sad, but you didn't come."

"Poor wee Isla. I'm sorry." Mother bent and kissed you. "There. You must be tired yourself. Ju-ju can drop you off at school, can't you Ju-ju? On the way to the Beauchamps? I was due there this morning."

· · · · ●·●· · · ·

You didn't get to go to the funeral.

Instead, you got farmed out with Hsiao Ling. I said it wasn't fair on Hsiao Ling to dump you on her at such a fraught time. Mother said it would be better for you, she said it would all be too much for a ten-year-old, though I thought the truth was she didn't have the emotional bandwidth to deal with your feelings in addition to her own.

As it turned out, the events of the next few days were to determine the course of all our lives, especially yours. Perhaps if things had been done differently, they'd have turned out better.

You kept your composure all the way to school, and then you had a little-girl weep before you got out of the car. Rose put her arms around you in the playground and you clung to her as I drove off.

On the way to the Beauchamp house, I rehearsed what I'd say. It all seemed perfectly logical. A maid showed me into the drawing room where Mrs Beauchamp was perched on an elaborate sofa, a gilded teacup poised in one hand and Aunt Connie in attendance. The formality of the silk-lined walls, heavily framed paintings, ornate furniture, and swagged curtains belonged to some other era. Before the war. Not my world.

"Oh," My godmother stopped leafing through the papers on her lap and put on her Constantia face. "Where's Maisie?"

In front of the two women was a walnut coffee table from which any hint of charm had been lacquered out. A glass vase of red roses at the perfect point of opening stood on top, long elegant stems in pristine water with just the right amount of foliage and blooms. But they had no scent. That came from the women. Someone had overdone the perfume.

"Unfortunately, my grandmother has died. Mother has to go up to Scotland." Their faces were inscrutable. "Today."

"But the wedding is tomorrow." Mrs Beauchamp lifted the wafer-thin porcelain cup to her lips and sipped. The rest of the world could wait on her convenience.

"Yes, and everything is taken care of." I had on my most mother-of-the-bride-reassuring voice. "All the arrangements are watertight. Our assistant will oversee the dressing and deal with any minor alterations. I'll be on hand at the church. Everything will be fine."

"That's not acceptable, Julia." Aunt Connie did superiority in shovel loads. An inclination of the head, a tightening of the lips, the slightest twitch of the nose. "The dressing is so critical. It's inconceivable that Maisie should miss it."

I didn't stand a chance. She made me feel a gibbering incompetent, and I wondered if she'd done the same to Mother over the years.

"She only has to delay her departure by twenty-four hours."

"It will make no difference. Her mother's already dead." La Beauchamp matched Aunt Connie punch for jaw-shattering punch. It was like being in a ring with two prize-fighters.

"Maisie could fly up straight after the wedding and be there tomorrow evening." My godmother was unrecognisable.

"Mother's distraught," was all I could find to hit back with.

"Guilt perhaps," said Aunt Connie. "She hardly ever saw her mother. She was neglectful."

"That's cruel." The words came out before I could stop them. The look my godmother gave told me I wouldn't be forgiven. I tried to backtrack. "Mother would be no use here. Her mind would be elsewhere. Mrs Tseng and I are more than capable of taking care of things."

"Tseng, did you say?" Mrs Beauchamp put her teacup down. "What kind of name is that?" There was a meaningful clink as the saucer made contact with the coffee table. "Where does this Mrs Tseng come from?"

The truth, Goddington, wouldn't be accepted. Mrs Beauchamp talked straight into my silence. "I'm not having someone like that overseeing my daughter's wedding."

"She made the dresses."

"Don't be cheeky."

My professionalism did a blip and for a minute it flashed across my mind that I could walk my twenty-six-year-old self out of this place.

"Maisie can't behave like this." My aunt's refined face went from slim to rat-like. Her eyes narrowed, her words spat out between even, white, clenched teeth. They cost a lot of money, those teeth. Just like her clothes and her expensively perfect figure. I remembered what Anna-Beth had said about contracts and wondered what exactly was at stake here and if there was more than self-serving venom on display.

"After everything I've done for your mother," said Aunt Connie, "When push comes to shove, she does a bunk. I suppose that's her sort."

"That's not fair. My grandmother died. Tragically. It's not Mother's fault she lives in Scotland."

"That's where she'd be too if it wasn't for me."

I didn't understand what she was talking about. There was nothing I could say. As it happened, there was no opportunity.

"That woman is not dressing my daughter for her wedding, and that's my final word on the matter." Mrs Beauchamp called time on the bickering.

My godmother stood up, lit a cigarette, took an elaborate drag, walked to the window, and made a theatrical display of thinking, then turned and blew a storm cloud of smoke in my direction. "You'll have to tell Maisie she can't go."

"I can't do that."

"Then I will."

As fast as I drove home it wasn't fast enough.

Mother was already on the phone when I ran in the front door. Her anguished "No," sounded in the hall. She was in the breakfast room, standing at the French windows with her back to me, looking into the garden, to where the white clematis was in bloom over the trellis she and Father had built, turning it into a snowbank of flowers. She was motionless with the phone to her ear.

"Jeremy married me because he loved me. Whatever came afterwards..."

Mother was speaking from the heart; I hesitated to interrupt.

"It wasn't convenience." A pause at Mother's end of the conversation. "He didn't lie to me." Another pause. "He wouldn't be so cruel. I know." Then a longer one. "No, no." Mother got agitated. "You'd destroy him."

Her pain was excruciating. When I walked in, she spun around. Her face was as white as the clematis flowers. "Julia's here," she said down the phone. "I must go. Don't worry Connie, I'll sort things."

· · · · ●· ●· · · ·

That's how I found myself on the overnight train from Kings Cross to Edinburgh. In the morning I got a taxi from Waverley Station direct to my grandmother's.

The tenements where my mother grew up had long since been pulled down. In their place the council had built a new housing estate with a children's play area on top of a landscaped mound which I suppose contained the debris from the slums. Some people romanticise the tenements, their teeming life and the community spirit it's supposed to have produced, but, looking at the new houses and the children playing on the swings and fighting over the roundabout in the evening sunshine, I could only see progress.

Mother had written out the new address. It didn't take long to find. Granny hadn't moved far. She'd decanted from the tenement to a block of modern maisonettes across the road from the playground. My high heels clattered along the concrete path across the front lawn. My grandmother's front door was locked, of course, so I rang the bell next door, where Mother said the neighbour had a key.

There was a scuffling sound from inside, and I felt someone look at me through the peephole, then the door opened and a man half-appeared. I say half because he merged so completely into the greyness of his surroundings that it was hard to tell where he ended and they began. Despite the heat he was wearing a thick cardigan with big leather buttons and trousers that sagged at the knees. All that stood out were his eyes that were small and bright.

"James Campbell?"

He nodded.

"Julia Stanhope. I understand you're the keyholder for number fifteen."

He nodded again and rocked forward onto his toes and reached up and took a key off a hook on the inside of his doorframe.

"I'll see you in." His voice was high-pitched and piping, like a child's.

"It's quite all right. I can manage. Don't you worry."

I held out my hand. He was reluctant to give me the key, and in the end I had to tug it from him. It had a bright yellow plastic tag and a label with "Flora Munro" written in a shaky, old person's script.

"Shall I drop it through your letterbox when I leave?"

That seemed to reassure him, and he nodded and gave me a smile, if you could call it that, with his funny lopsided mouth.

"Are you Maisie's daughter?"

It was my turn to nod.

"You don't look like her."

"So people say."

"You can call me Wee Jimmy if ye like." He giggled.

"Mmm." Somehow, I didn't think we'd have many conversations.

My grandmother's home was pristine. The front room had a big window with net curtains and in one corner a television set covered with a lacy cloth. On top of it was a silver-framed picture which I picked up and took to the window so I could see it properly. An old couple, arm in arm by a river with the Forth Bridge in the background. They beamed out of the photograph at me, matching smiles, shared happiness. The woman had to be my grandmother, dressed in a tweed jacket and a green cloche hat with a feather in one side. I couldn't recognise the man. He was wearing a flat cap, and I found one hanging on a hook by the back door. It was the only indication a man had lived here. He can't have been my grandfather, he was long dead. My mother had never talked about a stepfather, but then she rarely spoke about her family. The furniture was all spanking new and the décor and furnishings were in light blues and yellows so that the effect was of permanent sunshine. It was hard to feel sad in such a place. There was no trace of any regrets.

I put the framed photograph in my overnight bag. The house clearance people could deal with the rest. On my way out I dropped the keys back through the letterbox of number thirteen, then set off up the road to find a taxi.

By the time Mother arrived on Monday, everything was sorted. I'd phoned my Aunt Nancy, my other godmother, to check which church my grandmother had attended, and what kind of flowers she liked. Not that Mother appeared to care. She said you were furious at being left behind, and whether it was the emotions of that parting, exhaustion from the wedding, or some further showdown with the two dragons, she was still unable to make decisions.

Her numbness was over-powering. This was her home city, but it was as if she had a cocoon around her, as if she was shielding herself from something. We spent a lot of time walking. She became obsessive about it, along the Royal Mile, up and down more hills than I'd seen since Switzerland. One day we were walking down a road somewhere behind Princes Street, when she suddenly stopped and said, "This is where your grandfather worked." Her face scanned the row of shops with several floors of dark windows above. "It was one of these. He said he used to sit on a table sewing kilts. He took me there once. His friends all said he was a hero. One of them gave me a sweetie."

"You've never talked to me about him," I said. "Apart from the war hero stuff. You've never told me what kind of man he was."

The animation that had brightened her face flickered and dulled. The haunted wariness returned. She pulled her cardigan around her and resumed her walking. "Nancy's bringing her son to the funeral."

It was to be on Friday, and we'd catch the overnight train back to London. She held herself together at the service, hid her face behind a stylish black hat with a veil. It was the only thing that distinguished her among the black suits in church. Across the aisle from Mother there was an older woman in a black coat that strained at the seams, and a wide-brimmed hat that obscured her face, which she kept dabbing at with a hankie. The young man next to her looked familiar. He sat straight-backed in his pew, well-cut jacket, white shirt collar nudging above it. I leaned forward to try to get a better view of him.

Afterwards, the woman squeezed past an elderly couple at the little reception I'd organised in a staid hotel nearby and introduced herself. "I'm yer auntie Nancy, and this is my son, Dominic."

His suit was, as I'd guessed, well cut, although with a figure like his, it wouldn't matter. His shoulders were broad without being oafish, his hips slim, his legs long enough to carry off the flare of his trousers, which was just enough to declare himself trendy. He had black wiry hair that was brushed back from a face that looked at my mother with friendly commiseration, and at me with sexual magnetism.

"He's just started a new job with one of our big accountancy firms." Nancy's pride bellowed through the modesty of her voice. Dominic kept hold of my hand and gave me one of those "Mothers, what d'you do with them?" smiles while Nancy told me he'd got a first at "the University. You never went, did you Julia?" she asked. "Mind you, it's harder for girls."

Left to ourselves, he asked about our business. "Right time, right place. The potential must be limitless."

It was the first time anyone had talked to me that way. "You'll have to be our financial adviser."

"I aim to hit London before I'm thirty." He had the grace to laugh at himself.

After the reception, Mother said she wanted to visit Granny's place one last time. She said she'd get the key from Wee Jimmy. He'd turned up for the funeral in a faded black suit that looked like it was made a long time ago for a much larger man. I left her to it and went off for a drink with Dominic.

It felt as if I'd always known him. Our talk glided along at the bar of the forgettable pub down a stone-walled alleyway near the station. His university, my time in Switzerland, our Scottish mothers, his ambitions, my, well, what he called my successful business. I'd never seen it like that before.

"You should. There's not many women can build up a business like you've done." He knocked back his third whisky before adding, "I suppose your mother helped of course."

I liked that, even if the "women" bit grated. Since leaving school, I'd worked in what I'd always regarded as my mother's business. But now I thought about it, he was right, it was my business too. We were on our fourth whiskies when I plucked up the courage to ask, "Your father wasn't there today?"

"It's just my mother and me." From the way he twirled his glass and avoided my eyes, it seemed that he'd had to answer the question often enough before.

"I know how that feels."

"Do you?" He drained his glass and put it on the bar. "My father supports us. There's a lawyer who comes up from London every so often. Progress reports. But no contact."

He called the barman to pour him another drink and got my glass filled up at the same time. His eyes, which I'd thought were dark and warm, looked more slate-grey. They told me I'd done enough poking about in his feelings.

By the time we left, the light over the pub door shone into pitch darkness. At the edges of its glow, Dominic stopped and kissed me. He tipped up my face, "So I can see it properly," he said. "You're lovely." I'd not heard anyone say that before either. His face was in shadow, but I thought I heard a kind of longing in his voice that matched how I felt. We kissed until someone pushed past us in the alleyway, "Can ye no find somewhere mair comfortable?" I giggled, and he smiled, and we walked hand in hand to the station. Then Dominic pulled away. We found Mother standing with our luggage on the platform for the London train, anxiously checking her watch. Dominic helped us into our compartment and stood and waved on the platform as our train left.

"Nancy's boy turned out well," Mother said.

· · · · ● · ● · · · ·

A blast of five-spices hit us full-frontal when Hsiao Ling opened her front door to us the next morning. She didn't greet us but instead started rubbing at her hands with a piece of kitchen roll. If I'd bothered to register it, I'd have known it meant trouble. But you appeared behind her wearing an apron covered in flour, and I called out, "Isla," and pushed past Hsiao Ling and gave you a hug, and then you dragged me into the kitchen, spotless, newly fitted out with white cupboards and a black-and-white chequered vinyl tile floor. In the centre was a round white table with a bright yellow lemony design partly obscured by bottles of different coloured sauces and plastic packages with bright labels. Rose was at the cooker holding a fish slice over a smoking wok. For such young girls you seemed remarkably in control. At home you never cooked more than a sausage. By way of hello, Rose waved her fish slice at me.

"Look Ju-ju. We're making pork buns." You opened the oven door and pulled out a tray of soft white rolls.

"Would you like one?" Rose put one of the rolls on a paper plate on the kitchen table and then took the lid off a heavy iron pot sitting on the cooker. The smells that burst out of it filled me in a way that the flaccid British Rail eggs and tea that Mother and I had on the train back from Scotland couldn't begin to. I tasted the pork before Rose had even put it into the bun.

You frowned. "D'you think Mother might like to try one. It's not quite her thing, is it?"

Rose put one on the plate for her, but when I went back out into the corridor, Mother and Hsiao Ling had disappeared. I followed the sound of their voices into the front room. Mother was still wearing the black suit she'd had on at the funeral, crumpled from the journey. Hsiao Ling, hair tied back in a ponytail, hands on hips, body coiled in anger, was spitting rage across her elaborately carved coffee table.

"You humiliated me."

"No."

"You told me I would be in charge and when I turned up at the house, the maid sent me away. Said madam didn't want me. She shut the door on me. And then when I got home poor Isla was here with an overnight bag."

"I tried to call you about the change in plans. I left messages. I'm sorry. It's been a hard time." Mother rubbed her forehead.

All the whisky I'd drunk with Dominic made sure I went to sleep quickly enough on the train, but every time I woke up during the night, I heard Mother tossing and turning. She must have been shattered.

"She wouldn't have me because I'm Chinese."

"Did she say so?"

Hsiao Ling's eyes glittered, and I couldn't tell if it was anger or tears. "You don't need to have someone tell you when they say 'No' and close the door on you with that look on their face that it's because you're Chinese. You're good enough to do their laundry and cook the food they eat when they're drunk and do their cleaning and even make their wedding dresses. But only so far and then a great wall comes down and you're on the wrong side of it. Not white. Chinese." She made a clicking noise and turned her head away, which was when she saw I was there.

"You must have known about it, too."

"I didn't really think." I felt stupid standing there with the pork buns going cold on their plate.

"You're an adult now. You have to think."

"I'm sure Mother was only trying to do what was best."

"Best for who?"

"For the business." Mother had found a second wind. "For what's made our living and kept the wolf from the door all these years. What I've worked my fingers to the bone for just to make sure that we can pay the bills at the end of the month. I've had to pull myself up by my own bootstraps too, ye ken. From nothing."

"Nothing?" Hsiao Ling's voice shook. "I'll tell you about nothing. You always say how your father was a war hero. Well, my grandfather was a war hero too. But he never came home. He signed up in China because he was too poor to do anything else and then he was taken across the world by your people to fight in your war and he disappeared in it. No trace." Now Hsiao Ling's whole body was shaking. "My grandmother left her home to find him. Travelled right across the world. With my mother just a baby. She spent the rest of her life searching. He never even knew he had a daughter. And my mother had no memory of her father. That's nothing."

Silence. Footsteps went past on the pavement outside and there was the sound of women laughing. You and Rose were laughing too, peals of it rolled out from the kitchen.

"I can't change that." For a minute it seemed Mother would turn away, and I thought, oh god, what will that spark off? But she only went to the armchair in the corner and sat down. She opened her handbag and took out a packet of tissues, extracted one, and blew her nose.

Hsiao Ling watched her. "You can make it different."

Mother looked more flummoxed than I'd ever seen her.

"What d'ye mean?"

"You can make me a partner in the business."

Mother jumped. Visibly.

"Why not?" Hsiao Ling was unrecognisable from the mild-mannered woman who would sit up all night to finish a wedding dress. She stood up straight with her hands at her side and then shot, as it were, from the hip. "I've been making the clothes for you all these years, me and my sister and our friends. We've done exactly what you've wanted whenever you've wanted. Always good quality. Always on time."

"And you've been paid well for it."

"That's not enough. I want a share in the business."

Mother looked at me. I looked at my plate of food.

"Or I won't sew for you any longer."

The juice from the meat dribbled out of the white fluffy buns and congealed on the plate. The smell, which had been so delicious, now seemed slightly sickly.

"I've got a daughter too," Hsiao Ling said. "I don't want her to grow up seeing me being a skivvy, like I saw my mother. I want things to be better for her."

Something about what she said must have resonated with Mother. She stood up and took off her black jacket. "I think we can work things out."

· · · · · ● · ● · · · ·

That's how we restructured the business, sitting around the coffee table in Hsiao Ling's front room. Three directors, me in charge of marketing, Hsiao Ling in charge of production, and Mother in charge of finance. Hsiao Ling was happy because we each had an equal share. I was happy because I finally had a role of my own. Mother was happy because... well I'm not sure whether Mother was happy, or why; it was always impossible to decipher her feelings. But once we were all agreed, she smiled and said, "That's it then, we have a plan."

We celebrated with your pork buns, washed down with bright green fizzy apple juice out of scruffy bottles stacked at the back door, watching the Virginian on Hsiao Ling's colour television. Mother said the star reminded her of a friend. After that we endured a cringey children's programme that you girls found hysterical and rolled around with laughter on Hsiao Ling's new sofa.

You weren't to know at the time, but that day was a turning point for more than the business. I don't know how clearly Mother thought it all through, or whether it was instinct. And I don't mean her business instinct, but her instinct for whose side she was on, and who was on hers. Not La Beauchamp. Nor, in the final analysis, her old, now former, friend Constantia. Mother never saw her again. Goodness knows what our absent father Jeremy would have done in the circumstances. Dredging my memory, I came up with a picture of him standing by Constantia at his parents' funeral, and my holding Mother's hand on the other side of the grave, and wishing I was with my father. This was another such dividing line, and I guessed we'd probably be on different sides again. But this time I had no regrets. Not for either of us: you would never be part of any old guard.

While the television blared on, and I wondered what Dominic would make of our company restructure, Mother and Hsiao Ling reset their relationship. They chatted side by side on the sofa and munched their pork buns and Mother licked her fingers and her funeral frost melted. She seemed at ease. Just before we left, Hsiao Ling sent you girls to clear up the kitchen, and turned to Mother and said, "What I don't understand is why you didn't go straight away."

"Go where?" Mother was collecting up the pieces of paper with the jottings about the new company structure and putting them in her handbag. There'd be a visit to our lawyer—my godfather, Guy Forrester—sometime soon.

"To Scotland. I don't understand why you let a wedding dress stop you going to honour your mother."

CHAPTER FOURTEEN

JUNE 1975

Y ou woke me. Your screaming. Heart-piercing. Stomach-churning. Pitch dark. Freezing cold. My brain clicked into gear, my eyes focused. The green figures of my alarm clock showed 1.05.

In the corridor the night light glowed from its socket outside your bedroom door. Inside you were sitting up in bed, knees tucked under your chin, hands over your eyes, screaming like something out of a horror film. The bedside light shone on the fluffy pink rabbit nestled on your pillow and your favourite boy band, the ones in tartan trousers, looked down from the poster over your bedhead. Your windows were wide open, and the curtains flapped like things possessed. I already had goosebumps, and a gust of cold air made me shiver. I sat beside you on the bed and held you close. You were like an ice block. "You'll catch your death, Isla."

Another arctic blast hit us. I went over to the window to shut it. Outside the sky was black. No moon, no stars. At the far end of the garden, I could hear the wind, see the dark shapes of the trees flail, protesting the bitter gale, their branches writhing like desperate arms. The turbulence was disorientating. It made me feel sick. A squall of sleet stung my face.

We were alone in the house. Mother had gone up to London that morning to see Guy about the changes to the company, and then phoned to say the trains were in chaos because of the weather so she couldn't get home.

"There's snow on the way," she said.

"Not in June."

But it was, and now it had arrived, and it spooked me. That and your screaming.

"It's like the end of the world." You took your hands away from your face and I saw pain in it.

"It's only sleet." I pulled the window shut and drew the curtains. "There, it's gone."

"No it hasn't. It's still out there. The madness. I'm ten, I'm not a child any longer. Why does everyone treat me like I'm a child?" You bent over your knees and folded your arms over the back of your head and sobbed. You clenched your fists and your whole body shook.

I sat on the bed beside you and tugged in desultory fashion at the duvet to keep us warm. "This isn't about the sleet is it?"

You shook your head.

"What is it then?"

When you lifted your head, your fine red hair was stuck to your face with tears. I wiped it away. You didn't stop me. "Why didn't Mummy go and look for Daddy?"

That came out of nowhere. I pulled at the duvet in earnest and managed to get it around us both. "There, that's better."

"Why does everyone always change the subject? Why won't anyone talk about it? Why won't they tell me?"

"There's nothing to tell, Isla. He used to live with us, and then he'd come to see us, and then..." I didn't know what came next.

"Yes?"

"He stopped coming."

"Just like that?"

"Yes."

"He disappeared?"

"I suppose so."

"But when Hsiao Ling's grandfather disappeared, her grandmother spent the rest of her life trying to find him."

"How d'you know?" I hadn't thought you would have heard all the row at Hsiao Ling's house.

"Hsiao Ling told me. She said her grandmother took her mother when she was just a little girl like me and went all over the world looking for Hsiao Ling's grandfather, until in the end she came to London, and she got stuck here and died all alone in an attic by the docks all shrivelled up like one of those mummies. Hsiao Ling said her Granny died of the cold." I cursed Hsiao Ling, and the sleet. "Why doesn't Mummy try to find Daddy?"

"Perhaps she did."

"She can't have tried very hard. Or else he didn't want to be found." You screwed your face up like you were thinking through something very complicated. "Didn't they love each other?"

I thought back to when we'd all been together and tried to remember what it had felt like. At the time it seemed like we loved each other, that's what families did, even if they didn't always say so. I'd felt loved. I'd presumed that they did too. You only came along right at the end, and we all loved you. But by the time you were conscious of things, Father had disappeared. So, I suppose you'd never got to feel us all being together.

"Yes. They did love each other, I think."

"You only think." You blew your nose on the duvet. Now wasn't the time to remind you how much I hated the habit. "Even if they did love each other, It can't have been enough." You looked at me. Your eyes were intense, less of the baby blue.

You were right, you were growing up, and I hadn't recognised it. "Did Father love me?"

"Oh Isla, he loved you to pieces. He used to carry you around the garden singing silly songs with a big smile on his face. It was after I came home from Switzerland. The summer that Sergeant Pepper came out. My all-time favourite record."

"I have no memory of Daddy." We talked about him for a while. I got his picture from Mother's room, and you said how like him I looked, and after a while you lay down and cuddled your rabbit. When you were calm, I told you I was going back to bed. Even with the window shut it was too cold for me in my nightie. As I tucked the duvet around your shoulders, you suddenly asked. "How about Mummy? Does she love me?"

"Of course she does."

"I can never tell what she feels."

When I thought about it, neither could I.

· · • • • • • • · ·

That autumn you breezed through your eleven-plus exam and got into a grammar school. I thought you might have a melt-down under the pressure, but you seemed completely unper-turbed by it. Your only worry was that the secondary school you got a place at was girls only and you enjoyed the company of boys. "Not having any in the family," was your excuse. Rose, under pressure from Hsiao Ling got a scholarship to the same school. In the years that followed, you were inseparable. You shared clothes and make-up and homework. When you went out together, I knew you'd keep each other out of trouble.

Shortly before you finished primary school the heat, which had been excessive, burst into forest fires across the countryside. Smoke hovered in the air for weeks. When I hung the washing out, it dried to a crisp in minutes and smelt of burning. We sat at your bedroom window and watched the woodland behind our garden burn. The leaves on the trees had already shrivelled from drought. They looked so helpless against the flames that ate them up, however much they waved their branches in protest. There's something about fire that's apocalyptic. Even I had a sense of doom and I feared you might think the world was ending again.

You leaned your arms on the windowsill and gazed out at the burning countryside. "Things will never be the same, ever again."

"That's growing up, Isla."

You threw me a look.

Mother came in to view the conflagration. The fire jumped to the trellis that she and Father had built, and it disappeared in a rush of flames.

"Mercy me. The poor clematis." She bit her lip and stood with her hands on her chest, like she was clutching some pain in it, and then wiped a finger under her left eye. "The smoke got into it."

You watched her like a hawk. We all watched the fire brigade crash about in the remains of the woodland. Afterwards Mother replaced the burned down fence at the end of the garden with a brick wall, and had one built at the front too, fitted for good measure with electric gates. It changed the feel of the place, but like she said, things had moved on. The village was turning into a town. Our lane had become a busy road. We needed more security.

You insisted on getting to secondary school under your own steam. It was a tortuous journey by public transport, so we did a trial run the week before school started. A Greenline bus to Hampton Court, then a walk across the bridge over the Thames and a double-decker bus through Bushy Park. You insisted on sitting up top, right at the front, and held onto the railing and stared out through the big windows at the scrawny looking deer wandering about on the drought-blighted, fire-ravaged land.

"Freedom," you said.

......•••••

So it was for all of us. I hit my thirties. As marketing manager for our expanding company, I took on a PR assistant, a personable young man called Henry Mackintosh—Harry Tosh he branded himself for work purposes. He turned up in our boutique wearing a three-piece suit with his shirt collar unbuttoned and his hair in a mullet.

Mother said he was an extravagance. I pointed out we needed to develop new markets, and I was now older than most of our brides. And it was flattering to have the attention of a younger man who brought a frisson of sexual excitement, albeit work-distanced. He said I should vamp up my image and that with my height and colouring, which he called neutral rather than mouse, I could do padded shoulders and big hair and look like the fashion powerhouse I was. How about Mother? I asked him. She was "niche," he said, with her pared back chic and trademark red curls. Perhaps he didn't dare take her on.

You didn't have to vocalise what you thought of Harry. It was enough that you would turn up at the boutique whenever he was due in. Your school shoes would clump up the stairs to my office with "Marketing Director" written on the door, and then you'd hang around chewing gum and ogling him.

At the end of the '70s you marked your fourteenth birthday by going up the Kings Road with Rose and came back dressed in a leather jacket and black jeans ripped at the knees. Rose had bought a similar pair, and she went up to your bedroom to change back into her slacks before she went home. When I came up, she was smoothing down her torn jeans over a hanger in your wardrobe and you were replacing the tartan boy band with a poster of a punkish looking girl singer. One Saturday you got a perm. When I told you it made you look like Mother you went and got it all cut off in what you said was a buzz cut, but the school said it was too short and sent you home for a week.

We put a mock-up of a punk wedding dress, black corset above short white ruffles at the front, long slashed overskirt at the back and black lace-up boots, in our boutique window. It attracted lots of attention, but no orders.

·· • • • • • • • ··

The summer you took your O levels was the year Princess Di got married. Harry said that if we made an instant copy of her wedding dress, he'd get a picture of it in the local newspaper. You said you weren't going to stay in to watch a dress whoever was wearing it. So you went off by bus to meet Rose with a £10 note tucked into your strappy little shoulder-bag and your cropped red hair gelled into spikes.

Mother, Hsiao Ling, and I gathered around a giant TV monitor rigged up on the wall at one end of the workshop above our boutique. Dressmakers' dummies in varying stages of undress stood around the long, low room, waiting for their big day to arrive. Cutting tables ran the length of it and bolts of fabric in white, ivory, cream, chantilly, ghost white, bone white, Dutch white and anything else that would make white sound distinctive, lay on racks at the far end. Sewing machines sat on tables by the windows, three overlooking the carpark at the back and two overlooking the shopping parade. The sixth window was enclosed by my marketing office.

I went and unlocked the door and lifted the sash window. We'd hung discreet bunting along the front of our boutique. The rest of the parade was decked out more garishly. The street was deserted except for two women standing at our shop door. Hsiao Ling let them in; her sister and a friend introduced only as Jenny who had come to help with the dress production.

We were set. We were poised. We knew exactly what each would do. Mother would draw the designs, I would sort out the fabrics, Hsiao Ling would organise the production. All we needed was to see the dress. Mother, in an emerald outfit with her hair newly coiffed, commandeered one of the new tub chairs from downstairs and waved the remote at the television. Hsiao Ling stood by the big screen in one of her signature black tailored trouser suits, with her hair tied back and a slash of bright red lipstick as her one concession to the day. The two machinists stood behind whispering.

"Look." Mother leaned forward. A black carriage with big brass lamps at each corner appeared on the screen, driven by men in red and gold and surrounded by police on horseback.

"It's more like a funeral carriage," I said. "They could have loaned her a gold coach."

"You're as bad as your father. He always said they were stingy." Mother bit her lip.

Hsiao Ling darted in front of the television and peered at the coach. "There it is," she said.

"Hey, Hsiao Ling, we can't see," I said.

"Listen to them," Mother got up and opened all the windows and we heard cheering, not from the television, but from the houses and flats around about. Such a tidal wave of emotion. It made me feel quite weepy. Hsiao Ling was unmoved, rooted to the ground, her nose practically touching the big screen.

"Give over, Hsiao Ling. It's only a dress," I said.

"You don't understand." She was mesmerised. "This dress is something different. This dress will change the world."

She moved, but only when the cameras had switched to the Prince, sitting in a pretty open-topped carriage. She wasn't interested in him, and when the Queen appeared in a turquoise outfit, she turned her back to the screen and talked quick-fire to her sister and friend. Then the cameras cut back to the bride's coach.

"Look, look." Hsiao Ling pressed her finger to the screen, and I saw that the inside of the carriage was full of chiffon. No sign of the bride. Perhaps she'd bolted. No, the cameras zoomed in to snatch a glimpse of a veiled head. Hsiao Ling's running commentary reached fever pitch as the coach stopped at the red carpet up the steps of St Paul's Cathedral. Then the door opened and out it came.

Hsiao Ling shrieked. Mother's hand froze above her sketch pad.

The dress unfolded from the coach, billowing out like an airbag in a car crash. It had travelled to the top of the Cathedral steps before the train had even finished exiting the carriage.

"Bloody hell," I said. "We've not got enough fabric in the entire building for that."

Mother started drawing, prattling at Hsiao Ling who stood up close to the screen scrutinising every minute detail of the dress as it went into the Cathedral. I ran the length of the workshop as the wedding trumpets sounded the bride up the aisle and started sorting out fabrics. This was strictly business, I knew, but I did feel a tear prick my eyes, and that thump, thump, thump I always got when I saw a bride in her dress and wondered if it would ever be me doing what the commentator was proclaiming to be "her happiest walk."

By the time we peered at the peachy outfit she wore to go on honeymoon, our display was big enough to fill the entire shopfront. I moved the existing mannequins and then went into my office. The window was open and outside the day was mellowing into an evening awash with wedding bonhomie. A group of six men were walking down the road drinking cans of beer and waving union jacks and laughing. Two women coming the other way got entangled with them, kissed them, a passing car hooted. The women walked on, the men did a thumbs up at the car. It had to stop at the lights, and one of the drinkers walked up to it and stuck his head in the window and then staggered away laughing—the lights changed, and the car took off.

I lifted the phone, punched in Harry's number, and told him he could organise the photographers for the next morning. We'd be ready. He was jubilant. He was drunk. "I knew you'd do it. Mwaah." He kissed his phone. As soon as I put mine down, it rang again, so I picked it up. "Yes, Harry."

"It's me, Ju-ju. It's getting a bit dodgy here. Can you come and pick us up? And please don't tell Hsiao Ling where we are."

When you said where that was, I could see why you didn't want Hsiao Ling to know. The Excalibur, a splash of pebble-dashed aggravation in the dreary suburban wilderness of New Malden. The two of you were just old enough to be in the pub. But not old enough to be drinking. Let alone fighting.

· · · • • • • • · ·

You had hold of another girl's hair when I walked in. A large man in a light blue open-neck shirt had his arms around your waist and was holding you off the ground. You were kicking him and screaming, "You bastard, let me go." The other girl, whose top was so low her boobs showed, squealed.

Rose stood with an ice-bucket in her hands, her face screwed into a fury. The rest of the pub was gathered around to watch. Their shouts drowned out the noise of the royal wedding replaying on a big screen behind the bar. Some of the men were laughing, some were egging you on. The rest shouted obscenities. All were the worse for wear. Two barmen stood watching from behind the bar. One whispered to the other and went out the back. The younger women were screaming "Bitch" and "Cunt." One threw a glass of something at Rose who raised the ice-bucket and started circling it above her head.

"Rose. No." It was a superhuman effort to be heard above the pandemonium. Rose's head turned in my direction. Luckily, I'd caught her attention before she'd actually let go of the bucket, so all that happened was the ice went all over the floor as she let it down. When you saw me, your face registered relief. You stopped kicking and let go of the girl's hair. But the man didn't put you down, and the girl promptly bounced up and whacked you across the face.

"Stop that. Stop it now." I pushed my way up to the man holding you around the waist. He had stains all over his blue shirt and wet trickles running down his face. He was probably handsome when he wasn't snarling.

"You fucking little punk." He gave you a vicious squeeze.

"Put her down." I hoped my shoulder pads made me look braver than I felt.

But the fight had gone out of him. He was too drunk to hold a thought for long, let alone you. He lost his grip, and you wriggled free. I grabbed you and Rose and dragged you out of the pub. At the corner of the road, I let you go.

"Run, Isla." For once, you didn't argue. You pelted to my car. When I fumbled with the keys, you snatched them from me and held the front seat forward for Rose to jump in the back. We were just pulling away when we heard a police siren.

It was you who started crying. "They called Rose names." I told you where to find the tissues, and you got one out and blew your nose. "They said she was a... a..."

Rose's face in the rear-view mirror showed the same pain I'd seen in her mother the day of the Beauchamp row.

"And they made... they made..." You lifted your hands and covered your mouth with them, to hold back the words.

"You can say it, you know. It happens all the time." Rose's voice was harsh, like Hsiao Ling's had been that day. We were on the slip road to the by-pass, so I concentrated on my driving.

"It was that girl and her boyfriend who started it all," you said. "The one in the blue shirt. I don't understand how people get away with that shit any longer. And the whole pub was cheering them on. Rose threw her drink at him."

"Isla pulled the girl's hair." I couldn't decipher Rose's expression. Her eyes were fixed on the encroaching darkness out of the car window. "She was a real slut, that one."

"So I saw." The roads were still empty. We'd get back home in record time.

You dried your eyes. Rose, usually the first one to cry, didn't have any tears this time. She sat in untouchable silence and watched the suburbs slip by with a hardness on her face. Yours was red where the girl had slapped you.

"I wish I hadn't run away," you said. "I wish I'd pulled her entire fucking head off."

Chapter Fifteen

Summer 1990

Y ou arrived late with a man in tow. Through the ornate floral arch at the far end of the banqueting room with your lace-covered arm through his black-suited one, like you were making your entrance at your own wedding reception. My heart did a butterfly flutter. Then he turned his head in my direction and the butterfly turned into a crow. The man was Dominic.

You went up the aisle to the table where Rose was sitting in her bridal glory. She jumped up and, bless her, made a fuss of you, giving you a hug that enveloped you in ivory chiffon. Then she politely shook Dominic's hand. Rose's cautious face, the distancing of her body, the extension of her arm, showed a questioning of whether this was the right man for her oldest friend.

Rose's new husband, Michael Chan, greeted you with an engaging smile. He did the same to Dominic, beside whom he looked young, and gauche, with his sharp blue suit and open face. He grabbed Dominic's hand in both of his, laughing all the time, in fact he'd hardly stopped laughing the entire day. Dominic, one hand in his pocket, the other being pumped up and down in Michael's, started to laugh too, although it wasn't clear whom he was laughing with or at. You moved on down the bridal table and leaned over Hsiao Ling's shoulder. Bride's mother that she was, she extricated herself and addressed you with the intensity she normally reserved for her daughter. Your face was hidden from my view behind Hsiao Ling's elaborate hairdo. But when she turned around to point out our table, I could see the warmth of her affection for you. Had I forgotten how close you both were?

You weaved a slinky path, between tables where the exuberance of the clothes competed with the flamboyance of the food and the lurid drinks topped with frilly paper parasols. Scarlet lanterns beamed across bone white scented bowls of steaming deliciousness, platters of lobsters and chicken, whole fish, and sides of glistening pork. Scattered throughout were disposable cameras and, here and there, red and gold envelopes with gifts of money from guests. Rising above it all was the racket that predicted everyone at this wedding was going to have a very good time.

"Mummy." You bent and kissed Mother. "You remember Dominic, don't you?"

"Oh, mercy me, yes." Mother turned in her gilt chair, head poised, chin up, crimson lips in a carefully made-up face, curly hair thinner now and dyed a darker shade of red, fastened in a gold clasp. She crossed her legs at the knee and extended a hand to Dominic. She was doing her grand dame act which suggested to me that she had in fact forgotten.

"Nancy's son," I said.

"Of course." She examined him from the distinguished white streak in his black hair to the bottom of his tailored trousers. We all examined him; for me, curiosity was tainted with envy. Guy Forrester sat determinedly nursing a glass of water on the far side of Mother, and beside him was Harry Tosh, rebranded Henry Mack since his latest divorce. Dominic basked in the attention, although I noticed a fidgeting of his hand in his left pocket.

For a minute I thought he was going to kiss Mother's hand. In the event he only made a slight bow over it and then eased his way around the table, acknowledging me en route, a discreet handsqueeze of my shoulder which hinted at intimacy. I think I blushed. A couple of guests moved around so you could sit next to me, with Dominic beside you.

"What brings you here?" Guy sipped from his glass of water with awkward nonchalance. He addressed his words at Dominic, but not, it seemed, his affections.

"Isla, of course." He squeezed your hand, and I felt a pang. It was my fault, what happened. I understood that right from the start. Everything that followed was down to my emotional ignorance.

Dominic had succeeded in conquering London by the time he was thirty and we'd met a few times until he'd become too busy. It didn't take him long. Soon after he stopped returning my calls, you arrived home from university saying you wanted to work in financial services. He was the obvious go-to contact. So I overcame my hurt pride and plagued him for a meet-up. When it finally happened, the attraction between the two of you sparked across the ten-year age gap. I'd swallowed my now mortally wounded pride and left you both to it. You got your job, and I didn't follow up on anything else. This evidently was it. A waiter came and laid a fresh place setting for Dominic and poured him a glass of champagne.

Dominic turned to Guy, "I could ask you the same."

"Oh, that's easy. I'm the lawyer." Guy made it sound like he was a player in a murder mystery.

"And I'm the PR man." Henry leaned across the table, past Guy, and pressed a business card into Dominic's hand. "Pleased to meet you. I helped Hsiao Ling put this together. Wonderful event, don't you think?"

If Dominic had known Henry as well as I did, he'd have picked up the challenge. But Dominic didn't and wasn't interested either.

"And I'm the banker. Not theirs, I mean. In general." He slid the business card, unread, into his pocket.

Henry laughed. Guy didn't.

"We're not the dressmakers, I'm afraid." Mother was oblivious to the testosterone spat around her. "The clothes are all Hsiao Ling's doing."

"Well, that's the introductions done." You were busy organising the bowls and platters on the table. "Can we please move onto something else? Like this amazing food. Dominic, you must try this. It's abalone in case you're wondering. Hsiao Ling always said it signifies abundance." You held a tidbit to his lips with chopsticks and we were all transfixed as he ate—the two of you made it look like foreplay.

Dominic turned the attention onto Guy. "My mother sends her regards, I told her I might see you here."

Guy was caught with a mouthful of food, which he tried to swallow too quickly and choked, and then Dominic added, "She misses your little visits."

Mother looked from the one to the other. Guy blushed. Dominic smiled. For once I was glad I wasn't the pretty sister. I wasn't responsible for this drama.

"Oh fuck it, why do things always have to be so complicated?" You picked up a green cocktail, took out the dinky parasol in it, and snapped it in half. "Even the drinks aren't normal."

Henry ran around the table with a bottle and leaned over you. "Here you are, lovely lady. One completely normal glass of champagne."

You rewarded him with a giggle. "You're always such a star, Harry."

"Henry."

"Of course." You gave him one of those gushy smiles that you'd been directing at him since your teenage years and he grinned back.

What I wanted to know was why you were so spectacularly late. You never apologised, so I wouldn't have expected that. But I wanted to know how you'd managed to nearly miss the entire wedding of your closest friend. Instead, I said, "You look wonderful in that dress."

"Do I?" You must have known. It skimmed your figure with an expensive sheen and the lace in the arms looked handmade. You were wearing your hair up and with your delicate bones and pale complexion you looked like a china figurine. But there was a fragility about you, a need for approval that I didn't recall in the sister who'd stomped around the house in torn black jeans and Doc Marten boots.

"Dominic bought it for me."

"My mother used to wear her hair in a chignon," said Mother. "It suits you."

"You could come and model for us." Henry unwrapped one of the disposable cameras and pointed it in your direction. You did a smooch kiss at him over your green drink and, flash, he took a picture.

"There was a time she'd have done anything for you," I said. "When she was in her school uniform, and you were swinging Harry Tosh."

"Carpe diem." Dominic deployed his chopsticks. "You missed your chance there, Harry. She's mine now."

Henry scowled, the first time I'd known him to get so huffy.

Guy poured himself a glass of champagne, his first of the day.

Rose and Michael's tour of the reception took ages to reach us. They stopped at every table for effusive greetings, posed for pictures, arms around their friends, cheek to cheek, silly faces from the younger ones. The disposable cameras soon ran out and the shiny slimline variety appeared out of pockets and handbags. Much laughter, including at our table where Dominic and Henry sparked off each other, egged on by you and an increasingly tipsy Guy. Mother giggled along with them. The noise rose and mixed with the hot smell of food and perfume, now also tinged with sweat, formed a heady atmosphere punctuated with flashes from the cameras. Guy pulled a tissue from his pocket and wiped his expansive forehead.

When the bride and groom finally arrived at our table with their newly wedded bliss, the smart city lawyer and savvy businessman, I inspected the dress. It was a stunner, raw silk, ruched and pleated at the front, caught into a small bustle at the back, the top cut low, but with, I could see now, a delicate lace over the shoulders, stretching to the elbows, so fine that it was invisible from a distance. Her hair was intricately styled, with the lace veil disappearing down her back. Hsiao Ling had done her daughter proud.

Rose worked her way slowly around the table with many embraces and much picture taking until she got to Dominic.

"Dominic Gillies." Mother beamed with innocent pride.

"Not Gillies. Granville," you corrected her.

Rose and Michael didn't care. It made no difference to them and their happiness what his name was. They were busy shaking hands and Dominic was kissing Rose on the cheek and laughing, as if even he had lost control. But not so Mother.

"What did you say?" Her face didn't so much fall as crumple.

"Granville. His surname is Granville," you shouted above the racket.

"As in the dread Constantia?" Henry mimicked the accent, the aloof head, the angled nose.

I laughed despite myself, or perhaps because it couldn't make things worse. I should have worked it out. He was handsome Freddie, overlaid with wolfish Tim. Guy put his head in his hands. Then I remembered what Dominic had told me about the lawyer from London. The maintenance payments, the progress reports. Another of life's little messes tidied away out of sight.

Rose and her happiness floated off to the next table. "Shall we go to the ladies, Mother?" I asked, and took her arm, steering her under the floral arch and along the corridor into the hotel lobby where it was cooler and quieter.

"I don't need the ladies," said Mother.

"Neither do I." We sank into comfortable sofas with our backs to the hotel's front windows. Outside the London traffic thrummed by in the brilliant afternoon sun.

"Why didn't you warn me?" Mother asked.

"I didn't know. I used to call him Dominic Gillies. He never once corrected me."

"D'you think Isla's worked it all out?"

"We've not seen the Granvilles since Freddie's wedding."

"But Guy must have known."

I wasn't going to own up to what I knew about Guy's role in Dominic's life. "Lots of people have affairs." Like my own father, I thought, but didn't say, and wondered for the umpteenth time if that's why he'd disappeared.

"Aye, that's true, and Tim's exploits were legendary." Mother pursed her lips, and I wondered if she'd been on the receiving end of his attentions. "But with Nancy it was different," she said. "It was the only time that I ever saw Connie afraid she might lose him, apart from the war of course. Being Connie, she fought back. She told me 'the floozy' as she called Nancy, had been sent packing. She didn't spell out all the details, and I didn't ask. How old is Dominic?"

I affected nonchalance. "A few years younger than me, I suppose." It was five exactly, I'd counted those years so often.

"That would be right. It was just before you started school." She watched a waiter walk across the lobby with a tray of drinks. "Well," she said, and then à propos of nothing in particular, "Fancy that." She put her handbag on her lap and opened it and pulled out her powder compact and her lipstick.

"Is that all?" I was surprised that she took it so easily.

"Back then it would have caused a scandal. Nowadays no-one's bothered what people get up to. We've seen enough goings-on haven't we, in our business? It must have been hard on Nancy though. She was making a good career for herself in London. I hope Tim provided properly for her." She opened her compact, unscrewed her lipstick, and started to touch up her lips.

"Shouldn't we go to the ladies?"

"My brain may be a bit decrepit, but my bladder's still strong enough."

When we got back, Guy was sitting alone at the table drinking coffee from a tiny cup. You and Henry were dancing to frenetic music, you with the exuberance of someone trying to prove you didn't give a damn.

"He's done a bunk." Guy pointed at Dominic's empty chair. "A business function apparently. Those two are enjoying themselves though. So much the better. Dominic isn't a bad lad, Nancy's done a good job with him. But when it comes to women, he's lethal."

"He'll be getting that from his father, I suppose?" There were some aspects of Mother that hadn't mellowed with age.

Guy gulped down the contents of his coffee cup and put it back in the dainty saucer with shaky hands. "You've worked out who that is?" He refilled his cup from a silver pot on the table. Mother let the question hang till he answered it himself. "I was called in to sort things out. That's how I got to know Nancy." He loaded spoonfuls of pink and white sugar crystals into his coffee and stirred.

"It was vicious," Mother said.

"They were vicious times."

Mother wasn't letting him off so easily. "You let yourself be used."

"Connie insisted. You know what she's like." Guy gulped at his coffee. "Dominic's got a chip the size of an iceberg about it all." He took another swig at his coffee and then put the cup down. "Bloody demi-tasses, can't think why people bother with them." He patted at his mouth with a linen napkin. "I suppose we're the same, aren't we, you and me? Connie used us both over the years. But you were the one with the good sense to stand up to her." He got up and completely floored Mother by giving her a peck on the cheek. "Lovely to see you all, Julia, Maisie. Say goodbye to Isla for me. Remind her that amor bloody well doesn't vincit omnia." He waved in your direction, and you flung your arms around in the air like he was Tom Cruise and not lumbering Guy Forrester. Perhaps you knew.

Then the music stopped, and Rose and Michael reappeared. Rose shone in a red and gold dress, with a fitted bodice and full skirt, and matching jewellery threaded through her black hair. Mother stood up and began clapping. You jumped up and down and cheered. Henry put his arms around you to calm you, or perhaps to stop you falling over. Cameras flashed all around the room. Hsiao Ling and her husband looked fit to burst.

After they'd left, you staggered back to the table. "I don't feel so good, Ju-ju."

"D'you want me to take you home?"

You nodded.

"You take Isla; I'll look after your mother," said Henry.

It was a bit of a walk to the parking garage and I had to take your arm to keep you from bumping into people. You slid down in the front seat of my car and fiddled with the sound system until you found, to my surprise, some classical music.

"Soothing." You turned your back to me, and looked out of the car window, but then said, "God, so many people," and turned to face me instead.

"It was a lovely wedding." Getting out of the garage into the Saturday afternoon traffic took all my attention. I'd just traded up to a Porsche and didn't want it scratched.

"I don't understand why Rose did it," you burst out. Negotiating our way around Marble Arch was enough for the minute so I didn't answer. "We'd agreed. We promised each other. We were going to focus on our careers. Be twenty-first century superwomen." While I weaved through the taxis on Park Lane, you sorted your incoherence into sentences. "And maybe one day if we wanted a child, if we could fit it into our successful lives, we'd find a convenient man. Or use a sperm bank. I could puke."

"If you're going to do that, then stick your head out the window." I opened yours a crack and steered us past Buckingham Palace.

"Oh honestly Ju-ju, why d'you always have to be so practical? And now she's gone and done the whole meringue thing. Just like all those other stupid women in that fucking boutique. I can't get my head around it." You belched. The problem with champagne.

Across Lambeth Bridge, I turned left and headed off towards the cheaper part of Docklands on the south side of the Thames. "Perhaps she loves him."

"Huh." You reorganised yourself in the seat and the next thing I heard was a snore. I snuck a glance at you as I waited in the queue of traffic at Waterloo. A dribble of spit was trickling down your chin. When I stopped again at the lights at Blackfriars Road, I resisted the temptation to take a tissue and wipe your mouth like I did when you were little.

· · · · ●·●· · · ·

There was a parking space outside your flat in Rotherhithe, and I took the pound coins from the gadget Henry had given me for Christmas and pumped them into the meter. Then I shook you awake, pulled you out of the car and got you up the stairs to the second floor.

Your flat was in a grubby brick building without a lift, that had once belonged to the council. Now it was a private let that you shared with three friends, all of whom were out when we stumbled in the front door. The main room was stripped back white, with a minimalist sofa, two IKEA easy chairs, and a coffee table pushed against one wall with a television on it. A line of empty wine bottles stood under the window. It looked like it hadn't been hoovered in a while. You pointed down the corridor, we staggered along it into a bedroom, and I eased you down onto the dishevelled bed.

"I'll get you some water."

"And something to be sick in." You lay on your back, closed your eyes and rested an arm across your head.

There was an orange plastic bucket under the greasy sink in the kitchen, behind a desiccated sponge and some shrivelled remnants of soap. I couldn't find any clean glasses, so I took one from the crockery stacked expectantly in the dishwasher, ran it under a tap and dried it on a tissue from my handbag. Back in the sitting room I looked out the window at the unconvincing patch of grass behind the flats and the new high-rise buildings beyond. The ashtray on the coffee table was overflowing, and it looked like someone had been smoking more than tobacco. It was a lifetime from the comfort in which you'd been brought up, but it was your space and I envied you. I should have got my own place years ago.

You drank some water and were sick, then drank some more. I found a brush and smoothed back your hair. It had escaped from its chignon and fell around your face, which had lost most of its make-up and all of its pretensions to sophistication.

"I don't know what I'll do without her." You started to cry.

"Rose?"

"We were always there for each other, at school, at uni, always, until she met Michael."

It was hard to decipher your distress. I wasn't familiar with this emotional territory, not having been in it myself. "It was always going to happen. One day, you were bound to go your separate ways, for a while at least." I wished it was still as easy as giving you a spoonful of medicine and a kiss to cure your pain. "D'you want me to get a cloth and wash your face?"

"I'm not a baby, Ju-ju." You curled up on the bed. I found a coat in the wardrobe and spread it over you. You acquiesced. "Who do I phone now when things go wrong?"

"Me?" I thought it was obvious.

"You must be mad with me about Dominic." You had a furtive, hunted expression. My fantasy about the wretched man finally went ping. I'd promised to catch whatever life threw at you. But when it threw Dominic, I'd ducked.

Chapter Sixteen

November 1999

Y ou phoned at the most awkward times, in the middle of a show, or just as I was dropping off to sleep. I was negotiating the lease for our new branch in Sevenoaks when my handbag gave a telltale vibration. It was you about your latest triumph at work. Always work. You didn't talk about your personal life. If any self-doubts lingered after the Rose wedding debacle, it sounded like you buried them and climbed onto the back of the City tiger like you were going to ride it to death.

The wedding business exploded, and my forties slipped by in a haze of chiffon and confetti. It was in the frenetic final days of the millennium, when I was going through the design of our new website with Henry, that you phoned and asked if we could meet up.

Henry had morphed from PR executive into brand consultant and moved his company, Mack Creatives, into new offices behind Oxford Circus, enough streets back and enough floors up for it to be affordable. Theoretically it was paperless, with a row of computers and two young assistants managed by his latest wife, Emily. She was younger than him, pretty in an unthreatening way and very level-headed. I thought she'd last longer than the others. She came into the stuffy cubbyhole of a meeting room with a cafetiere and accoutrements just as my phone went.

I pulled it from my bag and slid it open.

"Isla?" There were times Henry was psychic.

I nodded. "Excuse me." Emily passed me a cup of coffee and I took it with me onto the chilly landing.

"When're you next in town?" You sounded in a state of great excitement.

"As it happens, I'm here now."

"So we can meet for lunch."

"I was supposed to be having it with Henry."

"He's such a darling, he won't mind, not if you explain it's something very special."

"Like what?"

"Can't say now." You gave me a time and a place and then, "Love you, Ju-ju," and you were gone.

I went back into the meeting room. Emily appeared effortlessly with a fresh coffee and slipped out again.

Henry was watchful. "Something to do with Dominic?"

"She wants to meet me for lunch."

"I understand." I'd seen Henry josh his way through every kind of situation, but now he seemed uncomfortable. "Isla needs to be careful. Did you ever manage to start reading the newspapers?" I grimaced. "It's about time you did, you need to know what's going on, now you're making serious money—who's up and who's down. Dominic's up, but some of the stuff about him isn't so flattering. It's not my call, but I wouldn't like to see Isla get hurt. She's entangled with him, isn't she?"

I shrugged. Non-committal. If only I'd known.

He picked up his coffee cup and took a sip. "Stone cold. I hate winter." He pulled a face and reverted to his Harry Tosh mode. "There. Lecture over. Back to your website."

· · · · · · · · · · ·

I found the restaurant with some difficulty. Your directions were never the most brilliant. Leadenhall, upstairs, bijou little place called Mljet. Tastefully understated, catering evidently for the City expense account market judging by the clientele, sleek men who looked like they counted money in billions. You were sitting at a table by a row of windows overlooking the arcade. You'd taken off your black jacket and your lime-coloured blouse showed off your hair which was cut in a feathery style around your face. Your designer handbag sat on the table, wide open of course. You looked up from the menu and gave one of those finger flutters that pass for a wave. You shone in your comfort zone, a flash of brilliance amongst expensive grey suits.

"How lovely to see you." You got up and kissed me, and then clenched your shoulders and scrunched up your face with unconcealed excitement. As I sat down and picked up a menu, a familiar face appeared behind you.

"Calypso."

"Welcome." She leaned over you and put a proprietorial arm around your shoulders and kissed you with an easy familiarity. "Your first visit here I think, Julia?"

I wished you'd warned me it was Calypso's restaurant; I might not have looked so gobsmackingly foolish. As it was, my jaw went slack as Calypso swung back her still long, still blonde hair with the same sultry rebelliousness she'd deployed in the bridal boutique in Sewell. Her laughter made the character lines on her face disappear. The suits turned to look. She still knew how to grab attention. "Not quite what you expected, back in the day?" She'd not managed to tame her voice, though. Still the cheese grater. "You guys did a great job on my dress, shame about the man. Not your bag though, was it?" She beckoned a waitress over, then winked at you. "Oh and fantastic flower girl."

You enthused about the menu, Calypso provided a running commentary on the sustainability of it while the waitress wrote and rewrote our order. I suspected that cost calculated per gram of food would make it among my more expensive lunches. You drank a lot of sparkling water, belched slightly, and asked after Henry. When I told you about the website, you asked when it would go live, then before I'd finished answering, you asked about the Sevenoaks branch. "Rose lives down that way you know. She's got a baby now." And then your attention flitted on to what Mother and I were doing on millennium night. You didn't listen to what I said about that either.

When our food arrived, dainty portions on big white plates, looking like delicate paintings in the centre of a sprawling blank canvas, you made your announcement.

"The thing is, Ju-ju, I'm pregnant."

I could feel my face going foolish again.

"Aren't you going to congratulate me?"

I tried to form my mouth around some suitable words, but all I could find was, "Is that what you want?"

You laughed. "Of course. Honestly Ju-ju, sometimes you're so out of the ark. I'd hardly be pregnant if I didn't want to be, would I? Look." You reached into your handbag and pulled out a little piece of paper. You gazed at it and your face glowed. "My baby."

When I first looked at the picture, it was no more than a mess of white and black swirls. Then at the bottom I saw a roundish, lightish blob that I worked out must be my future niece or nephew. I felt a stab of something—awe, yearning, envy.

"I heard the heartbeat this morning."

I peered at the blurry mass. "Is it a boy or a girl?"

"They couldn't tell. Perhaps next time."

"When's it due?"

"May."

"Who's the father?"

"I've got it all worked out. I'll get eighteen weeks paid maternity leave, so I can be off all next summer with the baby, which will be just divine. I'll have to move of course, but that's OK."

"Is it Dominic?"

"Does it matter? You know I said I'd use a sperm bank. I can afford a nanny, so childcare's no problem. It's what I've always wanted."

Not that I could remember, but you were so genuinely happy, I wasn't about to prick your bubble. Although, talking about pricks, Henry's warning came to mind. And then I thought, did it matter? My little sister was going to be a mother. Which meant that I was going to be an aunty. The grey suits spun around me and I grabbed the table to steady myself.

"It's wonderful news. I'm delighted."

Your cheeks flushed a pretty pink. "That's a relief, I thought you might be cross." You started to eat your meal which had sat looking immaculately beautiful in front of you. "It's so delicious, this food. It's all Calypso's vision. Dominic sorted out the financing for her."

"They're in touch?"

"They're good friends. Like minds, even though he's only her half-brother. She couldn't bring herself to ask Freddie for help and their parents are too stingy."

"So we'd noticed." We hadn't heard from Connie since Mother had pressed her over the last tranche of payment for her son's wedding. "Sounds like, you've got everything worked out."

"Yes. All except for one thing."

I got a sinking feeling about what was coming. "Mummy. That's what I wanted to talk to you about. D'you think you might find a way of telling her? You're closer to her than I am. I've always had a sense that she blames me for Daddy leaving. Oh, and Ju-ju, would you be my birth attendant?"

Forget the suits, this time the whole restaurant spun. Such an emotion-dump in the dispassionate swank of Calypso's restaurant. Despite myself, I had a little weep. "It will be the most special event of my life."

· · · ● · ● · · · ·

When I got home Mother was in her big wicker chair in the new extension I'd had built along the rear of the house with sliding glass doors, so in summer she could sit and enjoy the flowers in her garden. That evening it was in winter darkness, and all the colour came from indoors, from my orchids which I grew in profusion. They brought a touch of the exotic.

Mother was on the phone—the landline—she couldn't get the hang of mobiles. There was no need to ask who she was speaking to. Her accent was always stronger when she was talking to Nancy.

"Mercy me, he's done well." She caught sight of me and smiled, finished her call, and put the handset down on the glass-topped table beside her.

"I'll fetch our supper." She had her hair coloured a less intense shade of red these days. Up close it jarred with the papery tone of her skin. She'd lost weight and had developed a style of dressing in strong primary colours, so she'd taken on the appearance of a bright gem, hard, glittery, polished. She brought an intense glamour to her cameo appearances at the boutique.

We ate ready meals on trays in front of the television. Mother disapproved of the habit, but she wanted to watch EastEnders. It provided the right backdrop to tell her of Isla's pregnancy.

To my surprise, she was delighted. "I thought I was never going to be a Granny. When's the wee one due? Not till May? Such a long time away. Mind you, these days people tell you from day one, don't they?" And then finally the dreaded question. "Who's the father?"

"Isla hasn't said."

"D'ye think it might be Dominic? Nancy says he's off to a big new job." She went out to make us green tea and came back with a look of concentration which I thought was just the effort of balancing the teacups. But once she'd put the cups down, she asked me. "Why didn't Isla tell me herself?"

"She thought you might not approve." Mother's eyebrows raised. "You know, with her not being married."

"Oh goodness me. How many weddings have we done with the couple's children as attendants? And look at the fuss we all made about Princess Di's wedding, and how that turned out. As if a wedding ever made a difference."

You came over on Boxing Day, arriving by taxi in a bit of a fluster just before lunch. There was an aggressive smell of peppermint on your breath, and a whiff of alcohol on your coat. You were armed with your baby scan, and you and Mother sat out among the orchids and gushed over it. She'd never seen a scan before. There were lots of "mercy me's" while you went into graphic detail about how the ultrasound worked, and what exactly the picture showed. Mother took you up to her old sewing room and said we could turn it into a nursery if you wanted, which you did. Neutral colours, you said, none of that pink or blue stuff.

All went well until Mother asked you who the baby's father was. You retaliated by asking where our own father was. I wanted to know the answers to both questions but decided not to press the issue. Soon after I drove you to the station to catch a train back to town. It was freezing cold, and I didn't want you standing out on the platform, so we sat and waited in the car.

"It's not as if the father's relevant. I don't see why it matters." Your face was pensive. The winter evening had closed in, and a gentle drizzle started to fall. The streetlight lit up the water as it appeared silently out of the darkness, like some secret sorrow being squeezed out of the atmosphere. I didn't want to add to it.

"You'll be fine. It won't be as if you'll be stuck in a pokey flat on your own with a baby and no money."

"That's what I thought." Your voice grew firmer. "I calculated I'd got to a point in my career where I could just about get away with this. And if I hang about much longer, it'll be too late."

"Ouch." Rainwater trickled down the windscreen and I put the wipers on.

"Well at least you've got Mummy in your life, and you had Daddy. I mean, who've I ever had of my own?" I wanted to say "Me," but you were busy sorting through your emotional baggage. "This child is going to be the relationship of my life. The one that no-one can ever take away. Like, you can be uncoupled or unfriended or whatever. But you can never be unmothered."

It was the first time I'd understood the depths of your loneliness.

"I'm going to give this baby my complete one hundred per cent unconditional love."

Slosh, slosh. The windscreen wipers cleared an occasional sightline through the murk outside. It hurt that you had found our relationship of so little significance that it didn't even rate a mention. "Isla, you've always got me to fall back on."

"You're my rock, Ju-ju." You leaned across and kissed my cheek and then ran out through the rain and up the bridge over the tracks to the London platform. You were off into a world I didn't know anything about, driven by forces I couldn't understand, buffeted by emotions I would never feel.

· · · · ● · ● · · · ·

You were lucky. Your bump didn't show for some months. Pregnancy is supposed to make women nesty. It sent you into hyper-drive, as if you had to stake out all the ground you might lose while you were off work. Dominic disappeared into his new job at an investment bank. Big deal that, you said, it's where all the coming people were. Where you wanted to be too; for a minute you looked as if you'd rather be there than having a baby.

Your new boss suggested you might like a less demanding role, given your circumstances. When you pointed out that you hadn't so much as given up wearing the skyscraper heels the company expected of its women, he'd asked when you'd be taking your maternity leave. You fumed down the phone that what he was doing was only questionably legal. When I said perhaps you could work around it, you replied, "That's the trouble, that's what women always do." And so, in the end did you, because, you said, there was no point making a career-limiting fuss. It wasn't in your life plan to end up being a single parent in an employment backwater at the age of thirty-five. You were going to hop back on the nearest career ladder just as soon as you could.

Mother went with you for a final, late scan. You drove down the night before and the two of you zoomed off in high spirits first thing next morning. You lowered yourself into the sports car that you said you wouldn't give up for a family-friendly model until you were actually a family. "Elderly primigravida, risky, as they keep on reminding me," you said, clipping in Mother's seat belt. "What they mean is so bloody doddery you might lose it." I wasn't happy about the two of you driving in the rush hour rat race, but Mother was hell-bent on getting back into a sports car, if only into the passenger seat, you were still in tiger mode, and I had business to attend to.

Your pregnancy had brought you closer to Mother. She would listen for hours to you talking about every last detail of it. I'd find her sitting in her wicker chair contemplating the garden where the snowdrops had already passed and the daffodils were in bud, then they gave way to early roses, and there she'd still be with the phone clamped to her ear, a hand on her stomach and a distant smile on her face. As if she was recalling memories and feelings. When she wasn't on the phone to you, she spent most of her time knitting for the baby. It must have been good for you to have such unconditional support, given the conspicuous absence of the other parent.

With days to go you finally gave up work. "I can't be arsed with tottering around on high heels any longer," you said. "Besides this new man is just too boring. Dominic took all the buzz out of the office with him when he left." I'd arranged to take you for a shopping spree in Mothercare the following Monday. However, the baby had its own timeline, and on Sunday evening, when I was laughing along to Jack Dee's Happy Hour on TV, you phoned to say you'd called a taxi and were going in. "Take your time, Ju-ju, nothing will happen for ages." Mother said the same. But I knew you well enough to interpret the edge in your voice. More panic than excitement.

Where the A3 narrows going into London, I got stuck in traffic which inched its way back into the city after the weekend. The lowering sun cast long shadows. By the time I'd threaded my way through every last backstreet to the hospital, it was dark, and my nerves were shredded. The final stretch, up the lift to the ante-natal ward, was interminable, having to smile at people who got in and out while all I wanted was for once in my life to tell them all to fuck off messing about with the lift and let me find my sister.

You weren't in the ante-natal ward at all. The sister dispatched me with a cheerful smile. "They're downstairs in the post-natal ward."

They, you and your baby. I felt a surge of joy. But it wasn't two people I found in the post-natal ward; it was three. You were sitting up in bed drinking a cup of tea. The baby was bundled up in a white blanket and lying in the arms of Calypso. What? Yes, Calypso. I was doused with a bucket of undiluted jealousy.

"Look at her Ju-ju. Isn't she beautiful? I'm going to call her Skye." You put your teacup down on the bedside table. Calypso held the baby out to me and in that instant, I fell in love for only the second time in my life. All I could think of was the little head that showed above the swathes of white, her face bright pink, eyes clenched, her little mouth working away. She had on a dainty white hat that Mother had knitted. Then a tiny hand appeared from the blanket and flailed around, as if not sure what to do with all this space and freedom.

"It's all right, you can touch her, she won't break." You laughed, like giving birth had made you an instant expert.

She was the newest human being I'd ever encountered. I held her little hand and looked into her scrunched-up face for the likeness to you.

"You can hold her if you want."

I sat in the wooden chair beside the bed and Calypso lowered the baby until I was cradling her in my arms. I hardly dared breathe, let alone move.

You laughed. "Besotted Aunty Ju-ju." When I lifted my left arm so that the baby's head was close enough to kiss, she opened her eyes. They were a sharp turquoise blue. She glared at me.

"She looks cross."

"Don't be silly. You're only the third person she's ever set eyes on." Isla had taken on a 'believe me, I'm a mother,' aura.

Calypso meanwhile was putting on her coat and pulling on her gloves with the finality of someone who'd finished a hard day's work. She reached under the bed and pulled out a black patent leather bag, swung it over her shoulder, fluffed up her hair and said, "Good to see you, Julia. Give my best to Maisie." Then she leaned over and kissed you on the temple and said, "I'll tell him."

Chapter Seventeen

May 2000

A hormonal fug of motherhood settled over our house the day you brought your newborn home from hospital.

You insisted on arriving under your own steam—being a geriatric mother at age thirty-five didn't make you a complete incompetent, you said. I didn't argue. We had you for the summer, that was enough. I'd never imagined you as an earth mother, but that's how you looked when you stepped out of the taxi, swathed in a floaty cotton dress with Skye in a straw Moses basket. You exuded lush maternity.

"It suits you," said Mother.

You wafted into the spare room. Mother had got it painted in non-committal yellow and kitted out with a state-of-the-art baby changer and a cot with a monitor and nightlight. A mobile of smiling animals flew overhead.

"I hope they won't crash." Mother tapped the mobile and the little animals jiggled up and down.

"Why would they do that?" You laughed and laid Skye down in the cot, then plunged a hand into the front of your blouse and started fiddling with your bra. "Damn these leaky tits."

The fug found its way into every corner of the house. The kitchen was soon awash with its smell, milk, baby poo, talcum powder. It fanned through the sitting room, into the sunroom and billowed out of the sliding doors into the garden, where it wafted above the roses, slithered down your old slide, and curled up on the stone bench Mother had placed in the corner of the lawn where it trapped the evening sun.

We followed it outside. On fine days, Mother would spread a tartan rug on the lawn, and you'd put Skye in the centre of it and we'd sit around and admire her and not do much other than talk, to each other, and to Skye, not that she understood. But I like to think that our sun-warmed babbling provided a happy soundtrack to her first weeks of life. We wallowed in the sensual languor that attaches itself to a baby, like three graces luxuriating in an emotional steam bath.

Mother was the biggest culprit. There must be some kind of maternal reset button that gets triggered with a new genera-tion of baby. She'd find any excuse to pick Skye up and walk around the garden introducing her to everything in it in her gentlest voice with her strongest accent. At first I wondered if you'd get jealous, lazing in the sun on the tartan rug and watching the two of them through indulgent eyes and then I realised that of course all you had to do was to twitch that lifelong come-to-mother chord to reclaim her. She was yours. All yours. Unconditional love with no-one else to intervene. Not me, however much I wanted. And not Mother.

"You don't even have to share her with her father." I'd brought out a tea tray and put it down on the lawn, started pouring out tea for us all, and set out the glass of water I'd brought for you.

"Well, ours hasn't been much use, has he?"

Mother was cradling Skye in her arms, barefoot, her hair curled out like a coppery halo, her silky coral dress shimmering in the sun. She was smiling and making those funny clicking sounds that pass for talking to a baby. "It doesn't matter now, does it?"

"Sometimes it does." You lifted your sweatshirt and nestled Skye to your breast. "I have no memory at all of Daddy."

My memories of the sandy-haired man who sang silly songs and ate popcorn in the cinema were tinged with thirty years of nostalgia. The last time he was with us was in another such summer, when you were the baby on the lawn.

"You've got a photograph of him." Mother watched you feeding your baby, cocooning her little body in your arms on the tartan rug—she and I were both excluded by your intimacy with Skye. She watched with envy: I watched with awe.

"A photograph isn't a memory." You were concentrating on your baby and her rhythmic hypnotic sucking. "How d'you think I felt when the kids at school teased me about not having a father?"

"You did have one." Mother sounded mortified.

"That made it worse. Being abandoned by my father."

Mother still wore her wedding ring and twisted it around her finger. "I didn't realise."

"How d'you think it felt growing up knowing my father had taken one look at me and cleared off. End of. Has he ever even tried to get in touch?"

"There were circumstances. Things were"—Mother's eyes trailed off to the weathered seat at the end of the garden—"difficult." For a while I thought she was going to explain, but then you interrupted with a pain-induced wince.

"Hell's bells. Why does no-one tell you how much babies hurt?" By the time you'd got yourself and your breasts and your baby sorted out, the moment had passed, but you weren't letting Mother entirely off the hook.

"How about your own father? You never talk about him either."

"With good reason." Round and round went her wedding ring.

"Don't you think we should know something about our past? So I can tell her." You'd finished feeding Skye and were holding her to your shoulder and stroking her back. Her head was wobbling around, a puzzled look on her face, unfocussed eyes squinting at the world.

"It's not your past, it's mine." Mother started to collect up the teacups and put them on the tray, but then struggled to get up. "Some things are best left alone." It was the closest we ever got to an explanation.

"Our collective experience of fathers has been pretty dire." You gulped down the last of your water. "At least I've spared Skye that. Nothing to disappoint her."

· · • • • • • · · ·

I should have smelt a rat when Calypso turned up one Sunday afternoon with her half-brother Dominic in tow, but at the time I took at face value what she said about dropping in while in the neighbourhood. Mother went to answer the doorbell and appeared leading the two of them out of the French windows across the patio into the garden. You always said Mother had no feelings, but I'd worked out that wasn't true—she was just very good at hiding them—and I could see from the set of her chin and the way she walked with her hands folded in front of her that inside she was spitting teeth. You, meanwhile, seemed unperturbed.

"For my gorgeous—"Calypso stopped herself and then said, "flower girl's baby" and held out a gift wrapped in pink tissue paper tied up with a great frilly bow. Dominic held out a huge pink balloon bobbing on a silver thread which you promptly and deliberately let go.

"Oh dear," you said, and watched it float away above the trees behind the house.

Dominic looked like he wasn't in control of his own feelings let alone anyone else's. Calypso took the baby and cuddled her. "She's so beautiful and look how she's grown." He hovered, first behind you, then behind Calypso, his eyes fixed on Skye. He must have been in his mid-forties then, and his hair had silvered. Distinguished rather than old. His jeans had that expensive cut that has never seen dirt, much less built America. He can't have realised how much the longing showed in his face. Despite myself, my feelings did a lurch.

He arranged himself on the tartan blanket, contriving to appear casually comfortable. Calypso sat beside him, legs folded, boho chic sundress riding up over her tanned knees. You were trying to reclaim control over your body and had taken to wearing flattering tops over skimpy skirts that showed off your legs. That afternoon you'd also taken trouble with your hair.

We talked about everything except what mattered. Mother, immobilised in a deck chair, asked Calypso if she was going to visit her parents. There was a silence before Calypso said no. Dominic remarked on the traffic noise from the new by-pass behind the woodland and asked if we'd thought of moving. Mother said no. Calypso said her parents were indestructible. No-one could say anything to that. I wondered if Mother would ask Dominic about Nancy. Instead, she asked him about Guy Forrester.

"Oh God," you said and started to feed the baby. Dominic was transfixed. You snapped. "Come on, you must have seen your other children being fed."

Dominic looked away. I went into the kitchen and made up a jug of Pimms and stacked some tumblers on a tray. When I came back outside you were standing by the rose garden burping Skye. Dominic and Calypso watched you from the lawn. Mother was opining about Freddie. Dominic said Anna-Beth had got fat. Calypso jumped up and made a jangly clatter pouring out the Pimms. We hardly needed ice. You said you could do with a Pimms, just a weak one, but Mother said no to that, and then I took the chance to ask Dominic about his new job.

"It's going well," he said, stirring his drink, his face settling into the satisfaction of being on safe ground.

"What is it?" asked Mother.

"Assistant CEO, special products."

"That sounds very grand. What does it involve?"

"Growing the market. Making it safer for investors." A wasp whined towards him and sat on the edge of his glass. He flicked it away.

"Dominic's at the creative end of things." You were rocking Skye with that mesmerising swaying that mothers do when cradling young babies. "It's where the action is these days. Billion-pound deals."

"It's not quite what it sounds." So there was still a trace of humility in him.

Mother stared at Dominic, and I could see the thought going through her head: *This is Nancy's son.*

He was oblivious. "I mean if you're in my kind of business, CDOs, CDOs-squared, synthetic CDOs and the rest of them, the figures are always going to be big. That's just the nature of things."

I didn't like to ask what he was talking about. You surely knew. Calypso wouldn't care. It was left to Mother to say, "What happens if they fail?"

"Oh Mummy, honestly. You can't keep your money in a sock under the bed any longer."

"That's not quite fair," Calypso said. "Your mother understands money. Look at that brilliant business she's created."

Not that Mother was part of it any longer. As she'd disengaged, I'd taken over, but I'd been coasting since you'd come to stay. Hsiao Ling had moved down to Sevenoaks to be near Rose and manage our branch there. She'd supervised the extravagant productions for our string of millennium summer brides. Henry had made sure their glamorous photos were on the website. I'd provided what Henry called strategic oversight, which he said was enough, though I wasn't convinced. Lazing in the sunshine with you that afternoon, I was feeling guilty.

Dominic, meanwhile, having started to talk about himself, kept on going. From explaining how his business in structured asset-backed securities was remaking the financial world as we knew it, he segued seamlessly to ours in wedding dresses. Had we thought of opening a new branch? The market was good, interest rates were low, consumers were spending, everything was on a roll. He even knew of a shopping centre in the home counties that would fit exactly with our business model.

"You mean that new mall you financed for Freddie?" asked Calypso.

It only produced a momentary pause in the flow of Dominic's words. "You have to keep ahead of the curve."

Mother had drifted off to sleep and her teacup slipped from her lap onto the lawn with a tinkle. She opened her eyes with a start and seemed surprised at the group of people in her garden. "Mercy me," she said as if she hadn't expected to see them.

I was bothered by it. You laughed.

On the pretext of helping clear up, Calypso followed me indoors. Mother came inside too. We left you standing by the rose garden holding Skye with Dominic sitting cross-legged on the tartan rug, at a healthy distance. You looked like the one who was in control. Dominic was fiddling with his shirt sleeves. I almost felt sorry for him. Almost.

In the kitchen, Mother sat at the table with her hands in her lap while I stacked the dishwasher and Calypso chatted. Irrelevancies, food, clothes, David Beckham's latest haircut. Anything but the herd of elephants crowding out the room. Looking back, I wish we hadn't left you alone with Dominic. Then it seemed a tactful way to let the two of you say whatever was needed in what I assumed were the circumstances. But whatever words were exchanged between you had consequences beyond anything I could have foreseen.

· · · ● · ● · ● · · ·

I'd hoped the summer's bliss would last at least through July, but one evening soon after Dominic's visit, I arrived home from work to find Mother on her own looking after Skye. Mother was ecstatic, the baby was content, I fretted. You arrived back in a taxi piled up with disposable nappies, bottles, a steriliser, liquidiser and tins of baby formula which you unloaded into the kitchen.

"Best start as I mean to go on," you said. "I won't be able to breastfeed at work."

"That's ages off yet," I said.

"No." You set up the steriliser and loaded it with bottles. "I won't survive much more of this. I already feel like a milk cow."

Mother looked ineffably sad. "Don't go back to work yet. There's no need."

"The business is doing well," I said. "And I'm going to grow it. Keep ahead of the curve."

Neither of us pointed out the obvious, that you didn't need the money.

"You two really don't get it. I can understand that you don't, Ju-ju, but you should know better, Mother. I'm responsible for Skye. Me. Only me. I was talking to Dominic about it. I've been faffing around for too long. I need to pick myself up and reboot my career. He says he'll help me."

"Why d'you have to go to him for help?"

My unconditional love was bruised, but I didn't want to lose our newfound closeness. So when you said you wanted to go to view a new flat, I swallowed my hurt feelings and suggested we combine it with a visit to Freddie's shopping mall to scope out the potential for a bridal boutique. You borrowed my car, zoomed off into Sewell, and came back with a new suit and heels for the occasion. Earth mother no more.

The flat was a spectacular new-build on the posh north bank of Docklands. The agent started a relentless sales pitch as soon as we got out of our car in the gated courtyard. His broad chest strained the top of his suit jacket and when he touched the fifth-floor button of the lift, I noticed the back of his fingers were covered in thick blond hair. You avoided his efforts at eye contact. When he ushered us into the flat, you prowled it like an animal staking out a lair.

I was more cautious. "There's no garden."

"The balcony is exceptionally large." The agent put the key in the lock of the balcony door, pushed his shoulder against it and we piled out and looked across the cobbled pathway straight into the flats opposite.

"It's like being in a goldfish bowl."

"Honestly, Ju-ju." You rolled your eyes. "It's got the bedrooms I need, and the living room is large enough. There's space for a nanny. It's close to work. What more could I want?" You were being brutally practical. There was none of the joie de vivre you'd shown about your last chaotic flat. "What did you say the rent was?" You confronted rather than asked the agent.

"I didn't."

When he did, I gasped.

"What did you expect, Ju-ju? It was never going to be peanuts." You turned to him. "It's perfect I'll take it."

From there I drove us out along the A1 towards Freddie's shopping mall just outside the M25 in Hertfordshire. He'd taken over his father's development company and this was his first big project. It would have been a coming of age for him, except as you pointed out, Dominic had done the financing. "Making a point," you called it. We stopped for petrol and to pick up coffees en route. You sipped yours as I navigated the traffic. "You're right, that flat's not suitable for a small child. But I won't stay there long. When Skye's older I'll move."

You gave me my coffee and fed me a bit of sandwich.

"Your fingers smell of baby poo," I said.

"Yuck. It's ingrained." You wiped your hands with a wet wipe from your handbag and then sniffed them. "I'm going to get a transfer at work. Onto the trading floor. All I'll need are a couple of bonuses and I'll be able to buy a really fantastic house. So Dominic says."

"Is that what the two of you were cooking up that afternoon?"

"He says there's so much money sloshing around the City, I can't go wrong."

"And in return he gets?"

"Nothing." You stared straight ahead out of the windscreen. "He gets absolutely nothing."

"That doesn't sound like a Dominic kind of deal."

We reached the mall and parked in the underground carpark and then we got the lift to the shops. At one end was an up-market food hall with an outdoor terrace that looked away from the motorway and towards the countryside. It was packed with women having after-lunch coffee. There were a good number of buggies dotted among the tables, and a contented high-pitched chatter. They looked more the Mothercare than bridal wear market and I wondered whether Freddie or Dominic had mis-calculated, but you were impressed.

"Just the place for well-heeled urban escapees. Designer brands, posh décor, flowers, hairdressers, jewellers. Positively reeks of them. I can see you with a boutique here."

We promenaded the ground floor and went up the escalators that soared over an atrium where a fashion show was in full swing. Then we went to the second floor where, at the end of a walkway, past a couple of empty shops was a little unit, not much more than a cubicle. Brilliant lighting bounced off shiny white fittings and lurid pink walls. A doe-like girl with a soft face and limpid eyes stood in the doorway. Her white jacket and trousers gave her the air of a medical orderly. She pounced.

"Would you like to have your nails done?"

You held out your hands, dainty hands, with little pointed fingers that would have been pretty if it weren't for your nails that you'd spent your whole life biting.

"Please," the woman said. "My nail bar is new. If you like my work, you could tell your friends. It would be very good for me."

"You'll need to work miracles."

The young woman giggled. "I do." You followed her into the nail bar and sat down on a white plastic chair at a narrow table with a surgical style light shining onto it. I was planning to watch, but then another young woman who'd been sitting on a stool in the corner reading a magazine came up to me.

"I've never had my nails done before." I held out my hands. They weren't so bad, with strong fingers and square cut nails, varnished on special occasions, chipped now.

She took one of my hands in hers and stroked it with the back of her finger. It felt like a feather brushing over my skin. "I can make them nice for you."

I only had my nails filed and painted a deep plum. You had the full works, artificial nails attached to your stumpy ones and lacquered with swirling reds. While I waited, my beautician offered me a head massage. As her fingers probed into my scalp, I shut my eyes and calculated the risks of a new boutique. Upside, rich people, glitzy shopping mall, booming market. Downside, it could fail. But did I smell failure in the air? No. Only nail varnish.

"Look Ju-ju." When I opened my eyes, all I could see were your fingernails. Long scarlet talons. They belonged to some marauding she-devil, not my little sister. You were delighted. "Just the makeover I needed. No more life as a hormone-fest. I can scratch the City's eyes out with these."

CHAPTER EIGHTEEN

SEPTEMBER 2000

You had your new flat, new job and not so new baby. I had my new boutique. We snatched the sun's last fling of summer to wheel Skye around St Katherine's Docks. Sleek yachts jostled for position in the water, their owners vied for attention on the quayside, all in the heart of London, a short walk from your flat.

"She's very alert. She's starting to talk—the way she looks at me and makes sounds, I just know she's trying to communicate." You fiddled with the buggy's little parasol that shaded your daughter's face.

I couldn't see it myself. Skye seemed a contented baby, reclining in her buggy, gooing at the world as you propelled her through it. You'd got yourself back into shape. Even in the svelte crowd at St Katherine's, even with a buggy, you were noticed.

"She's quieter than you ever were, Isla."

"D'you think her hair is going to be as curly as Mummy's?"

"So long as she's happier than Mother, that's the main thing."

"Mummy's not unhappy."

Skye whimpered for a nano-second, and you immediately knelt down and fussed around her, ending up taking her out of the buggy and jiggling her in your arms, murmuring "Hey babe," which produced instant smiles.

"Not now," I said. "But she was when she was younger."

"Are you?"

"What?" You took me by surprise.

"Happy?"

You'd never asked me that before. In fact, no-one had that I could remember. I wasn't sure how to take the question, or what the answer was. It was a long time since I'd thought about happiness. "I suppose I am, reasonably."

You laughed at that. "Honestly Ju-ju. Whatever is reasonable happiness? I may not be everyone's idea of a mother, but I'm enough of one to know that my main job in life is to make sure my child is happy. I want my Skye to be ecstatic."

· · · · · · · · · ·

My final millennium bride would be the first big wedding to come out of our new Hertfordshire branch. She was the daughter of a hedge fund manager, an unimaginative girl marrying an ambitious civil servant. Her father needed help spending his money. I did our best to assist him, working my team flat out for weeks to deliver every last extravagance, drawing the line only at using real fur to line the bride's going away cape. Our brand wouldn't survive it; neither would the bridegroom's reputation.

"Good move all round," said Henry as he got his latest intake of bright young things to upload pictures onto our website from a string of summer weddings. "Brilliant pics. You're on a roll, Julia."

He on the other hand was suffering. Emily had defied our expectations and left him to set up her own design agency in Bristol. Businesswise it hadn't affected him, but on a personal level, for the first time since I'd known him, he'd lost his bounce.

The pursuit of my new venture came at a price. When I caught up with you again after a gap of three months, you had dark shadows under your eyes. St Katherine's Docks had lost its pizzazz, washed away in the wettest autumn on record. The fickle yachts had sailed south, and a group of ducks pushed their way through debris in grubby water.

I manoeuvred Skye's buggy inexpertly through the door of a half-empty coffee shop, leaving a trail of rainy tyre-marks in my wake. When you went to the counter to get our drinks, I saw it wasn't just that you'd lost your mummy tummy. Having spent so long looking at women's figures in and out of clothes, I could tell that under your baggy jumper and thick leggings, you'd got skinny.

"It's tough." You came back with an Americano for yourself and a tea for me. "It's not that Skye's a difficult baby. It's the relentlessness of it. She has a sixth sense for when I'm in hearing distance and it feels like she wants attention every minute of the weekend. I can understand now why men say they go to work to escape."

"I thought you had a nanny?"

You didn't say anything to that. Just gave one of your "Honestly, Ju-ju," looks. "At least work's going well. They think the sun shines out of my proverbial, so I should get a good bonus. I've built up a nice little line in credit default swaps. One of them involves that shopping mall of Freddie's."

"Ah." I squeezed out my tea bag.

"D'you want me to explain?" Your eyes were laughing at me.

"No bother." I retrieved Skye's dummy from under her buggy and dipped it in my tea, then stuck it in Skye's mouth.

"It's like an insurance in case the shopping mall goes belly-up. Not that it will, of course, but just supposing."

"So, Freddie would get paid out?"

"No, the owner of the swap would get paid out."

"That means you."

"Yes."

"But it's not your mall."

"No, but it's my risk. And Freddie doesn't really own the mall, anyway. The banks do."

"I suppose that means Dominic. He's in that business, isn't he?"

"Yes." You buried your nose in your coffee. I thought back to when I'd left you alone with him in the summer. Skye chose that moment to drop her dummy out of her buggy again. She fixed me with her eyes and gave a heart-stoppingly dribbly smile. I picked it up.

"Oh honestly, Ju-ju, you are a pushover. You shouldn't keep on picking up her dummy. It only encourages her." You tore open a sachet of sugar and sprinkled it on the table, then took the dummy from me, dipped it in the dregs of your coffee and rolled it in the sugar.

"That's disgusting." I wasn't sure which was worse, your sense of hygiene or business ethics—or who, in all of this, was being played for a fool. "I suppose you're making your fortunes out of it."

"At least she won't throw it out so fast. Here babe." You stuck the dummy in Skye's mouth and her little face lit up. "Come on Ju-ju, don't be so grim. It's only business. It's not war. No-one dies."

· · · · · • • • · · ·

Mother and I started to have Skye at weekends. It worked for all of us. I'd spend Fridays in the Hertfordshire branch. There was plenty of business to be done, even if it hadn't happened yet. I fixed with the centre management to hold a promotional show on the main shopping floor.

On alternate Fridays I'd drive home through London and stop off at your flat to pick up Skye. You grumbled about my taking your child in a sports car, but I said I wasn't giving it up for anyone, not even my beloved niece. I only wanted to dip a toe into parenthood, not jump into the raging torrent. Besides, my driving was always steadier than yours and my car was *vorsprung durch technik*. Built like a tank.

You'd come and pick Skye up on Sunday evenings by which time she'd been spoilt rotten, especially by Mother. She paraded Skye through the village first in her baby buggy, then as she grew older in her pushchair. Skye's red curls grew more intense, and her blue eyes sharpened, as Mother's faded.

One year you came when we were decorating the Christmas tree. Mother was sitting in an easy chair unpacking boxes of bobbles of such lurid colours that my poor orchids paled in comparison. Now in her seventies, age seemed to have overtaken her, and she fumbled trying to attach a green plastic hook to a bobble. Skye stood by her looking on with that concentration that small children have when watching an adult wrestle with fine motor skills. A late talker, Skye was trying out every combination of sounds to encourage Mother without actually managing to say anything. Finally Mother got the better of her fingers and gave Skye the bobble dangling on its hook.

You came through the door just as Skye toddled towards me holding out the bobble and beaming and saying, "Ma, ma."

"No Skye," you said, unwinding your scarf. "Not Mama. Ju-ju."

"Mama Ju-ju," Skye said.

I laughed. At the time it was the closest I thought I'd get to motherhood. You looked irritated. Mother, doing battle with another hook and bobble, didn't notice.

· · ◦ ● · ● ◦ · ·

The summer Skye was ready for school, you said it was time to move to somewhere bigger with a garden. I offered to help financially, but you said you had the money to buy a place outright. "City bonuses, dontcha know." It wasn't long before you phoned to say you'd found a nice house in Dulwich, close to good schools and some woods that reminded you of home.

"Can you be a darling and help me move in?" You had removal people booked for the Saturday and a shedload of furniture deliveries—Harrods, not John Lewis—and groceries coming from Waitrose as well as electricians and plumbers to connect everything.

"Mummy could look after Skye," you said.

Across the room Mother had withdrawn into herself under the guise of watching television and I thought of how she'd struggled with the kettle making our coffee after dinner that evening.

"Not a good idea," I said.

"D'you have a better one."

"Calypso?"

"Restaurant. Saturday." You made me feel silly for even suggesting it.

"D'you want me to ask Henry? He likes children, and he's always had a soft spot for you."

"However would Henry know how to take care of a child?"

Easily, it turned out. He was delighted to be asked. When I took Skye around to his flat in Fitzrovia, he'd put a pile of pink cushions and a ball pool in his spare bedroom, and a big fluffy white rabbit on the bed.

"Is it real?" Skye sat on the bed. The rabbit hopped off.

"There's your answer," said Henry. The rabbit loped behind the ball pool and looked at her with red eyes.

She laughed. "He's got floppy ears. He's funny." She didn't even notice when I left.

"Whatever are you doing with a rabbit in your flat?" I asked Henry as he showed me out.

"Company."

"It's unhygienic."

"No it's not. There's a hutch in the kitchen."

"Honestly, Henry."

"Between the rabbit and me, we'll keep Skye amused. See you Sunday." He leant on the doorframe, broad smile, arms folded.

"Thanks a ton." He looked so happy, more like the Harry Tosh of old, that on an impulse, I leaned forward and kissed him on the cheek. Under his languor, he blushed. When it sunk in what I'd done, so did I.

· · · · ●·●· · · ·

Moving in was a generous description of what you did that weekend. While I supervised the men unloading furniture, carting it up the stairs, levering it through doors, you were absorbed with your mobile phone. You'd hold it away from your face and whisper, "Sorry, work," and then follow me and the removal men around the house deep in conversation. Then it was a finger held up in warning, "Sorry, Dominic," and there'd be more of the same, you walking around in your own world until you spotted something the men had misplaced or I'd supervised wrongly, in which case you put your hand over the phone and it was, "No, that chair goes up in the main bedroom," or, "Oh for goodness' sake Ju-ju, that one's for Skye's room," as I directed them to take the third television screen into the study. And then you'd turn your back and carry on talking into your phone while the men grappled with the furniture, and I wished it was my own home I was sorting out.

In the evening, when the men and their van had gone, and the groceries had been stowed still in their bags straight into the cavernous fridge, we went out to recce your new neighbourhood. At the heart of it was a parade of chi-chi shops, with a primary school opposite, and trees everywhere, that gave it a countrified air, even though it was only a long stone's throw from the City. We found a restaurant with faux rustic tables outside.

"You can be happy here, Isla," I said.

"Mmm." You ran your finger down the menu. "Nice food."

"Did you hear what I said?"

You had one finger poised on the menu. You still had false fingernails, but I noticed they were shorter than the talons you'd had fitted at the nail bar in Hertfordshire, and they were painted a subdued shade of garnet. The make-up you'd been wearing on Friday night hadn't been replaced. Without it you looked, well, let's just say "happy" wasn't the first word that sprang to mind.

"I'm not deaf, Ju-ju. I've got a lot going on."

"Work not going well?"

You laughed at that. "It's going too well. We're coining it. In fact, it's hard to keep up with demand, not to mention keep ahead of the brat pack coming along behind me."

We ordered. The food was good—Italian artisan. You twiddled your pasta with disinterest.

"How's the bridal business?" You made it sound like you meant the bloody bridal business.

"Humming along. Especially online. Hertfordshire's slower, there's not the footfall in the mall. So, I'm rethinking my business model there. But we're still ahead of the curve. Just. Of course, Hsiao Ling's slowing down. And Mother needs more attention."

"Yes. Skye told me she dropped a cup in the kitchen. Mummy burst out crying. Over a broken cup for goodness' sake. What are you going to do about it?"

We, I thought, we. She's your mother too. But it looked like you had enough on your plate, with the job, and Skye and now a big new house.

"Does Dominic help?"

"Not really. I don't need him any longer, not now I've got myself going." You'd misunderstood me, and I wondered if it was deliberate.

We made up some beds, and in the morning I got a chance to take in the scale of the house. It stood fair square on a leafy-green plot, Georgian-looking brick at the front, modernist glass and concrete behind. A kitchen-come-diner-come-family room stretched along the back leading through an expanse of bi-fold doors to a big patio with a small, gated swimming pool. A beech tree towered in the far-left-hand corner of the garden with a swing hanging from a lower branch. Bucolic for London.

"You've done well," I said.

"Yes." You stood on the patio, sunglasses hiding your eyes, wearing leggings and a crop top that revealed a slim stomach with a dangly ring through your belly button. "Oh, fuck the unpacking. The nanny can do it. She'll be in tomorrow. Let's enjoy the day."

I stripped down to my bra and knickers. You stripped off completely and we lay on towels by the pool and plunged in every so often when it got too hot. You talked about Skye until

I dozed off. I talked about Mother until you jumped into the pool and stayed underwater for so long I thought you must have drowned. When you finally popped up, you wiped the water off your face and grinned and said, "So, did either of us ever actually fancy Henry?" You talked about Calypso's rift with Aunt Connie over Dominic, and I reminded you of Mother's bust-up with Connie over Hsiao Ling. And of course, we talked about Father. That part of our past seemed too distant to hurt either of us. We were both successful, we had nothing to prove, we were invulnerable, so I thought.

"He was a lovely man," I said.

"Did Mummy ever love him?"

"She must have loved him once, but I can't remember her showing it."

"She never showed she loved any of us," you retorted.

"But she did love us. I'm certain of it. I think she bottled up all her feelings and then somehow forgot how to show them. She loves Skye to pieces. She shows that."

"Not any longer. Skye said she got cross with her for not eating all her food up and stamped her foot at her the other weekend."

"That's age, not lack of love." I went inside and got us a couple of Diet Cokes. When I came back, I thought you were asleep, so I put yours down beside you and sat on the edge of the pool with my feet in the water, drinking mine.

You sat up and picked up your can. "Something terrible must have happened to make Mummy so unable to show her emotions. The dysfunctionality of it has been so destructive."

Now you put it that way, I could see what you meant, though I'd understood things differently. "Mother wasn't dysfunctional. She was busy."

"Perhaps you don't feel it, Ju-ju," you said. "You were always stronger than me." And then as I tried to process this, you added, "Did Mummy ever talk to you about anything that might have made her like that?"

I shook my head.

"It must have been something very traumatic. I wonder what it was." You pulled the tab off your can and took a drink.

"Does it matter? We've turned out OK."

You didn't answer me. At the time I thought you'd shrugged it off because you grinned and jumped into the pool again. With hindsight it wasn't so much a grin you gave as a wince.

Henry brought Skye back to yours on Sunday evening in one of those funny little cars that park sideways to the pavement. It was bright yellow, and he'd put a sticker in the back window, 'Princess on board.' As we stood on the doorstep in the twilight to welcome her to her new home, I felt the most profound happiness. This is it, I thought. Sisters.

"Honestly, Henry," you said, "how do you expect people to take you seriously when you drive around in a car that looks like that?" You were on teasingly good form, as if you were back to your old self. I didn't realise it was no longer there.

"My clients don't see it," Henry shot back. "Besides, the new lady in my life thinks it's wonderful."

He opened the passenger door and Skye climbed out with ketchup down her clothes, and a sparkling crown in her red curls.

"Hey babe!" You opened your arms and enveloped her in a hug that excluded everything and everyone else.

Chapter Nineteen

May 2007

A fter that you dropped out of view for a while. At the time it suited me, although later I regretted it. I got caught up with what looked to me like market turbulence, but what Henry warned was market failure. The Hertfordshire branch took a nosedive. The other two wobbled. With a lot of effort and a bit of luck, I reckoned we could run ahead of trouble. Just. But then the following spring luck, in the shape of Hsiao Ling, bailed out on me.

Rose emailed to arrange a meeting to talk about her mother's future in the business.

"I don't suppose there is one long term, is there?" We met in Rose's office in the City. It was the day after a young girl had been abducted from her parents' holiday apartment in Portugal. We'd seen the coverage of it on television and Mother had fretted away about whether Skye was safe alone in the house in Dulwich. Finally, I'd got cross and shouted at her that Skye had a nanny, even if her mother was as absent as she'd been in our growing up, and then spent the rest of the evening feeling guilty.

Rose's building was one of the steel and glass monsters that crowded out the narrow lanes around Moorgate. While I waited in the cool reception area, I paged through the Financial Times, thinking how I'd tell Henry I'd started reading newspapers, until a young woman in a smart grey suit came and announced, "Ms Chan is ready for you." Her office, six floors up, was huge, an immaculately tidy desk at one end with a laptop on it and a row of silver picture frames facing away from me.

"Julia, how lovely to see you." Rose got up from her desk and came to kiss me. She would have been in her early forties then, the same age as you, and was flawless, from her black hair skimming the shoulders of her tailored jacket, to her neatly turned black kitten heeled shoes. Her perfume was discreetly expensive. She gestured me to sit at a round table by the window and asked the young woman to bring tea for us both.

"Actually, I was thinking more short term," she answered in response to my question about her mother's future. "She's way past retirement age. She wants to step down, and we agreed it would be better if she came off the board as well. It's not good for her to stay on when she's not directly involved."

That was a blow. I'd envisaged some kind of exit for Hsiao Ling but not such a final break and I struggled to hide my disappointment.

"You'll find someone to take her place. You must have lots of younger colleagues who'd value the opportunity." Rose put her teacup down with such care I couldn't hear it touch the saucer. "Shall I deal with the paperwork for her resignation?"

I felt a carpet being pulled out from beneath me. "That would be helpful." And then to acknowledge the finality of it all, I added, "Thank you."

Rose smiled. The glass in her office windows had a greyish tint to it, so the world outside looked slightly unreal in an unquantifiable way, a bit like the atmosphere inside. There was something I couldn't quite put my finger on. I wanted to ask why Hsiao Ling hadn't told me herself. But Rose had already moved on. "How's Isla?" she asked.

"Very well. She's got a little girl, you know."

"So I heard. A bit younger than my son." She went to the desk and picked up one of the photographs. "Anthony. He's just starting secondary school."

She held it out to me. I could see Rose in the boy, the same pretty face and high cheekbones. I couldn't remember what her husband looked like, apart from his blue wedding suit. "You must be pleased."

"Yes." She looked at the picture with that maternal glow. "Michael's beyond proud. He wants Anthony to take over his business when he retires." She turned to put the photograph back on her desk, and then, while she still had her back to me, she asked, "Is Isla still involved with Dominic?"

I tried to sound non-committal. "Not particularly, why do you ask?"

"It's only..." She came and sat down again, and now her carefully managed reserve had gone. It wasn't exactly menace in her voice, but an edge, a warning. "I assume you know about his reputation?"

"No," I said. "Why should I? I don't work in the City."

"He's ruthless—I mean businesswise. In his personal life too, it's said, but I expect Isla's got the measure of that."

"I thought the City was generally cut-throat."

Rose was patient with me. "It's on a new scale these days and Dominic's an outlier. So far he's kept a step ahead of disaster, but he's left a few wreckages in his wake. I've had to deal with some of them. They're not nice. I wouldn't want to see Isla among them."

I assured her that you could manage Dominic and changed the subject. We talked about this and that while we finished our tea, promising that we wouldn't leave it another decade, and next time we'd ask Isla and Skye along. "Perhaps the two grannies could come too," I suggested.

"Yes." Rose's composure never faltered. "Say hello to Maisie for me. She was always such a character. And take care of yourself, Julia. You were my role model when I was growing up."

"Oh."

A surprise confession. Rose didn't elaborate. A final smile. An air-brush kiss. As I went back down in the lift, I tried to work out what had just happened. Outside the grey-tinted glass doors, in the natural daylight, everything seemed normal again. A sunny London afternoon. So why did I feel chilly?

· · · • •· • · · ·

It didn't take long to find out. After the last of my summer brides had EasyJetted off into the sunset, I arranged to meet Henry in a pub near his office. I wanted to sound him out about developing our online offer—another go at running ahead of trouble. While I was waiting for him, my phone rang. It was a banker from Hertfordshire cancelling on his daughter's wedding.

"Oh dear, did they have a falling out?"

"No, they're still getting married. She's just decided to scale things down."

I pushed back at him, until finally he lost his temper and said, "Do I have to spell it out? I can't afford it any longer. The money's gone."

The wedding was only due the following year, and he'd not actually signed on the dotted line or, more to the point, paid his deposit. But it was a hit I couldn't afford. When Henry turned up, I offloaded.

"Perhaps you need to refocus." Henry's hair had gone grey, which made him look distinguished, someone whose opinions were to be minded. His bluntness unnerved me. "The brand has got a bit... well... stale, I hate to say, and things aren't going to get any easier businesswise. Especially not for your present clientele. Eye of the coming storm."

"Coming what?"

On Friday of that fateful September, I arrived home to find Mother watching the early evening news. There were pictures of people queueing outside a bank, a girl in a light blue jacket with a rolled-up umbrella and a cup of coffee, older people in dull anoraks and scarves. Somewhere up north. The queue stretched up the road and around a corner.

"I'm worried," said a middle-aged woman, brown hair windblown. "Our life savings are in here."

"What's this?" I switched to another channel. Also showing the news. Different town. Same queues.

"The bank's failed." Mother sounded like doom.

I flipped. "How can you say that? It's not a moral failure. It's a tragedy for people who've lost money, but no-one's done anything wrong." I remembered your words. "No-one's died."

Mother folded her hands and puckered her lips. She was about to turn eighty. The white roots were showing in her hair; it was long past time for her to give up the struggle to pretend it was still red. Next time I took her to the hairdresser I'd persuade her to allow the colourist to let time catch up.

You phoned up that evening to ask if I could have Skye on Sunday because you had a barbecue on for your banking friends. Celebrating your bonuses.

"It'll be an adult affair," you said.

"That's gross, given what's happening."

"C'mon Ju-ju."

"Anyway, I'm spending the weekend taking a fine toothcomb to our figures. Things are tough out there in case you hadn't noticed."

"Sure, but you'll be fine."

"Says who?"

"You always are. It's what you do. Manage. Cope. No more than that. You ride the crest of every wave. My abfab sister."

"You've no idea, have you? Anyway, try Henry. He's always happy to look after Skye."

I hung up.

By Monday I knew it was over for Hertfordshire. In the morning I went into Sewell, still our flagship. The manager, an efficient young woman, well-spoken, charming, relentless—perfect for our clientele—said she had a new booking coming in shortly. "Ashleigh Cranford. She says her mother was at school with your sister."

"That's nice. What does her father do?"

"He's a consultant at Kingston Hospital."

"Public sector. Reliable. Good."

Upstairs, the Princess Di replica dress that Mother and Hsiao Ling had made stood on a headless mannequin in a glass cabinet in one corner of what was once the workroom. The sewing tables had been replaced with desks where eight young people wearing headphones sat at computers.

I phoned our solicitors to find out about getting out of the lease at the shopping mall. It was Guy Forrester's old firm, though he'd retired years previously to live on a smallholding in Devon. So in place of his reassuring tones, I listened to someone with an officious voice say they'd look into it and get back to me.

Things dragged on through the winter. Freddie turned on the Christmas lights at his mall with the help of a local radio station presenter, a listeners' darling who came and posed for a publicity picture at my doomed shop. But no amount of goodwill could make up for the empty units and the lack of a seasonal spending spree.

"You failed." Mother didn't make it any easier.

"Sometimes things don't work out," I said. "You know that."

· · · · ●· ● · · ·

At the start of February, I drove around the M25 to Hertford-shire. When I left home, there was frost on the ground and a nip in the air. While I was stuck in traffic near Heathrow, the sun came out. It beat down, brave February sun, and my mood lifted. By the time I got to the shopping centre, it was warm enough to go out onto the terrace to drink my coffee. The tables were deserted, apart from one. A semi-familiar figure hunched over his paper cup.

"Freddie? Can I join you?"

He gestured to all the empty chairs and forced a smile. "Might as well."

The years sat heavily on the face of Connie and Tim's pampered son. The extra weight had made his features sink and given him jowls. His grey hair was cut too short and made him look like an EastEnders villain.

"The centre's bust." Victimhood seeped through his posh voice.

"I'm sorry."

"Are you?" He turned on me with misplaced aggression. "Really? It won't affect you. It'll ruin me."

I wondered if the resentment I heard in his voice had always been there, lurking beneath his sense of entitlement. The boy who thought he'd always be on a promise. I decided to stick a knife in.

"You must've seen it coming. The place never took off."

"Dominic said it was surefire. Couldn't fail, he said."

"Mmm." I could imagine how that conversation went.

"He's all right mind. As usual. Walked away from the wreckage with millions." Self-pity is unattractive, especially in a man. Freddie wallowed in it. "I suppose your sister's done all right too."

"You leave my sister out of it."

A ghost of a smirk appeared on his grey face. He'd found a way to hurt someone. "Your sister. My half-brother. A right pair. Pity the kid."

"What a thug." It didn't start to express what I felt. "If there's one saving grace in all of this it's seeing you finally get your comeuppance. And for the record, you aren't the only person to suffer. Lots of people have, me included. So,"—I searched around for the rudest word I knew— "fuck you."

Swearing at Freddie was the best it got. I threw good money after bad trying to extricate myself from Hertfordshire.

I even called Rose about it, but she deflected me. "My mother's been off the board for months."

"Perhaps you could provide me some general advice on the options open to us."

"It wouldn't be appropriate, professionally." I pictured Rose sitting in her office, and wondered whether her desk was still as tidy and whether she was looking at the photographs lined up on it while she talked. "It's likely to get considerably more difficult, moving forward, especially as I'm guessing a lot of your customers work in the city."

"You know that's the case, Rose."

"I don't know, I'm not involved." Down the phone, I could hear the whoosh of air being sucked out of a room as a door closed and then the faintest hint of a click as the lock caught.

"I understand." It wasn't edifying. "Thanks Rose. Best to Hsiao Ling."

Eventually a charity shop moved into our unit in Hertfordshire. When I made my last visit, I found freshly laundered cast-offs hanging where once there'd been fine silk and lace. A woman in a black skirt and T-shirt with her glasses hanging on a chain around her neck jostled the rails of crowded coat hangers. She pulled out a cream linen jacket and held it up to the light with approval. "Barely worn," She picked an imaginary piece of fluff off the collar. "Would you like to take it with you?"

When the manager at Sevenoaks resigned, I didn't replace her. A burst of June weddings made me feel more hopeful. Our dresses were brilliant, our clients were ecstatic, but the weather was dull, and we couldn't get the usual sparkly bride pictures for our website.

"You can't leave it any longer," Henry counselled. We'd taken Skye out for a pizza followed by a ride on the London Eye. She had her nose glued to the glass wall of the capsule while it soared over the city and Henry sat on the bench in the centre of the pod lecturing me about my business options. He didn't like to admit he was afraid of heights.

· · · · · ● · ● · · ·

By the end of summer, the accountant in me was saying we might stagger through to the end of the year. The lawyer in me said we could then go bankrupt. The daughter in me said Mother wouldn't survive that. Even in her foggy state she'd spot what was happening. "I've failed," she'd say. So, I took a deep breath and in September I decided. Shut Sevenoaks, sell Sewell, lease back the first floor for an online business. Start again. Over Sunday lunch Henry said he'd do me a relaunch for free.

I cried.

On Monday morning, I gave the staff their notice. Monday September 15th. The date's written into my heart.

They cried.

That night the news showed pictures of young people pouring out of a London office block carrying their belongings in cardboard boxes. It was Canary Wharf. The scale of it even got through to Mother.

"Mercy me," she said.

My phone went.

"Hello stranger." You sounded hyper-excited. In the background was the sound of music and people.

"Is that your office on telly?" I asked. Some of the young people were laughing. More hysterical than happy. A glum-faced man with black eyebrows and white stubble appeared on-screen and started opining in a strong Scottish accent. Mother was mesmerised. I escaped into the kitchen to talk to you.

"Yes, but I'm not affected." You were burbling away. "I'm fine. In fact, I'm great. Never better." It sounded like everyone around you was great too. There was generalised laughter coming from your end, and then, from close up, a giggle. And then a familiar rasping voice called out your name.

"Well, I'm not."

"Oh dear Ju-ju. So sorry. Listen, could you have Skye this weekend? I've just put in an offer on the most fantastic new house and I'm taking Calypso to see it. Ultra-modern, architect-designed, lots of glass and an internal green space, fabulous garden, direct line to London, good schools. It's not far from that shop you had in Hertfordshire."

That's what made me snap. Why were you so emotionally tone deaf? I could just about take your partying with Calypso and bragging about your fantastic new house, but to chuck in Hertfordshire was too much.

"Have you any idea what I've been going through? Have you, in your making whoopee in the housing market, given it the slightest smidgeon of your attention?"

You faltered. "Oh. So sorry, Ju-ju. I knew things were a bit iffy, but—"

"A bit iffy? A bit? Isla, that doesn't even begin to describe what's been happening." Talking about it made it worse. "I've had to sell up everything, even the Sewell shop. Even that's gone. Everything. I've had to lay off fourteen people—"

"There's hundreds being laid off here."

"I don't care about hundreds. What I care about are the fourteen people I had to tell today that they're out of a job. Can you even begin to understand what that means when someone's worked their guts out for you and then you have to send them home?"

"But you're all right."

"So that's it, is it? I'm all right Jack, so everything's OK in the world. Isla, what is wrong with you that you can even think that? Besides, I'm personally not all right. In fact, I'm this far from disaster. We could go bankrupt and what would happen then? What happens if we lose our house? Mother's lived here half a century. How would she survive the disgrace?"

"She'd never know." Even down the phone, I could hear you smirk.

"You bitch. You absolute bitch. But then you'd have to be, wouldn't you, to gamble on your own sister's failure?"

There was a pause before you replied. Not a silence, there were still partying noises, and then you said. "Now what are you talking about?"

"You did, you know you did, Isla. You said so. You took a bet that the shopping centre would fail. That's what started all this trouble. You knew what was about to happen, and you made money out of it."

"Oh, for goodness' sake, you'll be all right. You're always all right." You weren't even trying to hide your scorn. "That was always your thing wasn't it. I was the unreliable one, crazy Isla, but good old Julia, Mummy could always rely on you to make things all right."

"What rubbish is this?"

"How d'you think I've felt always having to play second fiddle?"

"Who went to University? Who got her own home? Who got the baby?"

"I've had to fight for everything I've got."

As if I hadn't fought for both of us. I searched around for something I could throw back at you. "Come to think of it, I suppose it's my misfortune that's paying for your new house. For you and Calypso."

"It doesn't work like that."

"That's exactly how it works. You said so. You bet on other people's businesses failing. Cue disaster. You cash in. How immoral can you get?"

"Ju-ju." There was a touch of panic in your voice as I switched my phone off. In days gone by, I could have slammed down the receiver, which was much more satisfying.

Back in the sitting room Mother was watching coverage of the Battle of Britain celebrations. "The fighters won the battle, but the bombers won the war," she said.

"Now what are you on about?"

"Flying fortresses. Like the one that Roland flies. The most handsome man I've ever seen."

"Not now Mother, please, not now." I was shaking from head to foot. Anger, exhaustion, fear? I had no idea where all this would end.

"Has something upset you?"

"It's Isla. She's being impossible."

"Isla's always had her troubles, ever since she was wee. Be nice to her." She gave me her 'there's a good girl, Julia' look.

I went out and sprayed my orchids.

After Mother had gone to bed, I put my phone on again. There was a string of missed calls and text messages. From you. Variations of "Sorry. Please phone. Love you. xxx." Then one from Calypso. "Phone." No frills. You'd said something about taking her to see your new house. My curiosity got the better of my temper.

"Is she there?" Calypso's voice was cheese-grater harsh.

"And hello to you too."

"Don't fuck with me. Have you heard from her?"

Calypso's desperation collided with the dregs of my anger.

"She was fine earlier."

"Fuck fine. She was heartbroken."

I snorted. "Outrageous more like."

"You know how fragile Isla is. How could you be so vicious to her?"

There was something here I didn't understand.

"She should have arrived by now." If it had been anyone other than Calypso, I'd have heard the warning bells.

My phone went again as I was getting into bed. This time it was your au pair. "Is that you Julia?" A relaxed Australian, she'd normally follow up with a joke. But she wasn't relaxed and there was no joke. "The police are here. They want to talk to you."

CHAPTER TWENTY

16 SEPTEMBER, 2008

"You're my rock, Ju-ju," you used to say. And rocks aren't supposed to have feelings: those were your territory, not mine. Nothing had prepared me for what I felt that night.

My pain hollowed me out. Reduced my entire world to your life being played out on a hospital bed. My heart hooked to the monitor that tracked the fading beat of your own. My every flicker of consciousness willing yours to return. It was beyond endurable. You'd said childbirth was the worst pain, followed by the greatest joy. But this pain of mine would produce no joy. It would never end. I'd carry it for the rest of my life. The pain of losing my sister.

When I didn't pick up your calls, you got into your car. You must have been driving out to see me because, as the police so carefully worded it, in the dark night, on the Kingston by-pass, there was a road traffic accident.

So there you were, lying bloodied white, touchable but beyond reach. While I bled inside. And outside, outside, I wasn't even aware there was an outside to what I felt.

"Would you like a cup of tea, dear?"

The voice came from a long way distant. A woman with a round smiling face held out a saucer with a cup on it. I couldn't connect it with the pain I had become.

She held it towards me and nodded her head encouragingly, put the saucer into the hand that by instinct I must have raised.

It clattered. The chunky hospital teacup on its saucer clattered. It was uncontrollable. The saucer wobbled, the cup tipped, the tea spilt. I couldn't stop the clattering. Because I couldn't stop the shaking in my hand. And then it spread to my whole body, and I was standing, a shivering heap of pain. With the cup and saucer in white fragments on the floor in a pool of brown tea.

The next time I saw you was the last. You were dressed in your favourite emerald green surrounded by ivory silk in the oak coffin Mother had selected. The funeral director asked if we wanted a viewing. Mother didn't respond; I think she chose not to hear. I didn't like to think of you lying abandoned in a chapel of so-called rest, so, in some trepidation, I went on my own. The funeral director, dressed in an anonymous black suit with her dark hair held back in a clip, ushered me into the chapel, and then stood with sensitive discretion by the door while I stepped up to you.

"Her hair's wrong," I said.

"What?" The funeral director appeared, flustered, at my shoulder.

"Her hair's wrong. She'd never have it ordinary like that. When she was little, she'd gel it into spikes. Like a punk. Even when she was at the bank, she'd get bits of it tinted. And her nails. She liked long fake nails painted bright red."

"She must have been quite a character." The voice was professionally neutral.

Quite a character. You. Throwing toilet rolls at the boys at school, fighting in the pub in New Malden, getting drunk with Dominic at Rose's wedding, rolling Skye's dummy in sugar. How could such an anodyne phrase even begin to describe you?

I almost said, "She was." But I wasn't ready for the finality of it, so I just said, "Her name's Isla."

"I'll see to it," the woman said. "Would you like another visit?"

•••••••••••

There were two lives lost in that car crash. The other one was Mother's. The morning after the accident, I sat her down on a chair in the sunroom and knelt in front of her and held her hands and explained as gently as I knew how.

"She's dead?" Mother's blue eyes burned into mine.

"I'm afraid so. Yes." Her hands were icy. They felt like the cold claws of a dead bird. There was heat on my back. The sun was shining in through the sliding doors. Outside the roses were still in bloom, the flower beds were splashed red and white, and near the patio, a blaze of sunflowers. I didn't understand how they could be so alive. But then I didn't understand how I could be either.

"Were you there?" That piercing look again.

"Yes."

"I should have been."

"There was nothing you could have done. She never even came round."

"But I'm her mother. I should have been there for her." She played her trump card, then went outside to walk around the garden.

I watched her out of the kitchen window as I rinsed our breakfast plates and stacked them in the dishwasher. She never entirely came back. Of course, her body did, but her eyes had this vacant look, as if she'd left part of herself behind in the garden. Her soul, her spirit, I suppose I'd call it if I was religious. Whatever it was, she never got it back.

· · • • • • • • · ·

I feared how she'd manage the funeral. But she sat upright in the front row of the crematorium so close to your coffin she could have reached out and touched it, immobile in her black coat with a black hat and a veil over her face. She didn't need the veil. There was no sign of tears. Perhaps that's what she wanted to hide. I found the place in the service sheet for her and put it in her hands and pointed to the words. But she paid no regard, and under her veil, her lips didn't move.

Unlike Calypso's whose lips moved only too well. "How could you be so cruel?" She hissed in my ear outside the crematorium by the floral tributes.

There was a queue of mourners, and I was supporting Mother with one hand, while the other was pumped up and down by a succession of people who must have said their names, although I couldn't take them in. Some people kissed Mother, holding her with both hands as if they were about to lift her like a little china doll. It was a sullen day. I wished it would rain.

"Not now," I hissed back at Calypso.

"Yes now."

Calypso's long blonde hair was lacquered into place, but even her clever make-up couldn't conceal the lines down either side of her mouth or the redness around her eyes. "If you hadn't been so vicious to her, she'd still be alive." Her voice grated.

"It was an accident."

"It need never have happened." Her face twisted with the effort to keep her mouth under control.

"She was my sister. I thought the world of her."

"You, you, you. Can't you see beyond yourself?" Her face was working now, the lines in it deepened, her eyes narrowed. For a minute I thought she was going to hit me. Then Dominic appeared with a smooth deference suitable to the occasion and said, "This isn't helping, Calypso." He nodded to me and bent and kissed my mother and led Calypso away. Judas, I wanted to shout at his departing back, how dare you even pretend regret?

The exchange can't have lasted more than a minute, but it left me shattered.

"Are you all right, Julia?" A woman's voice. Its owner came into focus. Black coat, red hat, dark hair, flawless.

"We're coping."

Rose kissed me on the cheek. Her lips felt soft and warm. She rubbed my arm with just the right degree of comfort that it didn't make me cry. "We must keep in touch."

As she walked away, she took the hand of a skinny boy in a blue suit that was too old for him. He turned around and smiled at me, a pretty heart-shaped face like his mother's, and gave a half-wave. On their way out they passed Skye and her nanny. The cheerful Australian was struggling.

·•·•··•···

Finally, it was over. I took Mother back to the car and put her inside. The driver, a morbid-looking man in a grey suit shut the door. I was about to get in the other side when I saw an old man standing among the floral tributes. He had a walking stick in one hand, and in the other a joyous rainbow of flowers, unwrapped, which he bent down and laid amongst the others in their safe cellophane covers. There was something about his bearing that triggered memories. His beige-coloured mac was neatly belted, and although he leaned on his walking stick to get up, he had an agility, an elegance. When he took off his hat—the only thing about him that was black—there were sandy-coloured strands through the white of his hair. When he looked at me with warm brown eyes an emotional grenade exploded.

"Father."

Everything was in his face. Sadness. Joy. Relief. Fear.

My feelings were simpler. "Why?" I had so many questions for him. Why leave, why come back, why now, why so late?

"I didn't mean to intrude."

"That's not what I asked."

He winced. "I heard you were all doing so well. People said." He fell silent.

I wanted to clobber him with one of the bouquets, or my handbag, or a gravedigger's shovel. "Do you have any idea how much you hurt her?"

He leaned on his stick with both hands and swayed. For a moment I thought he might fall over, but I couldn't find it in me to pity him. Not yet. "Do you have the tiniest smidgen of a clue how much she missed you?"

He fiddled with his hat. Eventually he looked at me.

"She was the most beautiful baby. Exquisite. Your mother struggled to recover from the birth, so I had her to myself those first few weeks, until you came home from Switzerland. I'd feel her soft cheeks and count all her fingers and toes and couldn't believe how perfect she was. I'd sing to her—"

"No." I shocked myself that after a gut-wringer of a day, I still had the energy to emote. "You abandoned her."

He looked everywhere for an excuse. As if there'd be one tucked among the flowers or propped against a memorial or written in the clouds. But I wasn't going to let him off. "You owe me a reason."

"I couldn't stay. Not after Isla."

"Are you blaming her for it?"

"No, no. Of course not. She wasn't the cause. Her arrival only crystallised things." He fanned himself with his hat. "I'd spent my whole life trying to live up to other people's idea of who I was. I spent my childhood trying to live up to my parents' expectations of a son, and my adult life trying to live up to your mother's expectations of a husband. I tried, I really tried, to be a good father to you. And then when I held Isla in my arms, I knew I couldn't start pretending all over again. Not another entire lifetime of deceit. Not for her."

The last of Isla's guests left, curious faces watching our drama, discreet nods and waves as they walked to their cars. A new crowd was gathering at the crematorium for the next departure. A scruffy blue car puttered slowly along the drive and stopped at a tactful distance. A younger man got out.

"If it's any consolation, it hasn't always been an easy life. I lost my job of course. I set up a shop, but I didn't have Maisie's flair for business. A lot of my friends died."

"But we never heard a squeak from you. For so long."

"I sent letters, cards. Connie said they weren't welcome."

All those years that I thought he'd forgotten us. I didn't know whether to laugh or cry or curse Connie for her manipulative cruelty. Perhaps it was his fault for not pushing past his cousin's deception. It would take time to work out. For now I had only one more burning question. "So why did you come back?

"Whatever happened, she was still my child."

• • • • • • • • • •

The weekend after the funeral Skye came to live with us. The nanny drove her out. Mother and I stood at the front door as Skye stepped out of the car, clutching a white rabbit in her arms.

"Henry gave it to her. I hope you don't mind," the young Australian woman said. She lifted two suitcases out of the boot of the car and unpacked them briskly in the yellow nursery, then went out into the garden with a giant Ikea bag. Skye sat in the sunroom among the orchids, stroking the rabbit and talking to Mother with the unnerving self-composure of a child adrift on a sea of adult emotions. Out in the garden I watched the nanny assemble the rabbit hutch.

"Well, that's it." She stood up and wiped her hands on her jeans. "Time for me to make tracks."

Skye brought her rabbit out to the car to say goodbye. As the nanny drove out into the road, she gave a blast on the horn.

"Mummy says she shouldn't do that. It upsets people."

I took her around the back and we put the rabbit into its cage.

"It's not an it. It's a him," Skye said. "His name's Toshy. Like Uncle Henry's used to be."

She took my hand and we walked back into the house together.

Soon after that the rabbit's namesake moved in. Henry called us his flatpack family, fitted together out of bits and pieces. Convenience, not romance. Skye laughed. So, after a while, did I.

It's not that I forgot you, I still think about you every day. And the intensity of my loss hasn't diminished. It's just that there are gaps now between the pain when I can have other feelings.

"I"

2020

CHAPTER TWENTY-ONE

FEBRUARY 2020

I like to think of it as a homecoming. On my night flight to Edinburgh, soaring up among the stars, I try to imagine what it will be like to arrive at the place where my story started.

But then the plane breaks through the clouds, and I get my first sight of the city my grandmother left behind.

And there's nothing there, apart from pinpricks of light in a darkness so profound it blocks out all sense of place. There's no context. It's like my life. A yellow bedroom. A swing under a beech tree. An empty driveway in the morning sun. Bright spots in my memory, each significant in itself, but with nothing in between. No narrative to connect them with each other or with now. Below me the speckles of light spread and coalesce and turn into glittering buildings and streets and then we roll to a halt at Edinburgh airport.

By we, I mean myself—Skye—and Granny Maisie. Her ashes are in the overhead locker, to be scattered in what Aunt Julia says is the only place she'd want to spend eternity. "Your mother would agree." She always quotes my mother, Isla, on occasions like this and folds her hands and goes all quiet, as if that's how Mum would be too. "We were so close, Isla and I." But I don't ever remember Mum being like that. I remember climbing on her shoulders the times she picked me up from school and her singing, "You are my sunshine," and my thinking every kid in school must want a Mum like mine. In my head I can still hear Mum's voice and this time it's saying, "They're only ashes, babe, they'll be happy anywhere."

Granny meanwhile never said anything in all her years of speechlessness about where her ashes might end up. "You're the spitting image of her," Aunt Julia tells me, and I say how can that be when Granny stopped living years ago—only her heart kept on thumping and wouldn't let her die. Just because I've got her red hair and turquoise eyes doesn't make us the same. She was like a walnut with a hard, wrinkly shell, and no sign of any feelings inside. I feel everything.

From the airport I catch a shuttle bus into the city centre. I thought there'd be a sense of familiarity about it, some psychic recognition that part of my pre-history belongs here. Instead when I step out of the bus, all I feel is the shock of a cold arrival. My breath turns to mist in the night air, the Hogwartsian castle glowers from its mound, a spooky alleyway takes me through space and time into a mediaeval street lined with craggy buildings, one of which—I check my phone—is my hostel.

Under a stone archway, along a passage, through a door, I arrive in the reception area where an earnest guy called Ming Chung signs me in. He's a student, a second year like me, but having to work to pay huge overseas student fees, unlike me. As he hands over my keycard, he gives me a sweet smile, and directs me to my dorm on the first floor. And then it's up again, up never-ending stone steps where the sound of my footsteps spirals up ahead of me into a kitchen where a girl looks up from the stove.

"Heartfelt," she says.

The word hangs between us. There's her, all self-assured, smiley face, dark curls tied up in a green and gold head-wrap, black jumper down to her knees, bright red leggings, stirring her pot with a giant wooden spoon. And then there's me in my grey bomber jacket feeling ordinary.

The basics of the room are uncompromisingly white; walls, floors, cupboards glare at me. Trestle tables and benches crowd one end, and near them are noticeboards covered with scrawled post-it notes. Overhead light shines on condensation trickling down windows surrounded by climbing plants. The warmth unfreezes my face and my nose starts to run. A billow of chilli fumes hits me. My stomach grumbles. I slide my backpack onto the floor and unzip my jacket.

"Heartfelt," she says again, and then I realise what she's on about.

"Skye," I say. "My name is Skye."

· · · · ●· ● ● ● · ·

Later. After Heartfelt's beans have fed our whole dorm—two men from Newcastle, a Belgian and his American partner, three Bristol students and me; two Germans and the hostel cat decline. After we've followed the Belgian out onto the streets and into a gothic-looking cellar where we match each other shot for shot of whisky. Except for Heartfelt who's Zen and doesn't drink. "Y'areet pet?" asks one of the men and winds her up until she climbs on the table and wiggles her bum in his face to make her point. And we all laugh and shout the fundamentals of our lives to each other so when we stagger out to the next bar, we're like forever friends. And then the next and the next until eventually we climb back up the winding hostel steps that go on it feels like to the stars and our laughter rushes up and down the stairwell until we reach our dorm. Where the Bristol girls go "Ewww" at the idea of sleeping in the same room as Granny's ashes and insist that they—the ashes that is—get put outside in the corridor on a chair with a "do not touch" post-it note in bright red lettering. And to keep me happy, Heartfelt texts Ming Chung to make sure no-one, which means him, clears them away. And finally, after we get into our bunks, and the lockers get locked and Heartfelt's standing at the door telling the Belgian if he and his girlfriend want sex, they should have got themselves a separate room, she switches the light off.

After all that, much later, I can't sleep.

The ceiling swirls above me and I try to fix the shapes into something familiar. My aunt, my boyfriend, my dead mother. They all slide away. I try listening to the sounds of my room-mates. Soft breathing, snores. Someone farts. I sit up. I'm on the top bunk closest to a small turret alcove that has the only windows.

Heartfelt is on the bunk below me, her sleeping bag spread out and pulled up over her head, her back to the room, her big jumper folded neatly at the end of her bed. I climb down and pull it on and go to the window. Outside is deserted. A streetlight picks out white sparklets of frost. A figure stumbles across the cobbles. I tug at the sash. The window doesn't move. I crouch down and heave. The sash shoots up and I gasp at the coldness of the air. In the room behind someone groans. I pull the window back down until it's just a crack open, but it won't stay like that, and slides shut again.

Now I'm seriously awake. I pull on my socks and creep out of the dorm. Granny's ashes look lonely on their chair by the door, like a naughty kid put out in the school corridor. I stroke them in their box. "Love you Gran." In the kitchen the fridge hums contentedly. I take out a bottle of milk and pour myself a mug, then rummage through the overhead cupboard and find a battered tub with some dregs of cocoa powder, stir in a teaspoon and add some sugar and put it in the microwave. It comes out gross-looking, but it's hot and sweet and tastes of something. I've almost finished when I hear a noise from downstairs. So I rinse out my mug and leave it on the draining board. Upside down, to keep the spirits in.

Someone's crying. I pad down the stairs after the sound and find it's coming from behind the reception. Peering over the counter, I see Ming Chung, stretched across his desk, head on his folded arms, shoulders heaving with his sobs.

"Hey." No response, so I pull up a chair and sit down next to him. "What's up?" Still nothing. So I stretch out a hand and touch him on the back and he shoots upright. "Sorry." I feel crass about the intrusion.

He's got a toilet roll on his desk and rips a bit off and wipes his eyes, then hunches forward with his elbows on his knees and his hands dangling down between his legs. His tears drop onto the tiled floor. I don't know what to say. After a while he reaches out for more tissue and blows his nose.

"Did something happen?" Of course something happened, bloody stupid question, but what else is there?

"I got an email from my father back home. My mother's died." All the muscles on his face start to work and tears pour out of his eyes again. He leans over and covers his face with his hands.

"I'm so sorry." I know about this. It's my territory. I know what it's like, that breaking of the birth-bond. I've felt it myself, the terrible loneliness when the person who's brought you into this world goes off and leaves you behind in it. Passes, they say. Such a gentle word. As if that sanitises it. Fuck passes. They croak, kick the bucket, die. Like Ming Chung said. Like I'd felt it to be when my Mum died. A tearing away of part of myself.

And like I'd seen it to be for Aunt Julia. She'd tried to pretend when Granny died it was OKish, because Granny was so old, and had already forgotten her life, living in a nursing home like she was in a queue waiting for her turn to die. Except it wasn't all right. Aunt Julia went to pieces. All this goes through my mind while I listen to Ming Chung cry his guts out.

"I lost my mother too." The words are inadequate to contain so much grief. Ming Chung sits up and wipes his face on his sleeve and looks at me. "You know then?"

"D'you want to talk about it?"

By the time he finishes my head aches like it's out on a stalk. At one point he reaches out and grabs my hand, and then he won't let it go, and cries into it. He doesn't know why his mother died. He thinks it's a new virus that's going around. His father said she was taken away by people in medical gear and next thing she was dead. And all the while he squeezes my hand until the bones creak.

"I never got to say goodbye to her."

I can feel his pain. "I didn't with my mother either."

"You understand."

I nod. He doesn't need the details of how it was for me. Mum's empty bed, her laptop on the kitchen table, the missing car, my nanny's, "I'm so sorry," as if it was her fault. The nothingness. I know how it feels.

"I have to go home," he says. "I can't stay here."

How is that going to work I wonder, but don't like to say. How do you get to China in a hurry when you don't have any money and have to leave your job and studies and don't know when you'll get back? Ming Chung cries himself to a standstill and then I unfold my frozen self and climb back up the stairs and onto my bunk. It's still just about dark but there are some traffic noises starting up outside in the street. I'm almost asleep when I remember I'm still wearing Heartfelt's jumper. I peel it off and lean over and drop it onto her bed. It lands with a gentle "phut."

When I wake up the dorm's empty. They're all in the kitchen, sitting around one of the trestle tables, apart from Heartfelt who's cross-legged on the floor with her back against a wall, her hands palm-upwards on her knees and her eyes shut. She opens them as I walk past.

"Ming Chung's going home tonight," she says.

"How's he going to manage that?"

"We're doing a whip-round for him."

I get myself some coffee and join the others. Ming Chung's news has spooked them. They're googling viruses and China and following links on from there and now the Germans are on their iPads booking flights home. Ditto the Belgian and his American girlfriend, except they're debating whether that should be Belgium or the States. The Bristol girls are only here for a friend's wedding. The two guys from Newcastle have to go home for work.

"At least a wedding's more cheerful than getting rid of yer granny's ashes," one of them says. "Why don't you just put them in the bin and come out with us and enjoy yourself?"

"I know you don't mean that." He's not a bad guy, good-looking too in a blond hunk way. If I wasn't already committed, I could even be interested.

"Don't be so sure," he says. "Where are you going to tip them?"

"Scatter," says Heartfelt from her position on the floor. "You scatter ashes."

The guy laughs.

I take out my phone and show him the picture of my great-grandmother, the photograph that Aunt Julia found in her Granny's sitting room.

"It's that old bridge," he says. He taps on the screen and smiles at the picture. "Is that your gran'pappy?"

"No. My great grandpa was a war hero. He died years ago."

"In the war?"

"He had a heart attack throwing out some rubbish."

"So he was a fly-tipper."

"That's so rude." One of the Bristol girls grabs the phone and peers at it. "Is that your granny?"

"It's her mother, Flora. But it's the only picture we had of a happy place to scatter the ashes. The tenement where Granny grew up has been knocked down."

"The man's so obviously her lover. Look at the way they are together."

"His name was written on the back of the photograph," I say. "Robert Macpherson. But that's all we know about him."

"Secret love." She gives me a knowing look and hands my phone back,

Heartfelt gets up from the floor and sticks her head over my shoulder. "What a neat story." She takes the phone and cradles it in her hands. For a minute I think she's going to cry.

· • • • • • • • ·

The Queensferry train slides out of Waverley station. Edinburgh is sombre grey. Even the castle looks prosaic in the drab daylight. Granny's ashes are in the backpack beside me, Heartfelt is sitting opposite. She's zipped a tight-fitting leather combat jacket over her jumper. Her hair stands out from under her black beret like it's electric, and she's covered her mouth with don't-mess-with-me lipstick. I tell her she looks more urban warrior than ash-scatterer.

"That's an acute observation," she says. "It goes to the heart of who I am." She tells me about her work on a food project in New York. It makes me feel inadequate. She talks about her co-workers Finn and Precious, and it's a while before I realise they're her parents.

"I don't know who my father is."

She stops rattling on about her own. "Didn't your mother tell you?"

I shook my head. "He was never part of my life. For all I know he was a sperm bank. My mother didn't know her father either."

"Matrilineal. Independent women. That's something." She peers out of the train window. It's stopped drizzling, and the sun has appeared, a white smudge behind the clouds.

"Not exactly. Her father left home when she was just a baby. He only turned up again at her funeral. Aunt Julia said it was a bit late." It's a long story, so I use a shortcut to explain what happened. "I was his attendant when he married Tom."

"So what did your aunt make of that?"

"She said it was the sweetest wedding she'd ever organised. They had their picture in the paper and it said how he was one of the heroic codebreakers who won the war. He worked with Alan Turing, you know."

Heartfelt looks blank.

"As in the fifty-pound note?"

She's still blank.

"Anyway, Gramps was chuffed to bits. Tom's the only grandparent I've got left now. We're very close, he and I."

"That's quite a family."

"Complex, some people say."

There's a patch of blue sky when we get off the train. When we're part way down the road, the sun comes out, and then we reach the junction and there it is, the Forth Bridge, a great red dinosaur humping its way across the river in the watery sunshine.

That's when I feel a sense of connection. There are three bridges at Queensferry. The road bridges might be the bigger feats of engineering. Beautiful, bold pillars and fine lines, ethereal, if you can say that of anything made out of steel and concrete. But they look like they were dropped into the landscape. The old bridge looks like the one that defeated it, that overcame all the obstacles, powered its way over the river to give people a crossing. It's the old bridge that has the magic. I understand why, of all the places, my great-grandmother chose this for her special photograph. She must have loved Robert Macpherson very much. Whoever he was.

It takes a while to find the right spot to scatter the ashes. It turns out it's not as easy as showing up at the bridge and chucking them in. We find the place where Flora and Robert were photographed, a hotel with a terrace set with tables and chairs overlooking the river. It's deserted now in the pre-spring, but I can imagine them taking tea there in summer. Heartfelt holds up their picture on my phone. "The terrace, the river, the bridge. Just imagine, fifty years ago, and here you are, back where your great-grandmother came with her new lover."

And then we walk across the road to a kind of beach opposite. It's how I'd imagined it scattering Granny's ashes in the place where her mother had found happiness. There's even some sunshine. But looking at the shoreline, I don't fancy my chances walking out on the rocks. Further on down the cobbled High Street there's a little harbour which looks promising, and we walk out to the end of the quay.

"Perhaps I could scatter them here," I say.

"They'll just wash back against the quayside," says Heartfelt. "And then your granny will spend like the whole duration stuck to these stone walls."

"You're right. Granny deserves to be free."

We head back along the road towards the bridge. Practically under it there's a jetty. It's not the most romantic spot, but it's practical. Aunt Julia would approve. Heartfelt does, she says the tide of the river will carry the ashes away under the bridge and Maisie will become part of the boundless ocean that encompasses the universe. I don't like to tell her I think Granny's beliefs about the afterlife were strictly binary. Heaven or hell.

There are danger and deep-water signs at the entrance to the jetty, but nothing that says no ash scattering, so I take my shoes off, roll up my trousers, unpack the container of ashes and give my backpack to Heartfelt. Then I walk along the jetty, and where it disappears below the surface, step into a shock of freezing water. There's something about the sensation that goes beyond the numbness of my cold feet, but I park the thought and wade out until the water's nearly at my knees.

Ashes are unruly things. So I find when I start to sprinkle Granny's. They don't do what's expected, like fall gently into the place of my choosing. Some of them blow into the air and land back on the jetty, as if they don't want to leave solid ground just yet. Some blow up and catch the sunlight and sparkle like I'm told Granny used to do. A few land on me. Like Granny's blessing. Or perhaps her stardust. I shake the container harder. The rest of the ashes shoot out into the river and get washed away.

It's only then I start to cry, standing in the cold water bawling like a newborn. There's no reason for it. The trip was my idea. Uncle Henry said we could just bury Granny's ashes in Surrey.

But Aunt Julia said her mother would want to go home, that she had, after all, never lost her Scottish accent. And when she said she couldn't manage the journey, I'd offered to go alone, ash-scattering being, so people said, a joyous occasion. But it doesn't feel like that now. It feels like I've lost a part of my life. Another part, and I'm not sure which one is hurting me the most.

Am I crying for my Granny, Maisie, whose life sort of petered out after my mother died? I remember her being pushed around the village in her wheelchair by my grandfather Jeremy when he finally reappeared in her life. Too late, because she'd already, in a sense, vacated it. After he died, Tom wheeled her around. Perhaps he had some residual guilt for stealing Gramps away from her, or perhaps it was an acknowledgement that they'd both loved the same man. And lost him. Perhaps it filled an emptiness.

Or am I crying for my mother, Isla? But I thought I'd already cried myself dry over her. What I miss now are the memories of her that are losing their definition and will soon be gone. I remember how she'd put her arms around me and say, "Just you and me, babe, just you and me," and then we'd dance around like I thought we would forever. But now I can't remember exactly what her voice was like, or how she smelt when she hugged me. And there's so much that I don't know about why she died.

And then I recognise what it is that's so familiar about this moment. Sunshine and cold water. It's our pool at home on a hot summer's day, and us holding hands and jumping in and screaming, "Mum," and "Babe." It's myself I'm crying for, and what I've lost and how much I need to find. For the loose ends I thought I'd tie up here, but I haven't. For the loneliness I've felt and how I wish I could go back and interrogate my pre-mothers about their lives so that I could know what they went through and understand all the whys and wherefores that took them down the road that finally led to me coming here and tipping a pile of ashes into a river. That's when I let go and howl.

There's a sloshing sound in the water behind me and then Heartfelt's arms wrap around me, and I feel more than I hear her say, "Come on, honey. It's over."

· · · · · ● · ● · · · ·

My backpack's so much lighter on the train back to town, as if I've offloaded more than just the ashes.

When we reach the hostel, the Germans have already left. The rest of us take Ming Chung down to the station. Heartfelt gives him the envelope with our whip-round in. That makes him really happy. It's more than money for him. He's not sure how he'll get to China. There are travel restrictions and some places are in quarantine. We have a group hug on the platform. The blond hunk says "Aww, man," but I tell him to find his inner millennial. Or if he can't, then do it for Ming Chung, who can't decide whether to laugh or cry, so does both.

In the morning, the men from Newcastle pack up and leave, so do the Bristol girls once they've recovered from their hangovers. I plan to leave on an evening flight—the ticket's burning a hole in the top of my backpack—but before then I have one more visit to make, to the street where Granny grew up. Perhaps I'll be able to unpick more of the loose ends in our shared story. So I leave the Belgian and his American still arguing over which country they're going to go to, and head out on my final mission.

The sun's out again and I sweat walking up the hill out of the city centre. The crowded buildings have been cleaned up and glow creamy grey, stuck about with estate agents "For Sale" signs. There's a woman on her knees planting flowers in a little patch of garden outside a doorway to a chic tenement block. She looks up and smiles as I go past.

"Hot," I say.

"Unseasonal."

I consult my phone. A bit further up I turn right. The road is just as my aunt described it; the mound over the debris from the tenements where my grandmother grew up, the kids' playground, the row of maisonettes opposite. The sun beats down. A boy in a mucky garden throws a stone. A man with a dog shouts. I cross the road to look at the place where Flora's story ended. And that's when I see the face in the cracked window and an ancient figure comes running out.

CHAPTER TWENTY-TWO

FEBRUARY 2020

"I knew my Maisie wouldn't forget me." The old man with the baby face jiggles from foot to foot. The sun shines on his greyness and he blinks like he doesn't get to see daylight so often. Flecks of sweat appear around his face.

"You've come for your trunk." He shuffles off up the garden path, then turns and beckons to me with a gnarled finger. "Come on, come on."

There's a creepiness about this man as he scurries to his front door, like one of those grey creatures you find when you turn over a rock in the garden, which scuttles around until it finds some dark corner to crawl into. But he must have known my grandmother, and he has her trunk. What will happen if I tell him, forget how I look, I'm not Maisie? Perhaps he'll disintegrate. Perhaps he's past telling. I follow him inside.

Where the stench douses me like some foul steam bath. Air that's sodden with piss, decaying rubbish, souring sweat. Sunlight flickers through grime on the cracked window in the front room where the curtains are grey and frayed and held up with bits of string. It falls on bulging black bin liners and a sofa that sags under the weight of tangled fuck knows what kind of junk. A stained pillow, a rusted biscuit tin, a piece of rubber tubing that maybe was once some kind of bathroom fitting. The man stands among it like another bit of wreckage. Now I can see that the roundness of his face misleads; it's just his bones are that shape. In reality he's skinny as a rake. His cardigan hangs from his shoulders and his trousers look like they're hollow. A puff of wind and he'd be gone. I wonder where the social workers are.

He motions to me to sit down, and I start to lower myself onto what looks like the emptiest chair. Just as my bum's about to make contact there's a hiss, and the cat shoots out from beneath me.

"Don't mind her. Come here, kitty, kitty." The cat rubs itself against his legs and he totters and stretches his hand out and I think "Oh fuck, he's going to fall," but he just manages to catch his balance and stroke its tail. And then he asks, "Would you like a cup of tea?" and doesn't wait for me to answer before he lurches out the door.

To make things worse, he's got an electric heater going full blast, perched on top of a mountain of unopened mail. Hanging on the wall behind it, is a picture. It's the one thing in the room that's clean, silver frame gleaming, sparkling glass over a photograph from long ago. Two rows of children lined up. Boys in lopsided cutaways, girls in dresses that are too long or too short, all of them painfully thin and smiling in that heart-breaking way that children do to hide whatever's hurting them inside. At the front is a stunted boy who I guess became the old man whose home I'm in. Standing behind him is a girl who, even in the gloomy room, I can see is a mini-me. The same uncontrollable curls, dainty face—elfin my friends call it—mouthy lips.

"D'you remember that day, Maisie?" He holds out a mug of tea. He must have slipped in like a shadow, because he's standing right behind me with such a beatific smile on his face, I can't bring myself to tell him no I don't remember, how can I when I'm not Maisie? So I just nod and take the mug and beat a retreat to my chair and look at the tea and decide not to drink it. He pushes at the rubbish on the sofa. Some of it slides off onto the floor. He sits on what's left.

"I did like you said." He beams at me over his mug like there's some secret between us.

"Uh-huh." I've an urge to get up and run out of the house, slam the front door behind me and get away as far as possible before his patheticness lays some claim to me.

"You know. 'Watch over my Mam for me,' you said, and I did, Maisie, I did." He takes a gulp of his tea and rests his mug on the arm of the sofa. His grey cheeks take on a pinkish tinge, and I try to decide if it's the tea or whether my presence has triggered some inner joy.

"You see, I did nae forget. I tried to tell you last time. But ye were murnin' yer Mam that day. Ye never murned yer Pappy did ye? He were such a brute."

There's an edge to his voice. Something's unsettled the parallel world he's in, and he sits on the edge of his sofa, and clutches his mug so hard his knuckles shine white. I have no idea where he is or how to bring him back from whatever reality he's in. All I know is that this has nothing to do with me. I try to extricate myself: "I ought to go."

"Aye, he were a brute right enough." He radiates anger. Wherever this conversation's headed I don't want to go there. "I've got a train to catch." I feel inside my pocket for my phone, but before I can pull it out, he starts up again.

"Look at wha' he done to you."

There's cold hatred in his eyes. They fix on me, but they see Maisie. I want to scream, "No, not me, I'm not her."

And then he says, "That's why I killed him."

Everything stops. My hand fumbling in my pocket, my heart, my breathing. Nothing in the room moves except his lips drawn tight in his grey face.

"He always called me a daftie, your father. Simon Munro. War hero. So-called. 'There he goes, the daftie,' he'd say, and I suppose he thought I could nae hear him. Or I was too daft to understand." His lips contort. "But I could, I heered everything. How he hit yer Mam and made her cry. And I seen everything. How her never left the house without him and a bruise. And then he hit you. And it was the same all over again. I heered it and seen it and I understood. All along. I understood every-thing."

There's a silence in the room. Then the heater creaks. I take a gulp of fuck knows what's in the mug. The cat mews, winds its way through the piles of junk and sits at his feet. He looks down at it and it jumps onto his lap, curls up, and starts to purr.

"Eh, kitty, kitty." He fondles the cat's head. "So, one day he goes out to take the rubbish. With your Mam of course one step behind like always. And me following like I always do. To look after her like you told me to and like I promised you." He looks through me, to someone, someplace beyond, behind, long gone. "And I follow them up the hill, like they always go to where there's a drop that he throws the rubbish down." He strokes the cat and smiles at it.

"Ye're a guid wee kitty, aren't ye." Stroke, stroke the cat. My chest goes tight.

"And then when they get to the drop, yer Mam says some-thing to him and that's it. He hits her and hits her until she doesn't know which way to turn. And there am I, sneaking up and standing behind a tree and watching him hit her till he's fit to kill. And then I jump out with a shout. 'Stop Simon Munro.' And he gets a fright and cries out, 'Wee Jimmy.' He doesnae call me a daftie now. Oh no, he's feered of me now." The bones behind the round face stand out, and the hand that strokes the cat moves at double speed.

"And I shout out 'Run Mrs Munro, run.' And just in that instant she does. She runs right past me. There's fear in her face. And then I hear her say, 'Thank you Jimmy.'" He puts a hand on his chest and simpers, but then his voice hardens and the panic kicks in again. "And then the brute starts after her and I'm feered he'll catch her."

"And then?" My heart pounds. I'm not in the room any longer. I'm on the road up the hill by the drop where the rubbish goes down. And I'm seeing a dumpy young man with a round face and a woman running away. And the older man, the soldier—the war hero—my great-grandfather. What's he doing?

"He rushes at me, a big ugly devil, swearing that he'll kill me, and I know he will."

And now I'm beside Wee Jimmy, watching the raging man, the wife-beater, his tormenter, charging at us down the hill. "And then?"

"I push him." Wee Jimmy sobs. The swagger goes out of him, his pitiful voice comes back. "It was only a wee push. I only meant fer to stop him. But he goes over the drop where all the rubbish is."

And now I'm standing at the edge of the drop with Wee Jimmy and look over. And there he is, my great-grandfather, lying very still among all the bottles and tin cans and potato peelings.

"He doesn't look like a war hero any longer, in among all the rubbish," says Wee Jimmy. "But then he never was, was he? He was always just a brute."

So there's the truth lying down the cliff-side among the stinking ruins of his life.

"I'm no surprised you ran away." His voice drags me back to the clutter of the present. "Drink yer tea up Maisie, and I'll be fetching yer stuff." He gets up and goes out of the room. The cat jumps onto the warm spot he's left on the sofa.

Whatever's in the mug is cold. It's impossible to tell whether it was ever tea. Then in another room there's a bump, and the scraping of something heavy being dragged along the floor. It bangs against the wall, and my heart that's just restarted, stops again. Wee Jimmy appears in the doorway heaving at a tin trunk.

"Here y'are. I kept it like you told me that night you came calling after the funeral." He drops the trunk, puffing with the effort of it all and staggers over to the sofa and collapses on it next to the cat. "I'm thankful to yer Mam, mind, that she did nae snitch on me to the polis. Just said yer Pappy slipped and fell throwing the rubbish over the drop. So she told me."

Wee Jimmy shuts his eyes. His breathing slows to a steady in out with a wheeze in the middle. Then he sits up and looks at me and says, "Now you know what happened," and then his head rolls back and his mouth falls open, and he starts to snore. The cat slinks onto his lap.

It's not a proper trunk, more of a chest with a handle at either end, and covered in dust. It feels lighter than expected: I reckon I can manage it by myself. So I get out my phone and call an Uber. At the sound of my voice Wee Jimmy's eyes ping open.

"Are you away the now?" he asks.

I make do with a nod. Scared that any more might start him talking again, and God knows what else might come out. This isn't what I had in mind when I set out to find my roots: I understand now why Granny Maisie dug hers up and left. Wee Jimmy slumps on the sofa and goes back to sleep, the cat curled on his lap. I go and prop the front door open and come back for the trunk.

Just as I'm bending over to pick it up, Wee Jimmy says. "Give me a kiss before you go."

His voice wheedles its way under my skin.

"Last time you left, you kissed me. Kiss me again, Maisie."

Everything in me says no. Even if he's not a stalker, or a killer, at the very least he's not a man I would choose to kiss. Not out of affection, not for any old times' sake. There's no relationship between us to acknowledge, and I don't want there to be.

"Please."

On the other hand, he's very old and it can't make any difference to anyone but him whether he gets a kiss from a woman he thinks is leaving but is in fact already dead. Whose ashes I scattered on the river yesterday. It's the only thing, short of getting him a carer or cleaning out his house, that I could ever do for him. For the first time in my life, I feel I'm the adult in the room. I walk across to the sofa and lean into the fumes of piss and decay and kiss him on the cheek. His flesh feels slimy cold on my lips. The cat gives me a final hiss. At the door I pick up the trunk.

"Bye, Wee Jimmy."

He doesn't answer. His eyes are shut, his smile is frozen on his face, and the hand that was stroking his cat is perfectly still. I go out and put the trunk down on the kerbside. When I go back to shut the front door, I don't look in.

· · · ● · ● · ● · ·

My Uber driver says the trunk has to go in the boot. He doesn't want the metal scratching his upholstery.

"Bit of a battered old thing, isn't it?" He sits and chews gum in his driver's seat and watches me through the rear-view mirror as I slam the boot shut.

"You look like you've seen a ghost." Heartfelt runs out of the kitchen as I drag the chest clanking up the stone stairwell at the hostel.

"I think I did." I'm panting with the effort.

"What's in there?" She drags the chest into the middle of the kitchen, gets a wet cloth from the sink and wipes thick layers of gunge off the top. Her eyes light up and she reads the emerging lettering. "'*Simon Munro, Sergeant, 337100.*' The war hero."

"Turns out it wasn't quite like that."

She laps up my story about Wee Jimmy. "That's a much more interesting version."

"It's horrible."

"It's authentic."

The chest sits on the floor, swathed now in chilli fumes from the pot Heartfelt's got cooking on the stove. They condense on it and trickle down the sides like tears.

"Aren't you going to open it?"

"I haven't got a key."

She rummages around the kitchen, produces a hammer and a screwdriver and between us we deal with the padlock. When I lift the lid, there should be some blinding firebolt or at least a drumroll to mark the occasion. Instead there's just Heartfelt saying, "Is that all?"

A moth-eaten black coat. I lift it out and a china figure falls from between the folds and shatters on the floor. Heartfelt picks up the pieces and inspects them. "It's not the first time it's been broken. We can stick it back together if you want."

She gives me the pieces of china; a man in a kilt, a lamb, a dog, all criss-crossed with fine lines where they've been broken and glued together before.

"They must be full of memories." She says I should hold the pieces and close my eyes and feel their story. Which I do, but all I feel are jaggedy bits of broken china. No magic. Next in the chest is a folded page of newspaper and underneath it are two small bundles of letters and an army cap which I lift out. Its leather rim is worn soft, and the gold of the badge is tarnished, but its red flash shines bright.

"Look at this." Heartfelt's taken out the newspaper and is looking at a picture of a group of men sitting in what looks like the grounds of a hospital. Some of them are in uniform, some in anonymous hospital gowns. Two of them have legs missing, one has empty sleeves stuffed into his jacket pockets. There's a group of nurses with their perfect uniforms and starchy headgear and a doctor, gazing at the woman standing beside him. Even in the photograph I can see she's beautiful. Flora. With her hand resting on the shoulder of the man seated in front of her, army jacket over his pyjama bottoms, who has half his face missing. Who must be Simon.

"How awful."

"No, look at the caption. That's what matters." Heartfelt traces over it with her finger. "'Wounded heroes from the Somme, now recovering at Leith Hospital, Private Fergus MacPhail, Corporal John Fraser, Private Joseph Landsman, Sergeant Simon Munro and his wife with their nurses and Dr Robert Macpherson, doctor in charge.' It's him, her Robert. We've found him." She points at the figure on the right, next to Flora. "Look at them. Adoration. They must have loved each other all that time."

She walks me to the bus stop to get the airport shuttle. Out on the pavement, I heave my backpack onto my shoulders, and we stride off down the hill together. Her, all long-legged in tight red trousers and a black hoodie, with her aura of extraordinariness that makes people turn and look. Me, still in my grey bomber jacket, but comfortable with what I'm taking and what I've discarded.

Stuffed inside my backpack are the letters and army cap for Aunt Julia. Heartfelt insisted I put them in a plastic bag, biodegradable of course, in case of fleas. The newspaper is folded in there too. Heartfelt whipped out her phone and took a picture of it before I packed it away. "I like love stories," she said. The tin chest is parked under the window in the hostel kitchen, cleaned up and covered with plants, looking like it's found its happy spot. The black coat got bundled into a charity bag. The china pieces are in the dustbin. The past I can leave behind.

"I don't even know if what Wee Jimmy told me was the truth," I say.

"It was his truth—allow him that. It's probably the only thing in his life that has any meaning."

"But it's his truth, not mine." I adjust my backpack where it cuts into my shoulder.

"You sound like you know that for certain."

"Yes." As of now, I do.

"That's progress. You were so unsure of yourself when you first arrived."

I think of how Heartfelt was when I stood in the river crying, only yesterday, though it seems like a lifetime ago. She was like a sister then. And now, when I look at her, striding down the hill, all complete in herself, I wonder where that person went, or whether that moment too was not what it seemed. Perhaps all that matters is what I feel here and now.

We hug at the bus stop.

"Thanks for everything."

"Have a beautiful life, Skye."

"I'll follow you."

"Sure."

She makes no commitments, doesn't even say she'll follow me back. When the bus arrives, she waves once and then puts her hands in her pockets and her hair bounces up and down on her shoulders as she walks away.

· · · ●·●· · ·

Kit Ying meets me off the plane at Gatwick close to midnight. His mother Rose always calls him by his English name, Anthony, and I'd grown up calling him that too. But when he went to university, he said he wanted to be called by his Chinese name. And then he grew his hair and put it into a ponytail.

He kisses me. "You look different."

"I've had some thinking to do."

"Happy thoughts, I hope." He wraps his arms around me and kisses me again, properly, then swings my backpack onto his shoulders.

"I found us a free parking space."

He's good like that. He always manages to find a parking space. Like he always manages to fix the broken bits of my life. Like when I lost it and got drunk after I got D for my Maths GCSE. Aunt Julia said if I wasn't careful, I'd end up like my mother. He told her I wasn't my mother, I was me, my own person, completely wonderful, and all that said with his shining face that meant Aunt Julia couldn't get angry with him. Instead, she said she supposed I could re-sit, and it all ended up all right. When he, Kit Ying—Anthony as we still called him then—had left, Aunt Julia hugged me and said she hadn't meant it.

He puts my backpack into the boot of his car and opens the door for me to get in the front. The car's impeccably tidy and has a car freshener tree thingy hanging from the rear-view mirror. I hate them; it's about the one thing we argue over. This one smells of nauseating vanilla.

"So, what's on your mind?" he asks as he noses the car into the night-time traffic.

Chapter Twenty-Three

February 2020

Aunt Julia's in the sunroom at home next morning among the wicker furniture and bric-à-brac, misting the late blooms on her orchids. "Magnifique," she tells them. She's wearing a silky flame-coloured wrap, so busy with her spray gun she doesn't notice me till I put my arms around her waist and hug her.

She's been old ever since I can remember. She's still taller than me even now she's seventy. But I can feel that she's lost weight since Granny died. There's a vulnerability in the person who's always kept life at bay for me.

"There you are, dear." She pulls away from me and touches her hair into place as if she has a situation to retrieve, though I can tell she's pleased. "Anthony said to let you know he had to go to help his uncle with the restaurant. He was going to drop Henry at the station on the way. He said you had an interesting time in Edinburgh."

"Yes."

She holds out a cheek for me to kiss. "I'll make a coffee and we can talk. Perhaps you'd like a sandwich. I don't suppose you've eaten for a while."

I laugh. She pats my cheek and bustles off into the kitchen. Her house in Sussex is much smaller than the Surrey mansion.

She decided to downsize after she retired and moved us all to a modern place near a good secondary school for me and a kind nursing home for Granny. "To give us all a fresh start," she said. Uncle Henry put it differently. "A halfway house, between your grandfather and my work." At the back she added a sunroom which she's filled with orchids and mementoes of our life, my school pictures and souvenirs from family holidays with Henry. In the middle is the framed photograph of Gramps in his army uniform, peaked cap pushed back from his hopeful face, and behind that pictures from both his weddings.

My backpack's on the floor where Kit Ying and I left it when we got in too late to do anything other than crash into bed. It's open, and the clothes are in a plastic washing basket. I try to explain to Aunt Julia that now I'm grown up I can do it myself, but she says what's life for if you can't fuss over your family. The plastic bag with the hat and letters and newspaper is still in my backpack. I pull it out and sit down in one of the wicker chairs and plump up the cushions and try to decide how much I'll tell her about my trip. I'd said to Kit Ying that this wasn't a time for secrets, but he said if Wee Jimmy's story isn't true, why burden Aunt Julia with it?

She comes back with a tray set with a cafetiere, two coffee cups and a jug of hot milk. It's one of her things, hot milk in coffee, like what's the point of making hot coffee, she says, and then drowning it in cold milk. "He's such a nice boy, Anthony. I do hope he gets a proper job." She pulls out a little table next to my chair, puts a coaster down and sets a cup of coffee on it and then goes out into the kitchen again and comes back with a cheese sandwich.

I rummage around in the plastic bag and take out the hat. It looks even more moth-eaten in Aunt Julia's sunroom. It's like the romance going out of a holiday souvenir when you get it home.

"This was your grandfather's."

It's the first time I've seen Aunt Julia entirely drop her guard. Her eyes ping open and she sits down with a whup. She picks up the hat and turns it around in her hand, fingering the red badge with the flash on it, as if it will tell her something.

"I got it from Wee Jimmy."

Her forehead creases as she does a mental roll call, and then it registers. "That funny old fellow? I wouldn't have thought he'd still be alive. Not quite with it, I thought, though you can't say that now can you?"

"He was"—I try to find a neutral word for Wee Jimmy—"unexpected. He thought I was Granny."

She takes a sip of coffee and puts her mug down, concentrates on jiggling it so it fits very precisely on a coaster on the coffee table. "The last time she saw him was the evening of her mother's funeral. I didn't go. I went out for a drink instead..." she turns her coffee mug around, "with a family friend." Round and round goes the coffee mug. "It seems there was bad blood between Wee Jimmy and her father."

"He told me about it."

The guard goes up again. She picks up the coffee cup and takes a careful sip. "There was a lot of hurtful gossip at the time. You know how people are, think if they say something often enough that makes it true. But it was all hot air. My grandfather died of a heart attack. Natural causes." On the third finger of her left hand, she wears a huge ruby that Uncle Henry gave her instead of a wedding ring. It glitters in the sunlight. "The procurator fiscal said so." She puts her mug back on its coaster. If I'm ever going to tell her Wee Jimmy's story, now's the moment.

And then I see how the light catches the side of her face where she hasn't blended her make-up in, and I see how white and fragile her skin has become. Her uncertainty makes me hesitate. The moment passes.

"He also gave me these." I delve into the plastic bag again and pull out the two bundles of letters and put them on the coffee table. "There was more stuff in a tin chest, but I couldn't bring it on the plane."

I wait for her to answer, to object and say she'd have liked all the memories brought home for her to pick over. Instead, she says, "Very sensible," and takes up the bundles, turns them over in her hands, then unties the piece of string around one and opens one of the letters. She holds it up to the light.

"It's from my grandmother, Flora. They say she was a great beauty." Her eyes move down the letter, and then she leans forward as she reads out loud, "'I miss you more than I can say and long to see you again. The figurine you gave me is on my bedside table. Every night I tell my shepherd how much I love him.'" She smiles. "It's so touching. You can picture it, her tucked up in her bed and him in his trench."

I feel a pang of guilt about the shepherd. I should have brought him home after all.

She gives me the other bundle. "Here you read these."

I undo the thin ribbon, once white, now mottled grey, and unfold a piece of dull buff notepaper. It's covered in handwriting in black ink faded to brown, a jagged script that tells of days of muddied danger punctuated by sudden death. Then I come to a standout passage.

"Listen to this," I read it out to her. "'There was a break in the fighting. It was hard to bear, sitting and waiting. Sometimes waiting is harder than fighting. Some of us got the shakes. But now the fighting has started again worse than ever. Yesterday a cart came in loaded with men, dead and dying together. However long I live, I will never get the sound of their groans out of my ears. The stink is always the same, mud, guts, gunfire. I keep a picture of your face in my mind all the time. If it wasn't for that and the thought of seeing you again, I'd go mad.'

"Perhaps he did go mad," I say. "Perhaps that's what caused all the problems."

"Whoever said anything about madness?" She turns back to her grandmother's letters. Her lips move, but she makes no sound. Perhaps it's Flora's voice she hears. Finally, she holds a page up. "'My father's business continues to prosper. He still won't hear me speak of you. I hope he will be persuaded to give us his blessing when you come home. Your loving fiancée Flora McWatt.' So you see, she defied her father to marry her Simon. She must have loved him very much." She smiles.

I could press the point, show her the newspaper cutting which tells a more complicated story. But then I think, we've both got our understandings of what happened. They don't have to agree.

After coffee, she goes upstairs to change. I've just finished stacking the dishwasher, throwing away my cold toast, sorting my clothes and putting them onto wash when she comes back down in designer slacks and a cashmere jumper her favourite shade of cream, hair lacquered into place, and carrying a brown envelope in one hand.

"I started sorting through your Granny's things while you were away, and found these." She tips up the envelope and a stack of photographs shoots out onto the coffee table. They're old black and white pictures of a group of young people with a car, by a river, on a boat. They radiate that bright optimism of people sure of their place in life. They're all in uniform except for one man who's wearing baggy white trousers and stands balancing a punt pole in his hands like he's weighing up what's to his best advantage in the situation.

"Tim Granville, super-smooth even then," Aunt Julia says. "I think he had the hots for my mother. One evening after father left us, he turned up at the boutique looking for her. With a cheque, as if he needed to give it to her in person. Ha, ha." She holds up a picture of a group of them posing in front of one of those huge old cars like out of war films. "Here he is again, with Aunt Connie, gazing at him so adoringly when she thinks no-one's looking, meanwhile with cat's claws out at any woman who got too close, including your Granny."

"And that is?" I point to a tubby young man whose uniform is on the tight side.

"Guy Forrester. Everyone's lawyer, fixer up of life's untidy messes, especially for Connie, whom he worshipped by all accounts. You can see he's making eyes at her, as if she'd be bothered. He tidied away my other godmother Nancy after her affair with Tim, sent her packing off to Scotland. Her son Dominic is probably your father."

I grab the picture. She doesn't resist. These people who ended up making me, all wrapped up in their own lives without a thought for the consequences. When I was very little, I trashed my bedroom. It wasn't long after I'd arrived at Aunt Julia's house, and all I wanted was my old room in Dulwich with my mother and my fun nanny instead of people who were old and sad and didn't tell me things. I felt-tipped all over the walls and cut patterns in the curtains. Kiddy carnage. It made my point and made Aunt Julia cry. I have an urge to do the same again.

"Why are you only telling me this now?"

Aunt Julia's smile is like a rictus. "It's only a guess. We don't know. Your mother would never say." And then she turns back to the photograph.

"You can't close the matter like that."

"It's never closed for me. I live with your mother's loss every day."

There's a desolation in her voice that I'd never heard before. Perhaps she hadn't let it show, or perhaps I was too young to see it, or thought she was too old to feel with such intensity. She doesn't deserve my anger. I look back at the picture. Standing at the edge of the group is a slim young man with thick wavy hair brushed back from his face, clutching his army cap under one arm. Adrift from the others, he's smiling that gullible smile of his. It's the only likeness I can see to the frail old man I knew, the innocent expectancy of his expression that identifies him as my Gramps.

Next to him in the photograph is a young woman. For a second time I'm confronted with a picture of myself. This time it's me in a military uniform with my hair caught back into a bun, the curls escaping and falling around my face. Which looks so full of hope. It shows nothing of what I've seen, not the violence that I ran away from at home, or the destruction of the war that I ran into. I'm staring straight into the camera and smiling like I know it's for some future incarnation of myself. Before whatever shit it was that happened.

"And who's that?" I point to the figure standing next to me in the picture, a tall man of amazing beauty.

"He's the one. Capital T, capital O." She rifles through the pictures and pulls out a photograph of me/Maisie shoulder to shoulder with the man. He has a face of timeless beauty with black hair, a lock hanging down like a question mark over his forehead, and big melty-dark eyes. It looks like they're in a boat, there's a river in the background, and his arm is stretched along the seat behind her. His hand edges around her shoulders, and you can see from the bliss that pours out of her face even in the photograph that she's aware of it. Right on the cliff-edge of love. He bends forward like he wants to get up and on with life and she leans into him, so their heads just touch. And then the photograph's cut off.

"I loved my father dearly, but I don't think my mother did. I believe this was the man she loved. She talked about him all the time towards the end." She turns the picture over. "'Roland, Cambridge May 1944.' I don't know what happened to Roland, and I don't know why she ever married Father. It led to such unhappiness."

I'd never thought of Aunt Julia as being unhappy. My mother suffered. She told me how at school she'd make up stories about her absent father. Like when other kids said they'd gone to Mc-Donalds with their absent dads, she'd say hers owned a nightclub in LA and a weekend just wasn't long enough. But Aunt Julia has always seemed so in control of her emotions—even her relationship with Uncle Henry is one of great calm on her side. The ups and downs are all his.

"You've not been unhappy, have you?" I ask.

"I've had my moments." She fingers the ruby on her left hand. "Not now, of course, not with you and Henry, but earlier there was a time. So much of what I'd taken for granted turned out not to be true. In the end things worked out all right, in some ways they worked out very well. When my father came back and explained everything, it all made sense. It was too late for Isla, though. She had to live her whole life not knowing."

I hold my breath and hope she's going to say something more, but then there's a whirring noise in the kitchen. "Did you put your clothes into wash?" She always finds a way to change the subject when it gets onto my mother. It's like she has an emotional echo locator that warns her off when she's approaching something painful.

This time I won't let her go but follow her into the kitchen. "That's like what Kit Ying says. It's the not knowing that's the worst. He says Hsiao Ling can never accept not knowing what happened to her grandfather."

Aunt Julia takes my clothes out of the washing machine and puts them into a plastic basket.

"You know what happened to your mother," she says.

"Yes. It's the why I don't understand."

"Mmm." She loads my clothes into the tumble drier, shuts the door, chooses the programme, presses the start button with precision. But she won't talk about why my mother died. She's not going there. Not yet.

· · · · ●· ● · · · ·

I try again when Uncle Henry comes home from work. He's still handsome with cropped grey hair and stubble across his face and he dresses with suitably ageing chic. He's taken up cooking, says it's on his bucket list to do MasterChef, and Aunt Julia humours him. So while he dodges about the kitchen, talking about one of his clients—a singer, stuck on a cruise ship somewhere out east—and I unload the dishwasher, I press Aunt Julia again about my mother.

"She must have said something meaningful the last time you spoke."

Aunt Julia's setting the table. She lines up the knives and forks so precisely. "Not what you might think," she says. "We hadn't seen each other for a while. You know how things are, we were both busy and time slipped by." She always polishes the wine glasses before she sets them out and tonight she rubs them till they sing. "Your mother was at Calypso's restaurant that last night when she called me. I could hear the noise in the background, partying, there was always partying when Calypso was around, and then I heard that cheese-grater voice of hers close up. She was just like her mother Constantia, she liked to own people too." She puts down the last of the wine glasses, and her shoulders tense, as if she has to brace herself for what comes next.

Uncle Henry leaves off his cooking and comes and puts an arm around her and kisses her. "It wasn't your fault. She knew how much you loved her. You were always her Ju-ju. And you've given Skye such a happy life." He looks at me and makes a face that tells me I have to say something of comfort. On the surface these two seem so different, but there's this understanding between them. They can read each other's feelings.

"Yes," I say, and it's true, for all the ups and screaming downs, which have mostly been on my side. Plus which I can't bear to see this person who's been my rock fall apart.

But Aunt Julia won't be placated. "I said things I didn't mean. Cruel things. That weren't true…"

Uncle Henry kisses her again and holds her close like he's holding her together. "She'd have realised you didn't mean it."

"I'll never know."

"Didn't she say?" I ask.

"She couldn't. I turned my phone off. That's why she got in her car to drive out to me. So you see, it was my jealousy of Calypso that killed your mother. It was my fault."

For all I'm an adult, I feel my emotions are as simple as a child's compared with the complexity she's lived with for so long. In letting me have my story, she's had to confront the demons in her own.

Chapter Twenty-Four

March 2020

It takes a while to track down Calypso. When I call her restaurant in Leadenhall, the staff blank me. I spell out my name into the indifference down the line. There are pictures of her on social media. She knows how to work it. Always of the moment. Always poised, blonde hair, sunglasses or candle-light—sometimes both.

"She was always a looker, I'll give her that," Aunt Julia sniffs when I phone and tell her about the latest sightings. "So where exactly is she these days?"

That's what I'm trying to discover back at Uni, stripped down to my knickers in my stuffy room, searching on my laptop for Calypso. In the end it's Kit Ying who finds her. He texts me. "Look at Companies House. She's there," and sends me the link: Calypso Granville, Pulbright House, Netherbrook, Hertfordshire.

Just seeing her name and address like that gives me a handle on her. Makes me think I'm already there. Except now I've found where she is as well as what she's become, I get scared. Virtual sightings are one thing. A face-to-face encounter is something else. I lie on my bed and try to push my brain back to my life when Calypso was last in it, but it won't go beyond warm, fuzzy feelings of Mum.

"You must remember something," Kit Ying says. We're talking on the phone late one night. I should be working on a psychology assignment, but it's hard to concentrate when I'm caught up in this uncertainty of finding out who I am. "She and your mother were so close. There must be something about her that stuck with you."

"Perhaps when I meet her, I'll remember."

I reckon the best time to catch Calypso will be a Monday evening, when she's recovering from one weekend and building up her energy levels for the next. Kit Ying leaves work early and picks me up from the station at Watford. The days are longer in late March, and in the warm evening we drive with the windows down. There's early blossom out in the hedgerows. We take the scenic route and laze our way through manicured countryside. When we stop at crossroads, I can hear birdsong.

"Aunt Julia had one of her shops near here," I say.

· · · ● ● ● ● · · · ·

Pulbright House is set behind a high laurel hedge, carefully tended with a grass verge in front. There are elaborate iron gates with an entry phone set into a brick pillar on the driver's side. Through the gates there's a drive up a slope to a stylish white house. It looks like it was built to be happy, clean lines, big windows, carefully angled to catch the sun, but there's a creeper growing across the front and a stone lion sitting by the door. All the lights are off. If anyone's at home, there's no sign of a welcome.

"What if she says she won't see me?"

"Don't anticipate failure." Kit Ying reaches out and presses the buzzer. A light flashes, but nothing else happens. Kit Ying coughs and is about to speak, but then there's a click and the light goes off. Kit Ying presses again. The light flashes and this time I lean across him.

"It's Skye, Isla's daughter. You know, as in Isla Stanhope? I've come to see Calypso Granville." There's a rustling sound at the other end—whoever you are, don't hang up. "If that's possible." I put on my most grovelly voice. "Please."

The light goes off and the gates swing open. Kit Ying puts the car into gear. It should be a Rolls Royce, not a Nissan for a house like this. As the car chunters up the hill, we see the scale of it. There's a glass extension at one side that looks like it's an indoor garden with a pool at the far end. At the other side there's a lawn that sweeps down to a cluster of trees. There's a terrible squawking noise, and a peacock lifts its tail as we drive past. I feel intimidated, by the bird, by the house, by the gloom that's falling over us.

Kit Ying squeezes my hand. "Don't worry, you'll be fine."

He parks past the front door, and we walk back. What I had thought was a stone lion turns out to be a dog-like creature with a snaky medusa head. When I press the buzzer, there's no sound. Not from the buzzer, not from some door opening or closing inside, or any footsteps or voices. My hand is halfway to the buzzer to ring again, when the door swings open.

Standing inside in the shadow is Calypso. She looks like her pictures, slim, long hair that veils her face, pouty lips, pointy chin. She's wearing a beige silk top with long sleeves and one of those skirts with lots of little pleats that swirl around when you move. But they don't swirl with Calypso because she doesn't move. She stands, one hand poised on the door, the other on her hips, like a statue, an ageless golden statue.

"You look just like Maisie." She laughs. It sounds forced, controlled. I feel myself to be a child again—someone leaning over me, drapes of thick blonde hair cascading down, and then a face appearing through the hair to kiss me, and my turning away. And then I remember contrived laughter. "Come in," she says, and adds, "And you are?"

"Kit Ying," he leans forward and sticks his hand out.

"Don't tell me, Hsiao Ling's grandson. The indomitable Hsiao Ling."

She swings her hair and assumes control, of me, of Kit Ying, of the narrative, as easy as that. She heads off, knowing we'll follow. She sashays as she walks through the house, and her silk clothes shimmy. Inside is unlit, but not gloomy. The walls are white, so are the marble floors, and the sitting room is full of flowers. They're in big crystal vases, very beautiful, but they have no scent. If it wasn't that Calypso was so classy, I'd wonder if they weren't plastic. She leads us into a huge orangery, where she's got candles hanging in lanterns among the plants and vines with sprinklers going. It looks and feels like a rainforest, except for the smell, which is chlorine. The swimming pool, I guess.

"You'll find some seats around, help yourselves." She gestures around the jungle and then arranges herself on an exotic white chair set in front of the glass so that all we can see is a faint outline of her against the fading light outside. "Sit down, sit down." A honey-coloured dog, a Pekingese, wriggles out of the undergrowth and jumps onto her lap. "They told me at the restaurant that you were looking for me. I wondered when you'd turn up."

The dog settles its immaculately groomed self on her lap and wheezes. "What a pet." She strokes the dog. She knows we're mesmerised.

I'd talk if I thought she was listening. But I get the feeling that we're incidental to this occasion, an audience for her to play to. There's a click, and a small flame appears, then a glow as she lights a cigarette. She leans back and breathes out and a stream of cloying smoke appears above the exotic chair. Kit Ying squeezes my hand. The dog wheezes again.

Calypso carries on regardless. "Look at you, all grown up. What're you doing? A student I suppose. Clever, like your mother. The cleverest person I ever knew. And the best."

She's invisible in the darkness. The only thing that moves is the smoke curling above her chair. Kit Ying coughs. The dog sneezes.

"Poor Odysseus. We don't like smoke, do we?"

Fuck, she even involves the dog in her drama.

"I suppose you want to know about your mother." While Calypso talks, Kit Ying settles into his chair and crosses his legs, like he's getting stuck in for a duration of disbelief. "It was such a shame, quite shocking really, although I suppose, given the times, it was never going to end well. It was just so unfair it was your mother who had to pay the price for everything that happened."

I can't move, can hardly breathe, much less talk. She draws me in like she knows she can. "It all started with your grandfather being different, as Mother used to put it. She said she'd told her cousin Jeremy if he didn't get himself married off, there'd be a scandal, things being what they were at the time. So, when he showed no inclination to find himself someone, she did it for him. It wasn't very hard.

"Maisie walked in, bang on cue. She was pretty, she was biddable, she was a virgin which was a miracle. Bit below stairs of course, as Mother used to say."

The wispy tentacles of her smoke wind themselves around my throat.

"Maisie was so desperate to avoid going home after the war. It wasn't such a bad arrangement for her, Mother said. Jeremy was quite a catch, after all. The only problem was that Maisie didn't understand it was just a deal."

My lovely Gramps. His open face with all its wrinkles and his silly songs. He'd sing "Daisy, Daisy" to me in his quavering voice, only changed the words to "Maisie, Maisie" and he'd say I reminded him of her when she was young. And his brown eyes would shine. It can't have been an act. He must have loved her at one time, and I know he loved me, because he told me so. He would never be part of any deal.

Calypso's in her own world: "Maisie didn't seem to realise the truth of the arrangement until Mother threatened to expose him."

"What a monster." The words slip out.

"That's aggressive." Her mask slips and there's an edge to her voice. She hisses the last word at us, and her pointy face goes snakelike. There's a red glow from the joint and then a silence and then she says. "It was all Hsiao Ling's fault. She started the debacle with that whole silly row over Freddie's wedding."

This time it's me who squeezes Kit Ying's hand before he jumps in. Hsiao Ling's always been like family to me. There's nothing she'd do to hurt me. I know that. He knows that. And he knows I know that. Calypso drags on her joint and a stream of smoke comes at us across the jungle. Kit Ying coughs. Calypso smirks.

"Isla said things were never the same afterwards." Calypso's voice goes harsh. "Someone had died or something and Maisie threw a hissy fit the day before the wedding and threatened to bugger off to Scotland. Mother had to bring her back in line. Then Maisie dumped Isla with Hsiao Ling who turned bolshie and accused us all of being racist. Of course, Julia didn't suffer. How could she? After all, she had no feelings that anyone could ever detect. Besides, she went to Scotland with Maisie, favoured child and all that. Isla was devastated."

This time the cloud of smoke that comes at us is a thick fog. When it clears, the joint's gone, and she's stroking the dog that lies comatose on her lap. "D'you want to see her room?" Her gushy, managed voice is back.

This tears at my guts. It's as if this woman has some claim to Mum, holds some part of her life that I've never known. I nod. She unfolds herself from her chair and brushes herself down. The dog ends up on the floor and wiggles back into the undergrowth. Calypso saunters off, and then turns and says, "Come on," and beckons to me. Like Wee Jimmy, but spookier.

Kit Ying puts his hands on my shoulders and massages them as we walk along. "Loosen up," he whispers in my ear. "She's stoned, is all."

Calypso goes back into the hall and then up a circular flight of stair. She leads the way into a room, turns on the lights and quickly dims them to a boudoir glow.

Then she saunters around, plumping up the cushions on the double bed, purple and red, Mum's favourite colours, micro-adjusting the silver-framed pictures on the dressing table. There's one of Mum cuddling baby me in her arms. Then there's one of her and Calypso in a restaurant, Calypso bending over till her tits are nearly in Mum's face, one of Mum and Calypso with Dominic lurking in the background between them. Calypso picks up one of those sweetheart frames, all curly roses, and lovebirds, and shows me the picture in it of herself and Mum outside Pullbright House. The two of them have their backs to the camera and their arms around each other and Calypso is looking over her shoulder and winking. "Your father took that one."

"Bitch," Kit Ying mutters in my ear.

Calypso laughs like she's heard him, but it doesn't matter, he doesn't matter, nothing else does to her. "Dominic. A scoundrel, for sure, but he was the only one who kept his side of the bargain. No contact. No regrets. He saw you once and cleared off, like they'd agreed. He understood." She dangles him at me like a bait. But I won't take it. All he ever gave me was a strip of DNA. It was my mother who made me who I am.

She runs her finger over the picture and kisses it. "We were going to buy this house together. She was so excited. But then Julia shouted at her, called her all kinds of names, accused her of stealing their mother, scaring off their father, crashing the business, blamed her for everything including the mess that Julia had made of her own life. I was there, in the restaurant. I heard every last horrible word of it. All because your mother called to ask her to look after you for a day. She was jealous, of course, but it broke Isla's heart. That's why she got into her car and had that accident. So-called accident."

She puts the picture back on the dressing table and makes out she's jiggling it into place. But I can hear it squeak as she grinds it into the polished wood.

"Julia killed her. She was mine and Julia couldn't bear it."

The words, the gestures, the timing. This is too pitch perfect. She's acted it out before.

"That's rubbish," I say. "Aunt Julia was devoted to my mother."

"You'd think so." She drifts from the dressing table to a little desk that joggles memories of my old home and Mum sitting in her bedroom "doing the accounts," she'd say and groan. Calypso runs a finger along the top of it. Her skirt eddies around her legs like the tide.

"But Julia never understood her. How could she? She couldn't even understand herself. Isla was always fragile. She made a lot of noise but underneath she needed someone secure in her life, someone who would give her unconditional love. Her father abandoned her, her mother was as good as missing, locked up so tight within herself and that bloody boutique. For years she was farmed out with Hsiao Ling and then it was Rose who kept Isla going. But then Rose failed her. And then there was me. I was the only person who never let her down."

Kit Ying puts his arms around me. He's bristling at Calypso's interpretation of events. "Come on," he says. "You've found out everything you can from her."

I wish I could pack up the room and take it with me to remind me of my Mum. I look around, at least to capture it in my mind's eye.

And then I see it's not Mum's room at all. Her room would never be this tidy. She'd leave her clothes all over the floor. And even if she'd painted the walls boudoir colours, you'd never see it below all my schoolwork that she'd stick up everywhere with Blu Tack. She didn't have scatter cushions on her bed either. She had huge piles of squashy pillows and we'd lie against them on Sunday mornings, and she'd read books to me.

Even the pictures are wrong. Mum had lots of them. All of me. On my first day at school, at the beach on our holidays, as an angel in the school nativity play, getting a class prize. Every opportunity she took pictures of me and framed them in whatever frame she could buy in the gift shop up the road. Forget prissy silver. Plastic would do. And she didn't have to run her finger across the top of the furniture. She knew there'd always be dust there. It gave me resistance to bugs, she said.

Sometimes I'd find her crying, and she'd say it was about her mother or her sister, but everyone cries about their mothers and sisters, so it was never a big deal apart from her being sad. Sometimes she'd say it was in her genes, which I didn't understand. Then she'd laugh, and we'd go off on some wild adventure. "Let's be barmy, babe," she'd say, and we'd be happy and close, and things would be all right again. She didn't have to worry about unconditional love. That's what I was about. There's only one thing in this room which is true to my Mum.

"It's time for us to go," says Kit Ying.

I'm glad he's with me. Not just to extricate me. I feel less safe here than I did in Wee Jimmy's flat, and Calypso's truth is no more mine than his was.

We leave her standing with her false memories in the room that's not my mother's. Outside we get into the car and Kit Ying turns it around. As he does, the headlights catch Calypso coming out of the doorway. I can see now why the lights in her house are dimmed and why in her pictures she's always in the shade. She raises a hand to fend off the glaring lights. But she can't hide the anger that spews out of every last bitter line time has etched into her crazy face. And when she screams my mother's name, her voice is as harsh as the peacock's.

· · • • • • • • • •

Kit Ying stops at a pub to get a drink on the way back to the station. We've both been through an emotional wringer. I want to tell him that I'm sure about my story now, where it started and how I got to here. And that I know the only person who can define it is myself and that's what I intend to do moving forward. I know he'll listen and understand. He's at the bar ordering drinks when the news comes on the TV screen by the door and announces that because of a new virus, the country is to go into lockdown. Life as we've known it will end. I wonder where Ming Chung is now.

CHAPTER TWENTY-FIVE

JULY 2020

I make the drinks. Kit Ying takes the money and does the food. It works. We tried it the other way around, but people didn't buy that a redhead with an English accent can make pork buns and kimchi.

Our pitch is in a layby down a bank beside a river, near a south coast town. Morning sunlight steals across the water into the clearing where we park our SUV. Kit Ying unhitches the trailer. The grass is still bouncy with dawn dew. Birds sing into emptiness. The air here has a purity that makes you think that because you can see and hear and smell things more clearly, you can understand them better too. Kit Ying says it's our ground zero. But that doesn't work, I tell him. That would be an ending. Not an ending, a nothingness, he says. A place to start from.

'Coffee, tea, tray-bakes,' I chalk onto the display board we put out on the roadside. I draw floaty stars and underneath Kit Ying writes, 'Special—pork buns' and draws some fancy Chinese characters.

"What does that say?"

"That they're authentic."

It was hard explaining to Aunt Julia about the coffee cart. Every week she'd put on her make-up and do her hair for our zoom calls, and she'd say she was OK, whatever, but she couldn't hide her disappointment when I told her I was taking a year out from my university degree. It had been festering since spring and I couldn't make it relevant to where I was any longer. I tried to use words she could understand. So, finding a life that resonates with my new realities, became, "I need some space."

"What would your mother say?" Her question for every time she thinks I've made the wrong decision.

Don't let fate fuck you over, babe, is what I reckon Mum would say. But I can't say that to Aunt Julia, so I make do with, "She'd want me to be happy." It's also true, although what's essential is that I get to define what happiness looks like for me, which isn't the same as for my mother. Like Kit Ying says, I'm my own person. He says I have it easy, I've always been able to define myself—he's just starting out. I tell him he should try defining anything in the chaos that is my family. He says I should try surviving perfect parents. The coffee cart is a joint venture by two people in search of themselves.

The hot spell that started when I was in Edinburgh continues. It's an arc that connects then with now. Today promises more of the same. By the time I've got the coffee machine going, the sun's already burning off last night's freshness. The river moseys by like it knows it has to conserve energy for the coming heat. A couple of swans appear from under the bridge. They glide past. Untouchable.

Kit Ying runs down the bank from putting out the chalkboard on the roadside. I lug a couple of folded tables from the back of our SUV and set them up by the trailer. The milks and sugars and serviettes go onto one, the hand sanitiser onto the other.

Our first customer is a regular. Terrence. Not Tel, he says, never Tel. He waddles over to our coffee cart like a man who's always been plus-sized, although he swears his weight gain is recent. He takes his mask off to give me detailed instructions about exactly how he wants his coffee.

"Flat white, but with that bit less milk than most people have, and please make sure it's piping hot, without burning the coffee, and a few sprinkles on top. Please." Every day. And then he loops his mask back on and watches my every move while I work the coffee machine. And then leaves Kit Ying to put his croissant into a paper bag any old how. On his way back to his car Tel stops at the table and takes four sachets of sugar and then empties a whole lot of little milk cartons into his extra hot coffee and squashes the lid back on. I smile and wave as he pulls away.

I think of all the big picture issues that Flora and Maisie had to deal with, like war and death and mental health and stuff. And wonder what they would have made of me fretting about how Tel likes his coffee when the world's coming out of a pandemic.

Kit Ying and I have our coffee sitting by the riverbank. Kit Ying has his apron on, he keeps it tied around his waist all day. Sometimes I think it's to remind himself that he's not a physicist any longer. He says it's because he can't be arsed to take it off.

"Like the swans," he says. "Look at them. Nothing bothers them."

I wish I could feel as detached.

· · · · ● · ● · · ·

Tyres skid on the road. An engine revs up and then a people carrier swooshes into our layby. A door slides open, and an old man falls out, picks himself up and dusts down his white clothes. When I say old, I mean old, old. His face is wrinkled, his hair's gone, and it's like he's shrivelled up with age, like an apple that's been left too long in the sun. He smiles at me with an intensity that catches me off guard and I find myself smiling back as fiercely. Behind him comes another man, semi-old and then from the front of the people carrier a younger man and woman. Their shirts are so white they fluoresce.

They speak to each other, and then the younger man turns to us and asks, "Who wrote that sign?"

Kit Ying puts his hand up.

There's a burst of talk and laughter and then the driver asks him, "Five of your real pork buns please."

The old man watches Kit Ying serve up the food, and his eyes twinkle as he takes the first two buns and I hold my breath while he teeters back towards the people carrier. He struggles to clamber inside, and the young woman runs over and lifts him in like he's a doll. She takes a stack of serviettes and hands them into the vehicle and slides the door shut.

The group goes to sit by the riverbank and Kit Ying carries their order over to them. I bring them bottles of water and the young woman asks if I could give some to her grandparents.

When I slide open the door of the people carrier, I see that beside the old man there's an equally old woman. They've got layers of serviettes spread out over their white clothes and they're both chewing on their buns, grinding their jaws like I guess they've not got much left in the way of teeth. The woman puts her food down on her lap and smiles at me. The curve of her lips is picked up by zillions of fine lines around her face, so I get the impression of a thousand tiny smiles all directed at me. I feel myself smiling back.

"*Nei hou ma*?" Learning Cantonese is on my to-do list.

She doesn't respond, but the old man does and nods his head enthusiastically. It makes me wonder what I've said.

When I get back to the riverbank, the younger man explains that they're taking his grandparents on a day trip to France. "My grandfather wants to visit the Chinese war graves. He's been fretting about getting there before it's too late."

Kit Ying's sitting on the ground a bit apart from the group. He pulls his knees up to his chest and puts his arms around them. It's his way of keeping in difficult thoughts.

"My grandfather has an uncle buried there," the young man says. "The men in their village in China signed up for the Chinese Labour Corps in the First World War. The British Army shipped them away to work. My great-grandfather and his brother left together. My great-grandfather came back alone, with stories of their journey across the world, and how they dug trenches on the Somme."

Everyone else is tucking into their food, but Kit Ying's coffee cools on the ground beside him while the story unfolds. "My family used to talk about the lost brother, and my grandfather promised he'd visit his grave. If he doesn't go now, he's afraid he might never get the chance to honour his promise." The young man gets stuck into his pork bun, and then points to the swans and says something to the young woman who I presume is his partner.

Kit Ying's coffee is neglected beside him.

"I'll freshen it up for you," I say, but he's got that look of total concentration on his face that tells me he won't notice, even if I yell right in his ear. I nudge his bum with my foot. "Hey, you." He looks at me, but I'm not sure he registers. I wave my coffee cup in front of his face. "Freshen up?" He nods.

Something's stirring in him. After they've all finished, and the woman has retrieved the grandparents' paper cups and serviettes and thrown them in our bin, and I've said goodbye to the grandmother with her face full of smiles and mopped up what I guess are compliments from the grandfather on my/Kit Ying's pork buns, and the rest have packed themselves back into the people carrier and the young man has reversed out of our layby and I hold my breath because they nearly collide with a car on its way in, and they've zoomed out into the road, it feels like when I said goodbye to Heartfelt. Forever ending. No strings.

That's when Kit Ying says, "What if?" And I remember the story my mother first told me about Hsiao Ling's ancestor who disappeared.

·· ··•·•··· ·

Blink and you miss it. Turn right out of Calais and drive an hour down the main road, turn off that road, then off another, and another, and eventually I'm driving us through summer crisp fields in the middle of nowhere. The sat nav tells me to take the next right where there's a small sign by the road, "Cimetiere Chinois de Nolette."

We go through one of those orderly French villages that looks all certain of itself with a station at one end of the main road and a charcuterie at the other.

Even then, we've not arrived, but turn off into a hamlet that is seriously ungentrified with little farmhouses around muddy courtyards full of cows and chickens. There's an unremarkable signpost that points us down a gravelly single track that scrunches under our tyres. Rough wooden fencing on either side separates us from stubby wheat. And then opposite us on a small rise the cemetery appears, like a mirage in the wheatfield, surrounded by a white stone wall with an ornate archway and curious flat-topped conifers.

Kit Ying's got both hands on the dashboard as we bump along, and he's leaning forward peering around like he's landed on the moon. In fact, we're about as close to home as you can get and still be abroad. He videos out of the windscreen as I drive into the carpark, and pans around to take in the yellow crops, the white stones the intense blue sky. The colours are so sharp they hurt.

Then he puts down his phone and looks like he's going to cry. I think of how I felt when I took Granny Maisie's ashes into the river beside the bridge humping across the water, and how that journey led to so much more for me. And I remember how it mattered to have someone with me. I put my arms around Kit Ying and hug him and don't mind when he shrugs me off.

It's hotter here than at home. Outside, the air is thick with wheat dust. There's a choking sensation in my chest and I'm not sure if it's the heat or my emotions. I wonder which of the two's got to Kit Ying. There's sweat trickling down the side of his face and darkening the back of his T-shirt. He's put his sunglasses on so I can't tell about his emotions. Even in non-crises, he doesn't like to show them. He says it's to do with him being a physicist. He doesn't deal with emotions; he deals with facts. I tell him that's what caused all the problems in my family, not dealing with emotions.

In front of us is the cemetery with its rows of white gravestones, some still pristine, some mildewy, set out as blankly uniform as I guess the men were made to be in real life. It's a carefully manicured patch of isolation carved out of some French farmer's wheatfield.

I let Kit Ying walk on his own under the stone arch at the entrance to the cemetery, like Heartfelt let me walk out into the river to find whatever. I know how it feels. To look around and think, this is it, this is the place that makes sense of who I am. He looks so alone, in front of all those gravestones, I want to run after him and take his hand and go with him. But this is his story to discover, not mine.

Finally, he turns and walks to the first gravestone at the left of the entrance. He looks at it for what feels like forever and then squats down and traces over it with his fingers. I can't see his eyes behind his sunglasses, but I can tell from the way he scrunches his shoulders that this is difficult. Then he stands and bows at the gravestone and moves on to the next one, and then the next. I wait a bit before I join him.

"'A noble duty bravely done No. 9740 Chinese Labour Corps Died 13th November 1918,'" he reads out. "Not my relative."

"No name?" I ask.

"It's Pan Chung Shan." He points to Chinese characters. "In English he's just a number."

He moves on, along the rows, up the left side of the cemetery, faster now I guess the shock has worn off. The slogans are repeated, and I try to work out the number of them, and if there's a pattern. The reflection of the sun off the white gravestones hurts my eyes, and I start to get a headache. I go back to our car for water and give a bottle to Kit Ying. It's the first time since we arrived, he's smiled at me. Then he carries on, stopping only to check the names—I can see his lips move as he says each one. I follow him—gravestone after white gravestone.

Finally, the sun moves down the sky and a breeze blows in across the wheatfields. It carries a salty, earthy smell. Sea, or perhaps it's mud. This is, after all, the Somme.

When he's gone up and around the top and most of the way down the right side of the cemetery, I think, oh my god, his ancestor's not here, then what happens? I go to join him so I can mop up his disappointment. That's when he stops and takes off his sunglasses. His chest heaves, he opens his mouth to speak.

At first no words come out, and then he says, "That's him." He kneels in front of the gravestone.

"Chang Chaio Feng. My grandmother speaks so often about how he went away and was lost." He touches the engraved characters with his fingers. It's as if he can feel his ancestor in them, although he claims he doesn't go for that snowflakey stuff. Then he reads out the slogan, "'Faithful unto death.' That's very appropriate for him."

What gets to me is the date. Chiselled under 'No. 133724 Chinese Labour Corps' is 'Died 12th Jan 1920.'

"He didn't die in the war at all. He died way after it was over. He should have been home by then." It comes out harsher than I mean, as if I think it's his fault for staying away and I squat down next to Kit Ying and put an arm around him. "I'm sorry."

I know how this feels too. What happens when you believe one thing all your life and then you find out it's not true. Or more complex, because that's what life is. So, Chang Chaio Feng wasn't killed in the war, and he didn't go home either. Perhaps he died of hunger, or Spanish flu. Or perhaps the Somme broke his spirit like it did my great-grandfather's.

Kit Ying takes pictures of the grave with his phone and sends them to his mother, Rose, and then spends forever texting her. Meanwhile, I sit on the grass and wish I'd brought some flowers or a plant or something to leave behind to show that at least after a hundred years the family had found the missing brother, father, son.

I go back to the car and get one of our zillion serviettes and scoop up a bit of soil from around the grave. Kit Ying's eyes follow me while he listens to his phone, and he smiles when I wrap the soil up and put it in my pocket. "Mum sends her love," he tells me. "She says Hsiao Ling burst into tears when she saw the picture of the grave and can't stop talking. She says to take pictures of everything."

So he does. Of the graves of the other two men who died on 12th January the second year after the war ended. Of the wheatfield, where herbicide has killed off the poppies. Of the farms discreetly distant, and the woods that have grown back over the scarred battleground, where the sun is now setting. Somewhere among the trees I guess must be the river that gave its name to all this grief. He takes pictures of the interpretation board which we should have checked on the way in.

While he fiddles about focusing the phone so he can capture all the words, I read them out. "It says they came from Shan Dong."

"That's Shantung, where the silk comes from."

"No way. All those dresses that Maisie and Hsiao Ling made." I remember how my mother used to laugh about the brides dressed in their silk meringues. "D'you think they knew?"

Kit Ying shakes his head. It's like he's never going to finish taking pictures, and in the end, I get into the car and flash the headlights at him. We have a ferry to catch. He must have filled the entire e-cloud by the time he turns around. "I can't hear headlights," he says when he climbs in.

He reaches into the glove compartment and pulls out a bag of Haribo sweets.

"So now we know." He offers me a sweet, then puts one into his mouth. "You and me both."

"Yes." I start up the car. "Now we can move on."

ACKNOWLEDGMENTS

Some special people were part of the creation of this book.

Thanks to Ng Mee Ling OBE for talking me through the story of the Chinese Labour Corps. Theirs is one of the shocking, hidden episodes of the First World War. My Scottish grandfather, who served on the Somme, would have encountered the labourers. They were transported from northern China to work in brutal conditions, digging the trenches in which he fought and then recovering bodies and clearing debris long after he'd gone home. A derelict wall at Orford Ness on the Suffolk coast is the only remnant of their work in the UK.

Thanks also to Stirling Askew of Woodbridge Station Headquarters who was so generous in getting clearance and then showing me around what remains of the former Sutton Heath airbase. Pouring rain tipped down on us as we drove along the two-mile long runway carved out of Rendlesham Forest. But even that couldn't douse my amazement at the scale of the project or the heroism of those who served on it.

The wonderful City Lit got me started on my writing journey, and Jericho Writers picked me up and carried me along the way to this book. Thanks to them and the teachers, mentors and fellow students who were part of it. Thanks also to the

Olivier writing group who provided a sounding board for the many different permutations of the story, to the friends who have read and critiqued it, and especially to Zhui Ning Chang and copy editor, Mary Torjussen. Special thanks to the brilliant Lynn Andreozzi who designed the book cover and to Gwyn Garfield-Bennett who guided me through the self-publishing labyrinth with expertise and good humour. And also to Andrew.

If you are reading "She, You, I" with your reading group or book club—thankyou! There's a download with some suggested discussion points on my website at www.sallykeeblebooks. com.

The stories of Maisie, Isla and Skye are a complete fiction. Any resemblance between them, or other characters in this book, and real people is coincidence. The historical background however, was carefully researched, and you can find on my website the true stories that lie behind some of the scenes and settings. You might find the truth more astounding than the fiction.

Happy reading.

Sally Keeble

ABOUT SALLY KEEBLE

Sally writes about the things she's passionate about—the triumphs and tragedies of people's lives. It's what originally took her into journalism and then politics, and keeps her active there still.

Growing up in a diplomatic family, she spent much of her early years in the USA, Switzerland and Australia, returning home to the UK after working as a journalist in South Africa. She made the switch from journalism to politics, first as a South London council leader during the turbulent 1980s and then as one of the big intake of Labour women MPs who changed the face of British politics in 1997. She served as a minister for local government and then international development.

Itchy feet don't stand still. After losing her seat, she set up an international development agency for the Anglican Communion, and travelled widely, especially in Africa and South Asia. She's written nonfiction previously, but "She, You, I" is her first novel. Some of the storylines in it draw from insights gained from her personal and political life, but it's all fiction. Sally splits her time between Northampton, where she was MP, and Bawdsey, a village in coastal Suffolk close to her family roots. She and her husband Andrew have two adult children.

ALSO BY SALLY KEEBLE

Flora's Choice

Flora Munro finds herself free after her violent husband dies.
"It's your choice what happens now," says her daughter Maisie.
So what does Flora do with her newfound freedom? How does
she move on after the years of abuse? And what choice does she
make when a former admirer comes calling?

This novella takes a deep dive into the emotional life of one of
the characters from "She, You, I." And it also tells the stories of
Wee Jimmy and young Annie, who play crucial and unexpected
roles in Flora's recovery.

"Flora's Choice" will be sent free of charge to everyone who
signs up for Sally's newsletter.

You can find more about it and sign up on Sally's website at
www.sallykeeblebooks.com
or follow her on facebook at Sally Keeble Author
or on Instagram at SallyKeebleBooks

Made in United States
North Haven, CT
29 April 2023

35858551R00180